CHARLES BEADLE was a world traveler who was born at sea in 1881. When he was eighteen years old he expatriated from England and spent a dozen years exploring South Africa, Rhodesia, Zambia, Uganda, the Congo, Mozambique, Borneo, and Morocco. In his mid-twenties he organized an expedition to Fez and traveled there disguised as a dancing girl to interview the sultan of Morocco. In the 1910s he lived in Montmartre, where he befriended his neighbor Beatrice Hastings, the mistress of Modigliani and translator of Max Jacob. Modigliani later portrayed Beadle in a drawing titled *Le Pèlerin* ("The Pilgrim"), which may have been a reference to Beadle's first banned book, *A Passionate Pilgrimage*. During World War I he traveled to the United States, where he published stories in *Adventure* and in the *International*, a cultural journal edited by Aleister Crowley. He returned to the City of Light in the fall of 1919, where he lived throughout most of the 1920s, eventually moving to the French Riviera.

In 1938 Jack Kahane's Obelisk Press published Beadle's last novel, *Dark Refuge*: an unrecognized modern masterpiece that quickly fell into obscurity. It contains thinly disguised portraits of Modigliani, Max Jacob, Beatrice Hastings, Léopold Zborowski, and various other figures who haunted the Parisian demimonde of this period. Beadle's brazen portrayal of drug fueled pansexual orgies prevented the chronicle from being distributed in the Anglo-Saxon world despite its literary merit and lyrical beauty.

In 1941 Faber and Faber published *Artist Quarter*, a nonfiction work pseudonymously coauthored by Beadle with Douglas Goldring, which is still considered to be the urtext of Modigliani biography.

Although the time and place of his death remained a mystery until 2025, we now know that Beadle spent his final years in Nice, where he died on 27 January 1957.

ROB COUTEAU is a Brooklyn-born author and visual artist. His publications have been praised in *Evergreen Review*, *Publishers Weekly*, *New Art Examiner*, *Midwest Book Review*, and *Witty Partition*. In 1985 he won the North American Essay Award, sponsored by the American Humanist Association. His work has been cited in books such as *Ghetto Images in Twentieth-Century American Literature* by Tyrone Simpson, *Gabriel Garcia Marquez's 'Love in the Time of Cholera'* by Thomas Fahy, *Conversations with Ray Bradbury* edited by Steven Aggelis, and David Cohen's *Forgotten Millions*, a book about the homeless. His interviews include conversations with Pulitzer Prize-winning author Justin Kaplan, *Last Exit to Brooklyn* novelist Hubert Selby, Simon & Schuster editor Michael Korda, LSD discoverer Albert Hofmann, Picasso's model and muse Sylvette David, sci-fi author Ray Bradbury, film star and bibliophile Neil Pearson, and historian Philip Willan, author *Puppetmasters: The Political Use of Terrorism in Italy*. Couteau has appeared as a guest on Bob Barrett's *The Best of Our Knowledge* (WAMC), Len Osanic's *Black Op Radio*, and on Monocle 24 in Europe. In 2023 he published *Intimate Souvenirs*, a memoir featuring an Introduction by Robert Roper, author of *Nabokov in America: On the Road to Lolita* and *Now the Drum of War: Walt Whitman and His Brothers in the Civil War*. Since 2020 he has devoted himself to republishing annotated texts of important but forgotten authors such as Stanley Marks, Charles Beadle, and Francis Carco.

JOHN LOCKE has been fascinated by the pulp magazine era and its fiction, particularly in the 1920s and 1930s, for many decades. In the 1990s he started collecting information on the era, which led to writing historical treatments about the publishers, editors, and most of all the authors. Many of his findings have been published in his Off-Trail Publications books. Charles Beadle featured in two collections of Africa adventure fiction (*The City of Baal*, 2007; *The Land of Ophir*, 2012). In 2018, Locke jumped up to book-length histories with *The Thing's Incredible! The Secret Origins of Weird Tales*. He's currently completing a book about writers behaving badly in the 1920s.

The Lost Cure

Charles Beadle

Portrait of Charles Beadle, courtesy of Beadle's great-niece Patricia and her daughter Liz. An inscription on the back identifies it as a Christmas gift from "your loving son." Circa 1899.

The Lost Cure

Charles Beadle

Edited with Annotations and an
Introduction by Rob Couteau

Afterword by John Locke

DOMINANTSTAR

Contents

Author of "The Land of Ophir," "Gifts of Diamonds," etc.

PROLOG

CHATTER, laughter, and a subdued tinkle surged rhythmically against the brays and yowls and swoops of sound from the jazz band. Hard light gleamed on the curves of bare shoulders and was flung back in prismatic rays from manicured fingers and powdered bosoms. Waiters scurried like anxious ghosts. Oozy laughs accompanied the tinsel voices of the women.

At a table in an alcove formed by trelliswork screens of painted grapes sat two men smoking cigars. The smaller, who was leaning forward with his elbows on the cloth, was brown of hair, clean-shaven, with chiseled jaw and lips; the nostrils were wide and the eyes had the bird-like brightness of the magpie, a tense probing glance dominated by the prying instinct of insatiable curiosity.

His companion, Birskett, was a much bigger man, blond, broader of shoulder, wider of jaw, and with steady incurious eyes which always seemed loath to leave their objective.

"No," the big man was saying to his companion, Dr. Kirkton; "haven't been back three months from a trip up the Andes. Fizzled out. Went down to see the folks. You know what that is, doc. Then I got a hunch to hunt up something. Went down to see Griffiths, a mining engineer. He usually has something live on the move. But he wasn't in, so I went and sat in the sun on the Battery, wondering where Old Man Fate was going to push me off to next. There was a big bum sitting next to me. Blown in the glass. Noticed he was reading want ads.

" 'Looking for a job?' said I, wanting to talk to some one. 'Me too.' But he gave me a look as if I were a bull. Then he grinned. 'Gosh, mister,' said he, 'I've got a delicate constitution. Ain't strong enough for work, but I likes reading about them

Beadle's Plague Years:
An Introduction by Rob Couteau

"I never knew such a country as the African Continent for diseases of men and animals. It seems a wonder that anything is left alive."
– From the memoir of missionary John Moffat, 2 May 1903.

Although it's been widely documented in scientific writing, few works of literary fiction deal with the sleeping sickness epidemic that killed hundreds of thousands of Africans at the turn of the century. One notable exception is Charles Beadle's *A Whiteman's Burden*, first published in 1912, when the plague was still spreading and claiming lives.

While preparing to republish it for the first time in 113 years, I was informed by my friend John Locke that Beadle wrote another novel that also focuses on African **trypanosomiasis** as a central theme. Titled "The Lost Cure" and featured in *Adventure* magazine's 30 January 1923 issue, it has never before been published in book form.

The most devastating period of the epidemic occurred between 1900 and 1905, but a broader time frame spans the years 1890 – 1920. So, besides traveling through the most infected areas at the very peak of the catastrophe, Beadle composed his plague novels in the 1910s, while the illness continued to rage.

Here we have a rare opportunity to examine how Beadle explored the same theme first in a work of literature, *A Whiteman's Burden*, and then in a mass-market form of adventure fiction, *The Lost Cure*. Although *A Whiteman's Burden* represents a more sophisticated creative effort and ranks as one of his finest portrayals of tragedy, at its best *The Lost Cure* illustrates how Beadle always remained a cut above the average "writer for hire" of genre fiction. Though the writing in *The Lost Cure* is, at times, uneven, the author attains a level of authenticity rarely seen in the genre fiction from this period. In the words of John Locke, unlike some of *Adventure*'s other writers, Beadle's work resonates with acute authenticity because it's deeply grounded in life experience:

> You read it and you go: "OK, there's no way that he made all of this up." He'd obviously been there. So, I like the fiction with some authenticity built in. And with Beadle, it's also his authenticity of location. In *Adventure* you did get the case of, say, someone went to the library and read up on the Sahara Desert as much as they could and then just invented a story. That would fool most people if you did it well. But it would probably not have those magical quirks that you get if you had actually been there and seen the unique elements of life that would never have found their way into print otherwise. And for me, Beadle was one of those: the authenticity. To find someone who'd actually been places and seen things, that to me is kind of the holy grail. The fiction spoke for itself, and the content.[1]

The same can be said for Beadle's more literary novels. While reading *A Passionate Pilgrimage* or *Dark Refuge*, part of the fun is trying to figure out where fact intertwines with fiction. And, even more exhilarating, to witness how his reminiscence branches out, blossoms, and melds into a weave of creative transformation. The blurred boundary line between these two worlds proved to be a fertile ground for Beadle. Few authors have lived such an exciting life of travel and adventure in often-dangerous locales; fewer still are capable of leaving behind an oeuvre of such artful confession.

---

[1] Telephone interview with Locke, 22 July 2022.

THE LOST CURE

PROLOGUE

Chatter, laughter, and a subdued tinkle surged rhythmically against the brays and yowls and swoops of sound from the jazz band. Hard light gleamed on the curves of bare shoulders and was flung back in prismatic rays from manicured fingers and powdered bosoms. Waiters scurried like anxious ghosts. Oozy laughs accompanied the tinsel voices of the women.

At a table in an alcove formed by trelliswork screens of painted grapes sat two men smoking cigars. The smaller, who was leaning forward with his elbows on the cloth, was brown of hair, clean-shaven, with chiseled jaw and lips; the nostrils were wide and the eyes had the birdlike brightness of the magpie, a tense probing glance dominated by the prying instinct of insatiable curiosity.

His companion. Birskett, was a much bigger man, blond, broader of shoulder, wider of jaw, and with steady incurious eyes which always seemed loath to leave their objective.

"No," the big man was saying to his companion, Dr. Kirkton; "haven't been back three months from a trip up the Andes. Fizzled out. Went down to see the folks. You know what that is, doc. Then I got a hunch to hunt up something. Went down to see Griffiths, a mining engineer. He usually has something live on the move. But he wasn't in, so I went and sat in the sun on the Battery, wondering where Old Man Fate was going to push me off to next. There was a big bum sitting next to me. Blown in the glass. Noticed he was reading want ads.

" 'Looking for a job?' said I, wanting to talk to some one. 'Me too.' But he gave me a look as if I were a bull. Then he grinned.

'Gosh, mister,' said he, 'I've got a delicate constitution. Ain't strong enough for work, but I likes reading about them crazy guys who ask for trouble. Say, what's Looganda?'

" 'Loo ganda?' said I. 'What do you mean?'

"Then he shoved your ad under my nose. I left him feeling mighty happy."

"In this old burg," said the doctor, "you can find a man to speak any lingo under the sun. About two dozen showed up who could speak Swahili, but I was dead sure I'd find the Luganda man. Now, Birskett, that's all I'm at liberty to say at the moment. For the rest it's up to you. As far as I'm concerned I'm satisfied that you're the man we're looking for. We'll go along in a minute and see the old man. But one thing: don't get up in the air if he seems—well, kind of eccentric. You'll understand more afterwards."

"Oh, I guess I'm used to eccentric guys," drawled the big man with a slow smile. "I was a warder once in a real bughouse, doc. Had a wonderful time. I was real sorry to quit for I'd never met such a bunch of reasonable folk in all my life."

"Yes," returned the doctor, and his lips thinned to a line. "If all the half-witted idiots were where they ought to be, the rest of us might get on with our work without homicide and arson, theft and perjury, but, man, they'd fill New York, London and Paris and then some. Do you know that patriotism, war, success, are nothing but diseases?"

"Sure," assented Birskett, and his eyes laughed. "But say how about another drink before we quit? Mine's a dry state."

"Another damned disease!" snapped the doctor. "If they'd only prohibit people breathing foul air and fine 'em if they didn't take internal baths they'd do more good than driving 'em into swallowing fusel oil. Gosh, if some of these wise folk could only look eternity in the face, they'd need a drink to keep the cold of truth out! Say, waiter, two more and double 'em! Get that?"

"Well," continued the doctor, "here's to our better acquaintance, Birskett. Say," he added, "you're American born, aren't you?"

"You bet I am! But you are, doc, huh?"

"I'm a medical man. Science has no country."

For a moment the steady eyelids tightened, then came a slow smile.

"That's right, doc. Here's how!"

"Bughouse all right," muttered Birskett, as the doctor settled the bill. "But I like him."

On the curb waited a smart limousine, which hummed uptown and pulled up before a brownstone house in the eighties.

"This is my private 'yip' house," said the doctor pleasantly, as they descended.

He opened the door with a latchkey, and leaving their coats and hats in the hall, he led Birskett upstairs to a door on the right. A uniformed nurse was sitting at a table reading.

"Prepare the patient, nurse," he said briskly.

She rose and went into a room leading off and he followed her. Presently he reappeared and beckoned Birskett to enter. The latter saw a plainly furnished bedroom and a figure in the bed.

As he advanced he became aware of small feverish eyes which seemed to peck at him irritably, and as he stood by the bed a slight thrill of horror held him; for the heavy features seemed those of a dead and very old man, so emaciated that the skin, stretched over the cheek and jaw bones and the bridge of the nose, seemed about to split; even wrinkles were annihilated. The complexion looked in the electric light utterly bloodless.

The skull was nearly bald; the tufts of sparse hair suggested the mange. A big bony hand resembling a vulture's claw lay outside the coverlet.

"This is the man of whom I've spoken, Lörtzer."

The doctor's voice seemed strangely hard and abrupt to address a patient Birskett thought; even if he were a squarehead he was obviously very sick. The man's eyes glared peevishly for a few moments as if he were struggling to recall something, and then he said irritably in a whisper—

"*Kusema Luganda?*"

"*Manyi katono,*" (I know a little,) responded Birskett, a trifle startled at the familiar syllables.

"*Ovude wa?*" (Where do you come from?)

"Maine."

"*Omanyi Buganda?*"

"*Nali mukyalo.*" (I have lived in that country.)

Lörtzer continued to cross-examine him at some length in Luganda. As he spoke Birskett's steady gaze noticed that a film seemed to grow over the eyes of the sick man and the eyelids to droop. At length, wearily and with effort, he looked at the doctor.

"He will do—if you are satisfied," he whispered.

Once more he dragged his eyes, now scarcely showing beneath the lids, towards Birskett.

"If you—accept this job—you must—must swear—swear—sw—"

The eyelids closed, and the lips remained stiff in the shape of a kind of sneer, the shape of the last letter pronounced. As Birskett was staring, thinking that the man must have died, he heard the doctor saying vexedly:

"You didn't make it strong enough, nurse. He—"

"Shall I give him another, doctor?"

"No, no, don't bother him. He's done all that's required by accepting Mr. Birskett. He probably won't last another forty-eight hours. I'll look in tomorrow morning as usual. Good night, nurse."

He led Birskett upstairs and into what was evidently his private apartment. He indicated a chair and set a tantalus of whisky on the table and thrust forward a box of cigars.

"What's the matter with the old man?" queried Birskett.

"Old? He's not old, man. Thirty-eight."

"Phew! He looks about ninety odd."

"That's what you and I may look like in a few months," said the doctor with a short laugh.

Birskett gazed at the doctor for a moment questioningly; then his eyes opened.

"Sleeping sickness! Is that it?"

"Yep. Last stages. I've kept him going on the needle until this affair was fixed. Now it's no use to keep the dead alive."

"Lordy! It's ten years since I was there and it hadn't started much on the Nile then. Haven't they found a cure for it yet?"

"M'm. That's what we're going to find out." He walked over to his littered desk, drew a folded manuscript from a drawer and threw it on the table before Birskett. "I've got to go and look after some patients. Read that—but recollect, on your oath, you're not to divulge anything if you want to back out of the job?"

"Sure. That's what the old man, I mean that fellow, wanted to say?"

"Yep."

"Dictated by Dr. Adolph K. Lörtzer, in the presence of Dr. Fraser Kirkton and Nurse Patience K. Horniman," was written on the top of the first page.

The script proceeded:

"I, Dr. Adolph Kokstorr Lörtzer, do hereby swear that each and every particular hereinunder related is the truth and nothing but the truth, so help me God!

"In the Spring of the year 19— I left Berlin for Deutsch Öst Africa with a view to gaining the reward of 100,000 marks offered by the Imperial Government's Foreign Office for a cure for trypanosomiasis; also that of the British Government of £20,000; and that of the Belgian Government of 20,000 francs; but more with the object of winning the honor for the glory of the Vaterland, Science and Humanity. This I beg the reader, before he judge me, to bear in mind.

"While engaged at Muanza and district where the disease was rapidly spreading from the British end of the lake, in making most exhaustive studies, I met a fellow scientist engaged in the same laudable purpose, an American, Herr Professor Dr. Manfred Stoutt. He was on his way to the southwestern end of the Ruwenzori Range with the object, he told me, of studying the disease and the natives at one of the points of origin, namely the Congo, in the neighborhood of the lakes and swamps.

"This perspicacity was admirable, and despite minor theories which were undoubtedly untenable, he appeared unusually free from the stigmata of the western mind. I was so impressed by this that I actually offered to accompany him. Only then did he reveal the narrow-mindedness so conspicuous and regrettable among many alleged men of science. He refused. I saw of course that he wished to gather the honor for his own country and all the cash for himself; he feared that I might wish to rob him.

"Dr. Manfred Stoutt departed, and I continued my investigations. Some six months later he was reported to have written that he had already invented a formula which he hoped would be successful, but that he was not prepared to make any definite statements until he had proved his theory. The man had remarkable luck.

"The more I pondered, the more impressed I became by his theory of seeking at the source, which, as he had said himself, had been suggested to him by a young British doctor engaged at the clinic at Entebbe. Why then should he profit by what was not his own? If he could use that hint, why should not I? I determined to do so.

"I accordingly set out for the same district. After some considerable difficulties I succeeded in reaching the southwestern spurs of the Ruwenzori and heard that a white man was encamped high up on the mountainside. Through the fault of my native guides we became lost, and an extremely hostile tribe surrounded us. I understood that they had the impertinence to impede my progress. However, the next day appeared Dr. Stoutt—a most opportune meeting. He seemed on very good terms with the natives; in fact, as I afterwards found out, he had deluded them with an idea that he was of divine origin. He appeared to be in health and *very* elated.

"Concentration upon a given objective is the royal road to success. But this man seemed unduly gratified with the discovery of many unclassified plants. However, he informed me that some of this tribe who dwelt farther below, around the swamps had nearly been annihilated by the trypanosomiasis and that he had treated them with his formula or dope, he termed it. His expression and boyish optimism betrayed his unscientific method of thought.

"That night, while talking by the campfire, he stated quite seriously that so certain was he that he had discovered the remedy that he had deliberately inoculated himself with the trypanosomes, in order to test the action of the drug. I deemed that he was exaggerating, but he showed me the clinical charts upon himself and even the slide of the trypanosomes. I suggested that he should reveal to a brother scientist the formal results, but this he strangely refused to do. In fact he seemed to take my natural interest in extremely bad part.

"The following day he bade me goodbye and officiously stated that I would be free to wander where I should wish within the bounds of this tribe without injury. Very justly I was annoyed and reminded him that this was German territory. He exhibited very bad taste.

"I gathered from inquiry that he had a shack or hut of some sort high up in the mountain where the climate was fresh and bracing and where he carried out all his experiments, descending only occasionally to the valley for further investigation. Discourteously, he did not invite me to visit him.

"I ordered the chief to supply me with a hut in order to arrange my laboratory and pitched my tent within the compound. As I considered that nothing was to be gained by frequenting the swamps infested by the *glossina palpalis* I had several subjects sent up to me for investigation.

"At first I was tempted to ascend the mountain and to visit Dr. Stoutt, but considering his discourteous conduct I refused to honor him and his pompous theories. During my investigations here I conclusively proved that the crocodile is not the host of the trypanosomes, and also that the *glossina morsitans*, as well as the *palpalis*, is the host. At this time I was experimenting with a subcutaneous injection of C12 H12 O2 N2 AS2 2HCL and C10 H13 OHgOH, which I found very efficacious in arresting the development.

"Some months later, just after the rainy season, I was interrupted by the reappearance of Stoutt. He seemed to have forgotten his ill-bred behavior and was indelicately triumphant in his assurance that he had proved beyond question that he had discovered the remedy, and quite needlessly insulted me by adding that he rejoiced that American science would have yet another feather in the hat.

"I again with much tact implied that he should acquaint a brother scientist. Again he vulgarly refused, refused even to discuss technical matters; caused me to feel that he actually mistrusted me. He was, he said, going down to the swamps to make some last investigations, and after that he would return to the hut in the mountain and pack to return to America.

"In view of the statements to be made I beg the reader to recall this incident to mind, to feel and understand that by his vulgar manner and unnecessary words he had mortally wounded me in my tenderest feelings of patriotism to my country and science.

"Not the sum of the agony of Prometheus was comparable to mine. That this young American of scarcely any degree worth mentioning, should have the luck to stumble upon what his fathers in learning had sought diligently and with great sacrifice for many years, was unbearable. What interest had these Americans in Africa? None whatsoever! Whereas we Germans have the responsibility of many millions of black souls in our charge.

"That the country of Ehrlich and Wassermann should be compelled to bow the head in deference to an adolescent nation was unthinkable. Luck, that was all! Who was I that I should stand between the Vaterland and such honor? Was I a patriot? I asked myself. And as such I had no choice of action. I trembled with moral rage. I would go to him. I would wrest the secret from him in the name of humanity.

"He had gone to the swamps he had said. But perhaps he had lied to deceive me. I took my most trustworthy man, a

Munyamwezi, devoted to me, and ascended the mountain. I had some difficulty in locating his camp, for it was high up on the snow line, and the natives below, evidently influenced by that man, lied to me. On the third day I discovered it by means of a track through the bamboo forest. Stoutt was not there, but his records and notes were there. What preposterous luck the fellow had, for he seemed more interested in botany than pathology. Dozens of pressed specimens he had but exceedingly few notes. I began to hunt through them, trembling with emotion.

"Suddenly I looked up, and he stood before me. The rapidity of my intellect showed me that he would be stupidly stubborn. Yet the secret was here beneath my eyes. He was smiling, but he said a word that no man of honor could support. I had no choice. I fired.

"Two men with him as well as my *Munyamwezi*, I was reluctantly compelled to kill also. Then carefully gathering together his notebooks I hastened to bury the bodies in a ravine below the glacier. High up on the mountain none of the natives had heard the shots.

"Upon my return I informed them that Stoutt, his men and my own man, had been thrown down a gorge by a mountain demon, knowing that they were convinced of the existence of such chimera. I arrived at my camp without mishap, but deemed it prudent to leave immediately, which I accordingly did, with many expressions of good will between the chief and myself. I took the precaution to send a friendly message to their white god, as they called him.

"In order to follow the shortest route, I ventured across some of the swamps, very carefully protected by veils, infested by the *glossina palpalis*. Not until I reached Muanza did I find it convenient to examine the notebooks of the unfortunate Dr.

Stoutt. I regret to say that although the notes were copious and detailed, I utterly failed to find any clue to the actual formula; yet from the evidence of clinical charts it appeared almost conclusively that he had really discovered the remedy.

"In despair I returned to Europe, intending to study the records more carefully. On the voyage I suffered from an attack of fever which I took to be a form of malaria, but on arrival in Berlin I was surprized to discover symptoms which caused me some uneasiness. A biologist discovered the indubitable trypanosomes in my blood.

"I had contracted the dread disease and destroyed the cure.

"Hamburg treatment failed and I went to the Liverpool School of Tropical Medicine. They froze my spine, which arrested the disease but failed to destroy it. In desperation I determined to try America. Perhaps Dr. Stoutt had somehow communicated his secret to his colleagues before his death. On the voyage I experienced a great change of heart. I saw that I had been misled by my devotion to Science; I felt that indeed God had justly punished me. I bow my head to his Divine Justice."

Then followed a wabbly signature, duly witnessed.

When Birskett looked up from reading, the doctor was smoking in his chair.

"Well?"

"Poisonous kind of reptile!" said Birskett, grimacing.

"Yep," assented the doctor uninterestedly. "But are you going to risk the same medicine?"

"Sure. I said so, didn't I?"

"That's all right then."

"But what's the idea?"

"Endeavour to find the body and bring it home for Christian burial. That's his idea of reparation for past sins—murdering

Stoutt and leaving his wife and child destitute. Assured me that he had never known that Stoutt was so circumstanced, as he put it. Suppose he meant to imply that had he done so he wouldn't have shot him. But I'm out to find that cure. It's Stoutt's anyway. And if we can do that, it'll put the wife and kid on their feet, besides saving hundreds of thousands of lives and tacking a bit of tinsel on Old Glory."

I

The German boat *Marie Augusta*, of the Nord Deutscher Lloyd, which they had caught at Genoa, nosed away from cinder heaps of the Sinai wilderness into the desert of blue and steel of the Red Sea. Every ventilator hopefully turned its blunt ear toward the south. A corn-haired fireman, stripped to the waist, mopping his muscle-creased body with a lump of oily waste, turned bloodshot eyes on the line of passengers sprawling in chairs on the boat deck, in a murderous scowl. Past white shoes, blunt and pointed, scurried white clad stewards bearing trays of iced bouillon.

"Lordy!" commented Birskett, whose long legs nigh blocked the gangway. "These squareheads sure do feed a man. I thought I could eat, heat or no, but seven meals a day gets me beat."

"Nordic races require a greater supply of calories," responded the doctor, "but, in this climate it overheats the motor. Dietetics govern the race. Tell me what he eats and I'll tell you the man."

"What about the Chinese and the Arabs? One lives on a handful of rice once a day and t'other on a grab of dates, but if you can find anybody more overheated in the top story than they are, I'd like to have his address!"

"You know 'em?"

"Sure, I know 'em—and more," Birskett drawled lazily. "Say, doc, where d'you get that feed stuff?"

"Now, Birskett, I've given you straight and honorable warning that if you offend—"

"That if I kid any of your tabus you're liable to go after your guns! Doc, you're a funny guy. Why don't you laugh with your mouth like a he-man instead of your eyes? But say, have a look at this fellow," as the doctor continued his diligent study of Luganda.

Two men in whites passed, one a squat man with a notable paunch, a wispy beard and spectacles, who screamed Herr Professor, and the other, tall and slender, sporting a dark mustache, high cheekbones, and a curious eyes with a slight slit at the edges.

"Looks like a half-bred Chinese or Japanese," said the doctor pleasantly, when they had disappeared. "Who is he?"

"Search me! Seems interested in you though. Overheard him asking the purser which was you."

"You speak German?"

"Enough to get a drink with. Say, how about it? Sun's over the yardarm."

They moved along to the smoking room as, according to some abstruse astronomical calculations of the Herr Admiral of the fleet, drinks could not be served during certain magical hours upon the boat deck. They fortunately found a convenient seat in a corner near an open porthole.

"By the way, Birskett," said the doctor after a long pull at cool lager, "I've never thought to ask you, but what are you anyway?"

"I just hate you asking that, doc. I'm more sensitive about that than a woman of her age. If they knew, presidents would deport me, and kings crucify me. Ssh! I'm a professional adventurer! Scientists pass their lives in asking 'how'? Philosophers in demanding 'why'? I, in saying 'where'? But I say, doc, there's just one thing I'm set on doing before I die."

"Climb Everest or the South Pole?"

"No, sir. I'm going to make you laugh with your mouth."

"There's only one way to do that!" returned Kirkton.

"I know it, boy, and I'm going to do it. Talking about that, did you ever get Stoutt's notes from that pious ghoul?"

"Yep. But he was right as far as any definite formula or even hint of it was concerned. Seemed to me he must have suspected my humanitarian colleague; for he seems to have gone out of his way to omit practical details, and from what I've learned of him since he was a most conscientious worker. And again I think Lörtzer was right that the notes gave internal evidence that Stoutt surely had found the remedy."

Like a Congressman once started on election heroics, Kirkton swept eagerly on.

"A point that occurred to me is this: Apparently this thug murdered Stoutt right up on the snow line and buried him in, on, or beside a glacier, which implies that it's always freezing or near freezing point; and being on the equator the temperature remains the same practically all the year round. So there's more than a chance that the climate may preserve enough of the body to stand a biological examination.

"He said he had purposely contracted trypanosomiasis, and Stoutt wouldn't lie. If so, I may be able to get a clue. You see, just as any other form of organic structure, a microbe has a body. At the period which Lörtzer claimed he murdered him he had just arrived at the conviction that his remedy was right. If so, there should remain some trace of a dead microbe as well as that of the drug which— What the ——"

A violent kick on the shin stopped him.

"Say, guess you've left something behind in the burg, doc."

"What d'you mean?" demanded Kirkton slightly irritated at being interrupted.

"A nurse, boy. See that mirror, opposite. Well, that chink-eyed compatriot of Lörtzer was stretching his ears into a jackal's through that port there."

"But why?"

"Search me! We've got to find out. Now that theory of yours of parthogenesis, doc, 'smost interesting," he continued, and then added in a low voice: "If that son of a celestial don't take that ugly mug out of that porthole, I'll sure turn his nose into a potato. Go on, man, yap about something."

Yellow heat faded into blue heat, star scattered. Perim[2] came up like a rain cloud and dissolved astern. The southwest monsoon struck them, and people sighed and firemen jettisoned homicidal impulses for dreams of bad beer and worse women. Birskett who, as the doctor pointed out, was apt to take instinctive dislikes, tried every device of melodramatic sleuthism to find out whether the mysterious jackal-eared and Mongol-eyed German understood English. From the purser he found out that the man's name was Herr Doktor Hermanus Jacobus Friedlander.

" — — help us," he muttered; "another damned doctor! The woods are full of 'em!"

Then, getting mad at the irreproachable attitude of the suspect, he walked straight up and addressed him in English. A blank stare met him. Birskett apologized and retired baffled.

"You're a nice boy," commented Kirkton when he reported, "but you make me sorrowful thinkin' of home. Sure, I recollect you lived in a bughouse."

"Get fresh if you like," reported Birskett with an unusual display of temper. "But he who yips once yips all the time and don't you forget it."

Out of a curtain of tempered steel rose, like a jewel on a mirror, a vision of white houses and cool palms. Ultramarine

---

[2] Perim: island in Bab el Mandeb Strait at the entrance to the Red Sea.

water changed to cerulean, splashed with whipped cream. The grumble of the anchor suggested an invitation to a dance. The Tower of Babel was illustrated by the tones of those standing about the green valises and gun cases which had grown upon the deck as if in imitation of the tropical vegetation ashore, and those others still lounging in chairs or swilling lager in the smoke room.

Harsh Arabic cries rose from the water like sea birds. As steam began dull roaring like an impatient monster, Birskett strode from the companionway toward Kirkton, who was trying to communicate with the port doctor. Birskett grabbed him by the arm and shouted in his ear:

"Where's that chink of yours?"

"I don't know. Why should I?"

"Some one's gone through our kit. Every damned thing."

"Is there anything lost?"

"Not as far as I can see."

"Well, what about it?" screamed Kirkton irritably. "That doesn't prove that he did it. Why on earth should he? There he is, over there in that chair. Go and ask him!"

"All right, your funeral not mine!" growled Birskett, and went off to superintend the unloading of their baggage, particularly the cases containing the field laboratory.

The next morning they embarked for Kisumu on Lake Victoria Nyanza. On the train were some officials returning from furlough to Nairobi and some half-dozen fellows who were taking up land in the vicinity of Lake Naivasha, a movement at that time in its inception.

There was nothing particularly interesting to Birskett, who knew East Africa; but to Kirkton, who had heavily discounted articles he had read, the panorama of the country rising from tropical palms through the scrub hills on to the long plains of the Masai, covered with incredible quantities of game, even glimpses of the timid giraffe, impala, and small buck stimulated a dormant sporting instinct which almost overcame his feverish haste to reach the scene of his scientific labors.

On the train they passed over the summit of Elgon, nigh seven thousand feet high, demanding blankets for the night, and slid gently down to the lake. The next day the *Sybil*, more like a private yacht than a ferry, gently wafted them over summer seas to Entebbe, a town of small, red bungalows, tin-roofed and garlanded in flowers, squatting on a tiny, wooded peninsula.

On the jetty waited a bunch of rickshaws with their brown runners, garbed in pants and vests of white striped red. Near some white men in helmets and ducks and two women in lawn dresses was a black-bearded white priest, an enormous crucifix upon his white *soutane*. Near him stood a rival claimant for the brown souls of the country, a khaki-clad man wearing puttees and a sad blond mustache, talking to an official. Natives of both sexes in white robes tucked under the armpits, and some in the native dress of reddish-brown bark cloth, squatted and chattered over the excitement of the steamer's arrival; others bore on bare chests white metal crucifixes.

Here serious business began. Birskett sought the collector to arrange for porters, superintended the packing of the numerous packages brought by the doctor—at which he grinned but said no word—into loads and bought trade and other goods necessary for the expedition. Kirkton was furnished with an introduction from his American medical school to Sir William Bull, the head of the British Commission for the Investigation of Sleeping Sickness, who readily placed at his disposal the results of the experiments being undertaken at the local clinic.

"I see," said Sir William, as they walked from his bungalow, "that you propose following in the footsteps of the German Dr. Lörtzer. But why not here? Good Lord, we have enough of the *morsitans* as well as the *palpalis* to share with you Americans!"

"I don't know," said Kirkton diffidently, who had considered it wise not to disclose his true mission. "I met him in New York and there really seemed something in his theory of studying the disease at the source."

"Perhaps. Er—he's dead, isn't he?"

"Yes. Died just before I left."

"Um. Ah. Shouldn't have too much confidence, you know. We rather considered him an awful fraud. He claimed to have proved that the crocodile was not the host. Matter of fact we proved that some six months or more before he left Muanza. Believe the old devil simply heard that from a fellow countryman of yours, Stoutt, who passed through here. Very nice chap. Poor devil either died of fever or got wiped out by pigmies over in the Congo. You must know or have heard of him?"

"Oh yes," returned Kirkton politely. "He was thought much of in the States." Then he added slowly, "We've often wondered whether he might not have discovered something valuable before he died?"

"God knows. He struck me as being an exceptionally capable man. His death either happened in German or Belgian territory, or otherwise we should have made an investigation. Pity. Damned pity. Morning, Blake!"

Sir William nodded to a tall, fair young man, who passed slowly with an obviously depressed air. "That poor chap— another victim! Leaving for Liverpool tomorrow. Careless. Forgot a cut on his finger when he was dissecting a rat. Ah, here we are!"

At the back of a bungalow was arranged a long thatched building containing cages wherein monkeys were confined for observation in all stages of the malady. Some were still bright and perky, eager for nuts as respectable monkeys should be; but some moved restlessly, feverish-eyed and uneasy. One pathetically held his forehead like a caricature of a human on the morning after; others with drawn emaciated faces, squatted in corners, scarcely moving save to scratch lethargically; another fellow, mangy skinned, lay inert, filmed eyes half-open, yet asleep. A room of the bungalow was fitted up as a biological laboratory, where two young men and a middle-aged one were dissecting infected rats and mice.

Sir William, after pointing out items of technical interest, offered to conduct the visitor to the hospital where were five whites—two missionaries, a Government official, a trader and a sportsman in the early stages of the disease. There were also a few chiefs. They would have required a hospital twice as big as the Woolworth Building and a corresponding staff to deal with all the native victims.

"We've done something," said Sir William, "by cutting down some of the grass in the neighborhood of the lake and swamps, the home of the tsetse, but the great difficulty is to segregate the people. As you know, one of the early symptoms is a general restlessness and then they migrate and infect other districts. The mortality is appalling.

"The Sesse Island used to have a population of over a hundred thousand. I doubt if there's three thousand left. And it's spreading fast. The northern shores of the lake are nearly decimated—village after village is a charnel house. It's working up the Nile rapidly and is already down in North Eastern Rhodesia, using the *morsitans* as the host—a discovery, by the way, that your German fellow claimed again!"

He laughed slightly.

"Oh, well, that doesn't matter as long as it was found. The worst of it is that the *morsitans* are even more prevalent over Africa than the *palpalis*. Extend down to the Transvaal. If the disease is allowed to spread right through, the loss to humanity will be incalculable. However, we have hopes."

"If I'm not impertinent, may I know what the latest remedy is you are experimenting with, Sir William?"

"Certainly. Glad to give you all the aid possible. As long as a cure is found, what does it matter who gets the empty honor?"

They went over to the hospital and plunged into technical details. Kirkton lunched with Sir William and returned to the clinic. Towards five they strolled up the street to the club. On the veranda, happily ensconced with a whisky and soda, was Birskett.

"Well, Birskett, how long do you reckon before we can get a move on? I'm just wild to be away since I've seen what I've seen."

"Good for you. Not before four or five days. Collector's damned good sort, but he can't raise men out of the earth. He's sent off right now for porters. They carry as far as Toro on the Congo border. There we fix up for more men as far as the Semliki. But say, doc—" as Sir William was occupied with another man—"get a look at this."

He handed him a copy of the *African World* with his thumb on a paragraph.

> In connection with the award offered by the King of the Belgians for a cure for the dread scourge of Sleeping Sickness, we learn, on the authority of a German scientist now in the United States, that a distinguished American doctor, who is reputed to

have discovered the cure, has unfortunately perished at the hands of the pygmies and the secret with him. To deplore such a tragedy—

"Now, they'll be butting in," commented Birskett. "Wonder what that pious reptile has been saying?"

Kirkton glanced at the date.

"H'm. And that's six months old. Damn it, they may be on the spot by now. You're right. What has that sanctimonious faker been yapping about? I'd give more than something to know."

II

Dr. Fraser Kirkton had begun his first experience of the wilds, much to Birskett's amusement. Hitherto he had been of the status of tourist, traveling *de luxe* by boat and train. Now he had to march in humid heat; walk on a Coney Island switchback, as he grumbled good humoredly, for Uganda, or properly speaking, Buganda—as differentiated from Bunyoro, Busoga, and Buhima, each of which has its separate kinglet—is a jumble of small, conical hills, covered with long, rank grass.

The hills are about a mile in diameter and are separated by swamps of papyrus, across which run native corduroy roads of trunks and payayi stems. His town-bred muscles cried out; he didn't know how to sweat in the right places; but he knew how to swear, which apparently comforted his shrieking tendons.

In the interior there were as yet no tsetse flies, but there was the *mbwa* fly which, rising no higher than the waist, feeds for preference upon the wrist, causing large bumps of surprizing irritation and pain; also with the gentle jigger he made acquaintance, which burrows in between the toes and there lays eggs; and yet again with a small tick which, hiding in the grass, bites and produces a fever known as spirillum, for which there is no cure except time and cusses. And as master, yet fearful for his tyranny before the power of sleeping sickness, stalked malaria and his dread executioner, blackwater. Verily, as Birskett put it, a kingdom of bugs.

At last the everlasting hills changed, and they dived across a limb of dense jungle, abode of elephants and game. The next morning, as they sipped their coffee by the campfire, they saw the snow-clad spurs, carmine tinted, of the Ruwenzori peaks.

"Hanno must have heard of those when he talked of the Mountains of the Moon," commented the doctor, scratching diligently at bandaged wrists.

"Maybe he did and maybe he didn't," returned Birskett prosaically. "But I don't know whether you've noticed that all the prophets must surely have missed something when they were looking for plagues of the Lord!"

"But this doesn't go on all the time, does it?"

"No, sir. We change for a new set just beyond!"

"Gosh!" mumbled the doctor. "I'm beginning to have some respect even for that pious thug if he stuck through all you promise, Birskett."

"A hundred thousand dollars and sortie will do a lot as sticking plaster, doc. There she goes," he added, as with the rising sun a cloud settled on a mountain peak like a white-haired woman putting on her nightcap before retiring. Guess we won't see her again until we're kind of sitting in her lap. Haya! Haya!" he bawled to the seething mass of porters. "Get a move on, damn you!"

After the brief strip of forest the country broke into volcanic foothills set in the midst of which was Toro, a moated and palisaded fort almost under the shadow of the bamboo-clad slopes of the foothills of the Gamballagalla, as the natives call the mountains.

In addition to two Wunyamwezi they had engaged at Entebbe as personal servants, Birskett managed to secure two Sudanese ex-soldiers as guards and gun bearers. The Waganda porters had to be paid off and Wanyoro engaged, although they would only be required as far as the Semliki, two days distant, where they proposed to take canoes; nothing, presumably, except the defeat of the British Empire by land and sea, could alter these regulations, and that was all there was to it,

Official red tape and native obstinacy devoured ten days. Each porter had to be registered. But first of all he had to be caught, and as the country beyond a few miles was practically *terra incognita*, besides being reputed Belgian territory, reputed because the border had not then been settled by a boundary commission, he demanded an exorbitant price.

However, Birskett's winning ways and the soothing of the itchy palms of the *katikiro* (prime minister) and the tall ebony man who sported a khaki coat, called Kabaka Kasagama, which, being interpreted means King Kasagama, finally secured the necessary number of men. So they started at last, Kirkton's American sense of doing business fluttering round the boiling point.

"Say, doc," remarked Birskett as they padded past the conical formations of extinct craters an hour after sunrise next day, "you'd best quit that crab walk."

"Crabs!" snorted Kirkton, dragging his head away from the fascinating view of the mountains rising from the foothills to the clouds. "I want to get there, man, and not waste time sneaking round the damned universe."

"You'll get there all right!" retorted Birskett with a touch of irritation. "I guarantee that, even if it's your damn corpse. But see here, doc, if you don't smile once in a while I'll sure go bughouse myself. Damn you, a fellow always looks at a man's mouth to register a grin, not at his eyes! Look ahead man, and watch your step!"

The doctor did and stopped in his tracks. Immediately in front of him dropped an escarpment fully two thousand feet deep. Away to the northwest, under a faint haze, was the gleam of silver, Lake Albert; in front loomed vaguely the humps of the Congo hills, cleaved with dark masses; to the southwest meandered a thread of platinum through a field of corn at the bottom of what suggested the rut of a chariot wheel of the gods, tremendously banked on the south by dark masses of bamboo, shooting into crags mist covered. Over the edge dropped the safari like a wet rope into a well.

Kirkton, creasing his brows, sat stiffly but deliberately on a rock and lighted a cigaret. Without a word Birskett did likewise, except in the manner.

"I'd like to build a house here," said the doctor soberly.

"Fine!" agreed Birskett.

Then when they had finished they continued on their way. As they toiled along a path on a plain of grass and scattered euphorbia and palms, the doctor suddenly remarked loudly:

"Ow! What the deuce—" and clapped a hand to his sweat blackened shirt.

"Somebody stuck a needle into you?" inquired Birskett.

"That's what it felt like," Kirkton admitted, rubbing the spot. "What was it?"

"The patient you've come to diagnose," retorted Birskett with an unpleasant suggestion of humor.

"What? Tsetse?"

"Sure! I can't tell you whether he's the *morsitans* family or the *palpalis*. But cheer up, he only gets a bull's-eye once in four shots, according to local calculation."

"But," said Kirkton, with a note of consternation, "they can bite through a thick shirt?"

"You bet they can. I've been bitten right through a canvas hammock and a thick shirt, over there in Busoga. Wasn't sure for years afterwards whether I was due to grab a harp or no. Every damned time I get kind of sleepy I'd think to myself: 'Wow! There she goes!' "

"Then what's the good of veils?"

"Damned little," retorted Birskett, "as far as I know, and as friend Lörtzer must have found out. Except that they make you feel good."

That night they camped by the Semliki River, where it was about sixty yards wide and looking like a gouge mark through a cheese. By the morning the doctor's scientific interest had returned, and he dug out a special kind of bug-hunter's net to start in search of his first specimen. As he was leaving the tent, gloved, and veiled from helmet to chest, he saw Birskett sitting near the small village, superintending the payment of the porters.

"Why aren't you veiled?" demanded the doctor sternly.

"Oh, — —, doc! What did I tell you yesterday?"

"Never mind your layman's theories. Get your veil on!"

"Sure," agreed Birskett soothingly. "I'll get right along; but say, doc, this is where we strike Old Man Trouble," he added cheerfully.

"Why what's wrong now?"

"Go along and peek inside," said Birskett, jerking his thumb at the village.

Wondering, Kirkton entered. At first he saw what seemed merely an ordinary native village of a poor type, a collection of small thatched huts with one bigger than the others. No smoke drifted through the thatched roofs, all of which were ragged and in bad repair. Then his eyes seemed to grow harder and more magpie like.

He had seen a child lying on some matting in the shade of a hut. Instead of the usual potbelly of a healthy native infant, the stomach nigh touched the backbone and the ribs could be counted. Limbs were bones clothed in wrinkled skin. The eyes were a mass of flies, yet the boy was slightly alive, for he moved restlessly. But it was nevertheless a "case" to a man of medicine, and Kirkton examined him gently and with interest.

A sound from within drew his attention. A woman, evidently the mother, dragged her weary body through the low hole which served as a door. She was an adult replica of the child.

In another hut he found two men not so far gone. One was squatting and the other lying beside the cold firepit. As the white man stood waiting for his eyes to focus to the dark, neither moved, but the sitting one mumbled a salutation. Their bodies were not so much wasted as the woman's. The eyes of the man who had spoken seemed glazed. He immediately seemed to lose interest in knowing that a stranger and a white was there. As the doctor looked at the prostrate man he noticed that there was some raw banana—and a native always cooks his food—clutched in one hand, and between the lips was the piece he had bitten off; he had gone to sleep in the act of eating.

Unable to speak the language and failing to get any reaction from either of them, the doctor went out. He stopped curiously at another hut and peeped in. A stench of putrefaction stung his nostrils. Birskett came striding towards him.

"Pretty, ain't it?" he asked grimly. "Say, you can see there isn't a man here capable of swinging a paddle. Those that were left fit when they understood what was on, beat it—to infect another district and die just the same. I've a fellow out there. He's not so badly hit yet, but too damned tired to run away. He told me all this. You might give him a shot to wake him up, and maybe we'll get more out of him. I've quit paying these boys, for we may need 'em to take us back. Don't you think that's good medicine?"

"H'm, h'm," mumbled the doctor, absently gazing at the wreck of the woman and child, quite oblivious that his veil was hanging around the back of his neck. "Got to get that cure, by

——! Suppose it's no use wasting time trying to relieve these poor wretches? They're doomed anyway and don't suppose they feel much. That's one consolation to 'em. H'm. What did you say, Birskett?"

Birskett repeated what he had said, adding:

"What put it into your head to get set on coming around this way instead of following up Stoutt's and Lörtzer's trail?"

"Because that's through German territory," returned Kirkton. "Now they know that Stoutt did find a cure they'd block our path at every step, man. Don't you know enough to know that they're not going to let both the honor and the money be grabbed by another nation? The English may be half-paralyzed by red tape, but anyway they play the sporting game."

"Oh, all right, doc, don't get hot in the collar! You're the big chief, and I'll do my side all I know. You amuse yourself with this dime museum, and I'll go make a palaver."

The doctor, his professional interest now thoroughly aroused, hurried back to the tent for instruments and returned to his cases, who made not the slightest objection whatever he was disposed to do to them.

The midday heat in the Semliki Valley, in reality a vast crack in the earth's crust running from Lake Albert Edward to Albert, with the Ruwenzori Mountains and the Buganda Plateau at four thousand feet on the one side, and the Congo hills on the other, was intense; the nerve-sapping heat where the air is stagnant and denuded of oxygen, seeming to shrivel the lungs and stew the flesh. Before the haze of noon arose, the faint blue streaks of the peninsulas of the Ituri forests, the home of the pigmy, were discernible up the river.

The plain, stretching some seven or eight miles on each side of the river, was as flat as a floor, dotted with Phoenix palms and euphorbia. To the north, only visible from the top of either escarpment, some twenty miles away the River Semliki petered out into vast swamps as it came to Lake Albert, swamps which afforded a nursery for the tsetse fly.

Sweating and slightly temper cracked, as he was not yet acclimated, the doctor returned from his labors to the tent to wash his hands in disinfectant and safely put away blood specimens he had drawn from various of the afflicted natives. Birskett, who was still holding an interminable *shauri* with the porters near the village, he did not notice in his absorption of details of his beloved cases. Presently the latter came over and sank, mopping his face, into a camp chair.

"Nothing doing, doc," he reported with his usual irritating cheerfulness—or so Kirkton found it at first.

"What d'you mean, 'nothing doing'?" he snapped.

"The *munyampala* (head man) of the porters can be bribed, but his men won't listen to anything. They say they were forced to come, which is more than probably true, by the *kutikiro*, who also probably gets half the dough or more. They swear that wild elephants or a tusk apiece won't keep 'em in this valley overnight, much less make 'em go down the river which, the *Mwami* adds on his own, is certainly haunted by demons as well as flies."

"——!" swore the doctor. "And at the very beginning too! What are we to do?"

"Make a camp here I guess, and leave some of our own men, if the sons of guns will stop alone with the tsetse, and trot over to the Congo side and see if we can scare up some men there. But then probably they won't be paddlers. But we could work down trail as far as the Congo forest, which they surely won't enter for fear of the pigmies. Maybe we'll strike another river village before then. That's the best I can think up for the moment."

"Aren't there any canoes here?"

"Saw one or two. But for the gear we want at least two very large ones, and who's going to work 'em?"

"Can't we float down with the stream until we find another village as you suggest?"

"Don't float the right way, doc. She flows into Albert on the way to the Nile." He eyed the sluggish stream. "She don't look very fast, that's true. They're off, damn their moldy souls!"

He pointed to the line of porters stringing out on the back trail. The doctor was moodily chewing a cigar in his vexation.

"D'you think that our men will stick it through?" he demanded. "If they go back on us we'll be up against it."

"Yep. I'm pretty sure of 'em. Our two Sudanese anyway. They've been trained and have transferred some of their superstitions from demons to the whites. Emin Pasha found 'em the most trustworthy of any of 'em. And I think Matana and Kubi are all right. They're Wunyamwezi, and I took care that they were not Christians. Hullo, what's hit the porters?"

He referred to the line of departing porters, who had suddenly halted in a bunch. He snatched up a pair of glasses.

"Now what's up?" he added. "There's an askari among 'em, and now they're all coming back."

"Perhaps it's a message from Toro," suggested the doctor. "Mail or something sent on—although the what-d'you-call-him didn't look as if he'd be so obliging as that."

They sat and watched them until a tall Muganda in the Government uniform came up. He saluted smartly and handed them a letter addressed to the doctor.

"Government seal! What's this?" he muttered as he tore open the envelope. A swift reading creased his brows and was followed by a sharp oath.

"Of all the nerve! Read that!" he snapped angrily.

The letter was official and addressed from the chief magistrate's office at Entebbe.

> Sir:
> On the representation of the German vice-consul, who is instructed to prefer a serious charge against you, I am compelled to request your immediate return to Entebbe.
> I have the honor to be, Sir,
> Your obedient servant,
> JAMES FIRTH.

"Now do you appreciate why I didn't try the German route?"

"But this is bosh!" scornfully ejaculated Birskett. "What charge, for Heaven's sake? Tell 'em to go to Hell!"

"Sure," assented Kirkton more quietly. "But don't you see the game? Any excuse to hold us up. I suppose the British can't help themselves in making the request. Anyway, by — —, one soldier can't take us back, and by the time they try any other tricks, we'll be out of their territory. Yes, sir! But what I can't figure out is, where did they get the stuff?"

"That jackal-eared chink on board," said Birskett, and for once the doctor made no objection. "He must have got enough—merely caught the name of Stoutt—and guessed the rest."

"But what's set them after it?"

"Perhaps that pious thug talked more'n you thought he did. God knows, and we're not likely to hear."

III

Kirkton was for writing a formal refusal and despatching the messenger forthwith. But Birskett strenuously opposed the suggestion.

"Don't reply at all, doc, and keep the fellow as long as possible. That will give us longer to get out of this hole. No; send a letter and address it to this guy in Entebbe and merely enclose your card, with your compliments. For one thing that'll get him puzzled, and secondly it will take this askari straight through to Entebbe; but if you send nothing at all, that solemn guy at Toro may have a brainstorm and act by sending a bunch of the K.A.R.[3] to persuade us to go back."

The Government messenger they ordered to wait and began to discuss the situation. Suddenly Birskett laughed.

"What, may I ask, d'you find so humorous about this?" snapped the doctor. "You don't seem to realize what is at stake."

"Sure I do, doc," returned Birskett, controlling his inopportune mirth. "To tell the truth, I was thinking of a story I read—yep, right in Uganda in the *East African Standard*. The editor put a proposition to those writing guys: Suppose a fellow had his gun broken and was chased by a lion up a tree, and while the damned lion waited for him at the bottom he discovered a boa constrictor coming down the trunk from the upper branches! Then, what in — — would he do next?"

"I suppose," said the doctor, with graven lips, "that he married the lady and lived happily ever afterwards."

Birskett stared at him for a second and then laughed again.

---

[3] [Author's note: "King's African Rifles, stationed at every fort."]

"Damn you, doc, I never can remember to look at your eyes! But talking allegory, I'm going to hypnotize the boa constrictor or do a Daniel stunt with the lion, but I'm — — if I'm going to Hades as you suggest! See here, doc, if we stop mussing about, scaring up porters up there on the Congo hills, the British lion's liable to grab us, and if we go back the German constrictor'll sure constrict all he knows. We'll shove a river into that tableau and make the hero jump in and swim on a crocodile's back — meaning canoes. Get me?"

"But you said that we couldn't without paddlers?"

"Sure, but since then I've got all het up, as they say. We'll just have to abandon everything not absolutely necessary — and there's lots of your stuff ain't — and teach these men of ours to paddle against time. When in doubt, take a chance. We may strike a village within a few miles."

"But what if it's wiped out as is this one?"

"Never can tell. But mor'n likely it won't be. That Mister *Morsitans* or *Palpalis* who bit you yesterday comes up from the Albert Swamps, so there ain't many of 'em around here. Now let's push this fellow off with the envelop and the card right now so's they can get to the escarpment by night. That'll give us a good few days anyway to lose our trail. Then after *chakula* I'll go and hunt up what canoes there are. As soon as they've gone with the porters — I'll not forget that — we'll break the sad news to Matana and the others."

The askari made no demur, having doubtless never received other instructions than to deliver the *barua* (letter), the magistrate probably reckoning that they would receive it at Toro; and anyhow that they would not dare do otherwise than obey the summons.

After *chakula* of canned salmon in vinegar, canned *pâté de foie gras* and biscuits, which the doctor fondly believed to be the usual fare of the tropical explorer, Birskett went down to investigate. The first thing he paid serious attention to was the river. A slight survey showed him that they had a stroke of luck in their favor in that the river seemed unusually low. At first he was puzzled; but a little reflection showed him that in all probability the wet season on the southern side of these mountains might easily be earlier or later than that on the plateau of Uganda and East Africa. Whatever the cause the fact remained, which meant of course that the current would offer less resistance to inexperienced paddlers.

He found seven dugouts, two of which were split, having been left high on the bank in the sun. None of them was very big. After surveying them he overhauled the contents of the loads. He returned to the tent where the doctor sat smoking, dividing his mind between the silly physical obstructions, as he considered them, and speculation on pathological problems. Birskett ordered coffee and settled down to wait patiently until the porters had gone, which he knew would not be until about two, giving them just enough time to reach the escarpment by nightfall.

"Phe-ew!" groaned the doctor. "New York in July's a piker to this heat. If I had to live here I think I'd prefer trypanosomiasis! Not even a fan!"

"All in the cause of science!" Birskett reminded him solemnly.

"Of course, of course!" assented Kirkton a bit hurriedly. "I'm not grumbling."

"Of course not, of course not!" mocked Birskett. "Not yet!"

"What d'you mean?" queried the doctor, sharply. "It's going to be worse?"

"Some! Forest, doc. Never mind, the pigmies like it."

"Pigmies!" snorted Kirkton. "I'm not a pigmy. What use are they anyway?"

"I dunno." Birskett's incurious eyes stared speculatively at the Ruwenzori high in the mist. "Guess the Guy Who made all that didn't see much difference between pigmies and other folk."

The doctor's eyes brightened as if a film had been torn from them, and he peered at Birskett.

"Thought you had more of a sense of proportion," he said coldly. "I'm here to find out something for the benefit of humanity."

"That's what the pigmy witch doctor says when he pokes his nails into your guts!"

Birskett rose, and added:

"Well, now those guys have cleared out I'm going to fix things. Say, doc, I guess we'll be shifting tomorrow morning."

He strode off with a wicked grin on his face.

"Doc's a great man," he mused, "but the Lord sure ran short of springs when he made his face."

He called up Matana and Kubi and the two Sudanese, and made them haul out all the loads. Then, still with his malicious smile, he deliberately began to sort them; various packages containing anti-mosquito soaps and lotions, portable camp lamps and electric torches, together with the heavy refill of batteries, two sporting rifles fixed with telescopic sights and their ammunition, Alpine boots and stocks—

"Lordy," he muttered, "does he think he'll find Mister *Palpalis* tobogganing in the tropical Alps!" Various other articles he callously condemned to be placed in an abandoned hut of the village. His own tent, when struck, he gave secret instructions to be left also.

The only cases he didn't touch were those containing the field laboratory. The others he reduced to very little food, the trade goods and an express rifle apiece. Two of the sound dugouts they had found were ample to contain all the loads left.

When he returned he found the doctor, regardless of *morsitans* or *paipalis*, sitting with his shirt half-off, and, above a dirty scrub of a beard, an eye stuck to a microscope. But Birskett said no word of the massacre to him.

Before dawn Birskett was up and kicking the camp into life. While the whites drank coffee and ate some of the few biscuits the remorseless Birskett had left, the boys struck camp. Afterwards the doctor was shown the two canoes. He had on his veil, but had forgotten his gloves.

"You take that one," instructed Birskett, "with Matana and Zapoko. I'll take the other with Kubi and Abdul."

"Say, Birskett," said the doctor, peering around, "have you got all the baggage in these two canoes?"

"Sure!" lied Birskett. "I'm the seventh wonder of the world in packing! Come along, get aboard, man!"

"Ouch!" murmured Kirkton as he crouched down in the dugout.

"Forget it, doc," said Birskett. "You'll be an athlete when you've finished. Exercise the legs and then the arms! *Mukwate mugolomoli eryato mwena—a!*" (All aboard! And shove off, you!) he yelled.

Like amateurs rowing a skiff around an artificial lake they began, but they all were game to try. The cranky canoes, as sensitive as an automobile to the wheel at high speed, careered and swerved as if bent on charging the bank. The Sudanese and the Wunyamwezi laughed uproariously at their own mistakes; for the African is fundamentally a happy race. Apt at mimicking they quickly picked up the idea from the taller white man, whom they had named, "He-who-laughs!"

Wabbly, but still going, they made their way close into the bank to avoid what current there was, with Birskett's canoe in the lead.

The banks were not high except from the point of view of canoe men—six to ten feet perhaps, enough to give the impression of traveling in a sewer. But they crawled along, diligently following the windings of the eastern side.

Kirkton at first was inclined to set a terrific pace; but a combination of Birskett's advice, the rising sun and his own muscles, cooled his ardor. At noon the river, with the refraction from the water, seemed like the interior of a frying pan of sizzling fat. They halted awhile on a sandbank, from which three crocodiles obligingly but lazily made room. Both whites' clothes were black with sweat from head to foot. Birskett climbed the bank.

"There's a herd of buffalo about a quarter of a mile away, doc," he reported, "and some *pookoo*. Feel like fresh meat?"

"I don't think I do," said Kirkton, meditatively gazing at the dark of the Ruwenzori.

The afternoon was a continuation of the forenoon. They camped for the night on another sandbank. When there appeared but one tent, the doctor did not even inquire where Birskett's had disappeared. He was really suffering in the morning, The next day was the worst. But Kirkton, although he had grown unusually quiet, said nothing save for the eloquent expression of his tortured brow, and Birskett, knowing and watching, persuaded him to rest frequently.

Their progress was slow, but they made time against the sluggish current. That day they painfully crept by a washout in the bank which had formed a swamp, the extent of which they could not judge. They did not see or feel any tsetse flies, but beyond they came upon a small village with some abandoned canoes, containing nothing save skeletons long since picked by vultures and jackals.

So for three more days they plugged on with diminishing speed, the blue of the Congo forest growing denser. They had reckoned roughly, according to the map, which was very hazy in details, that the southwestern spur of the mountains, where Stoutt had camped, might be eighty or a hundred miles due south as measured by compasses, but whether that was doubled or even trebled by the windings of the river and the possible detours to be made, they had no means of estimating.

The Semliki at that time had never been mapped or even ascended to its source in Lake Albert Edward. Two explorers had reported that they had been held up by the difficulties of the route and the hostility of the pigmies and the natives generally; and Stoutt was not the first man who had officially been "missing" in that district. Shortly before he had come to the country, the report of which may have decided him to take the German route, a famous English explorer, Stratton, and an American, Varden, had disappeared. Also, by reason of the decimation caused by the sleeping sickness, Birskett and Kirkton had no chance of securing a guide from one of the river people who at least might know the river as far as the land of the pigmies.

Birskett realized all this thoroughly, but he said no word to Kirkton, who seemed sublimely indifferent and appeared to imagine that all one had to do was to paddle on for a space, get out, take the turning on the left and the first on the right and be there!

Birskett noticed as they progressed that the country was changing as well as the formation of the river, the former becoming more humped and with greater belts of vegetation, and the latter narrowing with outcrops of sandstone showing among the silt of the banks.

They had just crossed at a sharp bend from one side to the other to avoid the current and had entered a deeper pool than usual, when Birskett spotted a turmoil of water ahead and shouted to the doctor to hug the bank. Clamorous yells answered him. Even as he watched, the bow of the doctor's canoe was thrust up on the snout of a hippopotamus.

Zapoko and Matana immediately flung themselves overboard and swam for the bank, but the doctor, dropping his paddle, seemed helpless in the canoe. The canoe fell back with a splash without overturning.

"*Wunjula eryate! Goba mu mwalo awo!*" (Turn the canoe round and make for the bank!) yelled Birskett at his men. "*Leka! Leka!*" (Stop!)

As he scrambled up the bank, rifle in hand, he saw the beast break water again and charge. Then the doctor, half-lying on his back where he had been thrown, fired straight into the cavernous mouth some three yards distant.

"Jump, man, jump!" howled Birskett, expecting the wounded animal to crush the canoe to slivers with his tusks. But as suddenly as a released stone sinks the brute disappeared in a swirl. The doctor, jerking his lever, rammed in another cartridge and waited while the rocking canoe began to drift out into the current.

"Jump, doc, for God's sake!" Birskett bawled again.

A terrific swirl of water, some twenty yards downstream preceded the huge mouth, followed by half the vast body. Two rifles cracked simultaneously as the bulk crashed back, sending up waves of water.

"Get your paddle then, you damned idiot!" yelled Birskett, now afraid that the canoe would drift on top of the stricken beast.

Then the doctor pulled his jangling nerves together and cautiously paddled into the bank.

"Why the devil didn't you jump?" demanded Birskett. "You can swim and the bank wasn't three yards away. It would have crushed you to pulp!"

"But," objected the doctor, squatting in the canoe, "there's all my field laboratory in this canoe. Why," he added aggrievedly, "did he attack me?"

Birskett laughed.

"Guess he didn't choose you specially, doc! But as a matter of fact they seldom do charge unless— Sure, there's the reason!" and he pointed downstream to where the comparatively small, piggish head of a calf broke water. "Mama was cross, that's all. Come on, all aboard! And don't forget to hug the bank, doc."

They resumed their interrupted labors amid the excited chatter of the Sudanese and Wunyamwezi whose observation of physical peculiarities and admiration of coolness was revealed in the name they bestowed upon the doctor, "One-whose-mouth-is-of-rock."

"Say, doc," yelled back Birskett, "I think I have spotted a village from the bank. If it isn't wiped out like the others we may scare up some men."

Two hours later, seeing no signs, he sent Kubi on to the bank to reconnoiter. Kubi cried back that there was a large village.

"*Wala?*" (Far away?) inquired Birskett, conscious of the sun low over the Congo hills.

"*Neda, mwami, wampi nyo.*" (No, chief, quite near.)

Twenty minutes later they saw the village close into the washout of the bank. The absence of canoes was ominous. No smoke nor signs of life were there. Kubi scrambled up on the bank, but he soon returned at the run, shouting:

"Afudo bufi! Mongota-a!" (They're all dead! Sleeping sickness!)

The doctor, who understood the word *"mongota,"* wanted to disembark to investigate, but as the sun was so low, Birskett wished to get on to another place to camp to avoid the pestilential stink which hung about all these small towns of the dead.

"The whole country seems to be annihilated," said the doctor as they got under way again.

"The north shore of the Victoria Nyanza in Busoga is just the same, only that for one here there are or were fifty villages there. I guess it's creeping up from the swamps of Lake Albert and probably also from the other side from Albert Edward."[4]

---

[4] "In the five years between the close of 1900 and the end of 1905, sleeping sickness killed over a quarter of a million Africans in the British Protectorate of Uganda. This tragedy sparked off one of the most dramatic chapters in the history of medicine.... Southern Busoga was soon considered the chief focus of the disease, and by the spring of 1902, local African chiefs reported that nearly 14,000 people had died." "From Busoga the disease spread rapidly east and west, and by the end of 1903 there were over 90,000 deaths. By November 1904, it was epidemic as far west as the shores of Lake Albert, which bordered the Congo Free State. Official calculations of mortality rates varied, but [David] Bruce, a reliable witness, claimed that in Busoga, with a population of 300,000, as many as 200,000 had died! In 1905, one member of the Royal Society's commission estimated that in the past three years sleeping sickness had caused an annual mortality of 100,000 in Uganda. Another reliable source, Brian Langlands, later asserted that in Uganda between 1900 and 1920, deaths from the disease numbered between 250,000 and 300,000. All the colonial powers in Africa took note of events in Uganda. We will never know the total mortality for certain, but it is obvious why administrators of all African territories were alarmed." Maryinez Lyons, *The Colonial Disease: A Social History of Sleeping Sickness*

"But how is it that we don't see any tsetse flies?"

"Maybe they only come—luckily for us, doc—after the rains when this valley is pretty well flooded."

About a mile above the village the river began to narrow quickly, naturally making the opposing current stronger and reducing their speed to a mere crawl as they painfully dodged from bank to bank. The trees also were growing more forest-like, many of them overhanging the banks. There were no more sand banks.

"Guess we'd better camp, doc," said Birskett, and chose a spot to land on the Congo side.

Birskett, who was first up the steep bank, suddenly dropped on his knees, yelling:

"Down! Down, doc! *Mukotekote! Ogirete bunduki! Mangu! Mangu!*" (Crouch down and get out your rifles! Quick!)

The words were followed by three tiny arrows which nicked into the water, and by the crash of Birskett's express.

The men and the doctor slithered up the bank on all fours.

"Pigmies!" said Birskett in answer to the doctor. "They're in that large tree in the jungle there. Look out!" as another flight of arrows sped just over their heads. "Give 'em a volley!"

In reply to the roar of their guns came a wild, harsh yell and a scuttling in the branches and bushes.

"I guess they've quit," said Birskett, after listening intently, "but we'd best camp on the other side. "No, no! Don't go along peeking now. Maybe they're still hiding in the bush, and those arrows are poisoned, remember!"

---

in Northern Zaire, 1900-1940 (Cambridge, UK: Cambridge University Press, 2002), pp. 70-71.

IV

"Dandy little outfit, ain't it, doc?" said Birskett, when they had landed, holding up a slip of an arrow about a foot long, having leaves instead of the usual feathers. "Watch out for the tip. Just a scratch and you're finished," he added, as the doctor began to examine the weapon curiously.

"What poison is it?"

"Dunno. Some say they have a knack of emptying the glands of a snake, Indian fashion, by kidding him to sting a piece of meat; others say it's vegetable. But the effect's damned swift, believe me!"

"Ever seen a death?"

There was that cold prying light in the gray eyes again.

"No. But we're likely to if we're not mighty careful."

"I should like to see one and analyze the blood," responded Kirkton gravely. "Extremely interesting. Many of these Indians—I mean savages of any continent—employ most valuable specifics did we only know them. Quinin, for example, which the Jesuits learned of from the Indians. M'm."

The place they had chosen on the Ruwenzori side had the advantage of being open for some sixty yards or more about them, affording no cover for an attack. However, Birskett took the precaution to put the Sudanese into watches, taking one, the last and most dangerous, himself. They had just pitched camp on the edge of the bank as the sun dived like a bloody godhead foremost into the ocean of green forest.

By the light of the lantern the doctor was busy packing various instruments and cases in waterproof satchels and in reply to Birskett's flippant question, gravely responded that he wasn't taking any more chances for his invaluable gear from hippos.

Zapoko awoke Birskett. He took up his watch in a chair alongside the tent. The night was sticky. The peaks of the Gamballagalla to the east were vaguely discernible against the stars which, although brilliant, seemed hot. Listening intently, he distinguished beneath the seethe of the forest a continuous plaint like the distant murmur of violins.

"There's a cataract not far off," he said to himself.

Now and again came a harsh squawk telling of a parrot surprized by a snake or other enemy. The shrill, irritable yelp of jackals floated from afar. He noted the direction. "End of the plains, beginning of the forest, and trouble if I'm not mistaken."

Presently started a commotion across the river, although it sounded close by. Shrill squawks, cries like a baby in pain, and angry chattering, a tale of forest victory and defeat. Birskett listened as if inhaling. "Gosh! Can't that guy swear!" he thought admiringly.

One star, looking as if it were falling down the slope of a sepia peak, went out. Followed others, one by one, as if a celestial lamplighter were putting out the lamps of a street. A warm glow was hinted and then like a prairie fire the mountain tops were alight. Birskett suddenly jumped and shook the shoulder of the sleeping doctor, who quietly rose up.

"Well?"

"Look at that, man!" exclaimed Birskett, pointing to the east.

Kirkton looked.

"Dawn," he said as a statement. "Are the men up?"

"Oh, Lordy!" exclaimed Birskett and laughed, tugging at his half-grown beard. "Sure," he added and retired to his chair, wondering.

During their breakfast of coffee and the few remaining biscuits the doctor wanted to go across and investigate the pigmies, but Birskett wouldn't consent, guaranteeing all the pigmies the doctor might require before long and then some.

"But what's the hurry?" demanded Kirkton.

"A whole damned heap! These fellows will be bringing up all their brothers and cousins. Take a tip, doc. In this country, if trouble comes along, fine! Go to it! But don't *ask* for it! You'll get a belly full before you're through, believe me!"

Before consenting to leave, the doctor solemnly propped a shaving mirror carried by his boy Matana in a satchel and shaved, using a special cream not requiring water.

By the time they got under way, the Ruwenzori peaks were shrouded in mist. The river continued to grow narrower; the slit of the Semliki Valley gave place to granite and sandstone. The going was hard and slow. The forest crowded upon them on both sides, and suddenly the river left the rocky formation and split into half a dozen channels between islands massed with palms and thick growth.

Birskett in the lead chose a passage at random—one was as likely as another for all any of them knew. The channel grew narrower until the branches of the great trees almost interlaced overhead, shutting out the sun, until they were continuously traveling in shadow. Kubi suddenly began shouting his fears of the pigmies to Matana in the rear canoe.

"*Lekerao!*" (Shut up!) commanded Birskett and threatened to throw him to the crocodiles.

The boy whimpered to the Sudanese, but Abdul promptly cursed him into silence. The only advantage here was that the current, being diverted into many channels, naturally lost power so that they made better speed. In the boughs about them their passage excited troops of monkeys, funny little fellows with wispy beards, who followed, traveling like trapeze artists from bough to bough and swearing terribly. Birskett joined in the cusses, for he knew that the commotion would give a certain message to any lurking pigmies.

The forest grew denser and the passage narrower, suggesting that it might develop into a swamp. However, Birskett pressed on, hoping for the best. He was still sure he had heard the sound of rapids in the night and was puzzled to account for their absence. The only feasible explanation was that it had resulted from some stream rushing down from the snows.

Roots, stretching like water pythons across the muddy stream, began to worry them, and the stench of rotting vegetation in the intense heat was almost overpowering.

"Owa! Zawata!" (Oh, the tsetse fly!) exclaimed Kubi, smashing blindly with his paddle.

A gray fly, about the size of a horsefly, swirled away from Birskett, who shouted a warning to Kirkton. The next moment, in the excitement caused by the dreaded insect, he ran aground on a snag.

"Is this the Ituri forest?" inquired the doctor as his canoe overtook him, much as if a stranger standing in Broadway were saying brightly, "Is this the Woolworth building?"

"Bet your life it is!" responded Birskett grimly. "And it don't look promising, believe me."

"But where's that tsetse fly you were talking about?"

"In — —, I hope," responded Birskett a bit roughly. "But anyway he probably isn't dangerous, as this district doesn't seem populated and therefore infected. But, see here, bring your canoe alongside and take Kubi and Abdul so's we can shove her off."

He instructed Matana and Zapoko what to do, but no sooner were they afloat and trying to pass, than they jammed again.

"This damned snag runs right across the river, I guess," said Birskett. "Say, we'd better land and have a look ahead. I'm scared of this channel petering out."

They backed off and made for the bank, or rather the octopus-like roots of a great tree. Birskett landed, and the doctor and Kubi scrambled after him. They struggled from root to root for some thirty yards until they struck firmer ground. The undergrowth was so dense that although they could force a passage they could not see farther than a yard or so.

Fighting on, they came suddenly upon a short glade or opening, into which the rays of the midday sun penetrated. As they stood peering they noticed simultaneously a splash of bright color upon the moss covered bough of a great tree a few paces from them.

"Curious kind of fungus," remarked the doctor, picking one which was a deep purple with slight stripes of vermilion. "The shape reminds me of Indians' pipes, except for the color. Don't know much about botany, but I'm sure it's unclassified. I wonder if Stoutt found any. Look, that's curious. Many of the stems have been broken—as if some one had been picking them."

Both were examining the strange growth when Kubi, still within the jungle behind them, gave a low cry of warning and pointed. Following his outstretched finger Birskett saw in the gloom of the opposite side of the tiny glade what at first seemed a gigantic human figure sitting against the bole of a tree. As it stood up, another but smaller rose and fled up into the branches like a shadow. The doctor was bringing his rifle up.

"No! no! For God's sake!" whispered Birskett. "Not until four yards!" and he stepped out in front of him.

The strange beast advanced on its hind legs with a waddle like a deep-sea sailor. Then stopping, it raised its snoutlike head. A sound resembling distant thunder reverberated through the dank forest. Raising its hands it beat upon its breast like a great drum.

"Good God, it's a gorilla!" he heard Kirkton saying.

"Keep quiet and don't make him rush," whispered Birskett.

The brute, with a horrible resemblance to an ugly drunk, lurched on again. Then it stopped and roared its challenge once more.

Through the spattered sun rays flickered several shadows which struck the great hairy chest—pigmy arrows! The small eyes under the craggy brows, glittered with insane rage and the enormous canines gleamed. Deliberately, as if convinced of resistless power, the ape came on slowly but stopped again. Then the white man saw that they were not the gorilla's objective. But as a mighty bellow thundered out Birskett fired.

The sound was choked in its throat; the beast swayed for a moment, and then pitched sideways. As Birskett stood waiting to see whether the gorilla was quite dead there came a subdued chattering and the rustle of branches.

"Pigmies!" whispered Birskett. "Look out!"

But no arrow came. At first he could not detect any sign of pigmies. Then a cry from a great tree not five yards from the dead gorilla attracted them. Birskett advanced cautiously.

From a tangle of roots and vines he made out a small chocolate face with a smudge of gray on the chin. At first he thought it was a monkey, but as the figure rose he saw that it was a pigmy, an old man who was chattering and grinning, evidently making friendly overtures.

Birskett spoke in Luganda and then Kiswahili, but was not understood. As the old fellow stood upright, scarcely to Birskett's chest, he saw that one leg was drawn up, to which the man pointed. That there were other pigmies in the trees he knew, but the gestures were so undoubtedly grateful for having killed the gorilla when the pigmy was helpless to escape, that he called over the doctor.

Very interested, his eyes prying into the strange little man, the doctor examined the foot.

"Ankle dislocated," he pronounced, and forthwith deftly jerked it into place.

The pigmy grunted but seemed to understand that that was what was required. Tearing a strip of cloth from Kubi's shirt—to his indignation—for a bandage the doctor bound up the foot.

When all was done the pigmy jabbered something incomprehensible and pointed to the forest.

"He wants to make a date, doc," said Birskett, "and take you out to lunch."

"Extremely interesting," said the doctor watching the man.

"Sure," assented Birskett hastily, fearing the doctor would want to accept, "but leave it open till we're disengaged."

Replying in Luganda, as it sounded better, he handed him several cigarets. Then the little man hopped on one leg to a tree and hauled himself up.

"Almighty!" gasped the doctor watching him disappear monkey fashion into the foliage. "But Darwin was a great man!"

"Sure," grinned Birskett, "but let's have a look at our older brother here."

Reminded of the rival interest the doctor walked forward as if to attend to the next patient and bent over the huge form.

"Shot through the heart," he pronounced as Birskett came up.

"I sure meant to, doc," returned Birskett. "I've never even seen one before, but I've heard of his ways and that once he rushes you'll never have time to reload."

"Magnificent beast!" murmured the doctor and produced an aluminium measure from a pocket. The head, with brows as low as a baboon's and the enormously powerful maxillae, was set almost into the body without a neck; the black short-haired chest and tremendous arms, long enough to touch the knees, formed a mass of corded muscle: yet he had a belly like an alderman.

"Six foot two!" exclaimed the doctor triumphantly. "I don't suppose we can preserve the skeleton."

"Preserve the skeleton!" ejaculated Birskett. "How in Hades are we to carry that as well as the other stuff?"

V

The doctor assented reluctantly to the impossibility of carrying the corpse of the gorilla. Fortunately Zapoko, Abdul, and Matana had succeeded in dragging the canoes past the obstructing giant root. After a hurried council they decided to take a chance—to push on rather than go all the way back to the entrance to the channel.

Although they kept rifles ready and a sharp lookout on the left bank, they saw no more pigmies.

As the water became more sluggish they made even better speed than on the open river. In places, the boughs, festooned with mossy ropes of creeper, were interlaced overhead. Farther along another troop of monkeys picked them up and to their annoyance insisted upon following, chattering and screaming at them.

Parrots added to the uproar so that their progress must have been advertised to jungle society for a mile or more around. Other brilliant-hued birds darted about here and there. The doctor, searching for more of the curious fungus, a sample of which he had kept, noticed orchids which seemed to glow in the humid twilight.

Some time in the afternoon they came out suddenly, as if emerging from a green tunnel, into the river again, a real river some forty yards broad, with a fairly appreciable current flowing through high banks in open country, which gave a reassuring view of the Gamballagalla. The western sun tinted the mists as with blood and the slopes and ravines in vivid green and deep purple.

From their camp on the Ruwenzori side they could see a wide extent of undulating grass country with scattered light timber, and beyond in the depressions the dark of the Ituri forest, which seemed to sweep in rollers like the sea breaking among the foothills of the mountains and even splashing over and higher up the slopes.

The two whites ascended a hillock several hundred yards inland in order to try to get a clearer view of the range to estimate how far it was to the southwestern spurs. But from what they could see any attempt to form a judgment was but a wild guess. However, close beneath, they spotted a herd of buck of the impala species, and Birskett brought down one for the larder.

Now that the doctor had nearly recovered from the stiffness of his arm muscles, he promptly found another pest in the shape of the *bukukini*, a tiny fly, smaller than the *mbwa* of Uganda, which also attacks the wrists, and causes as painful and irritating bites.

"I told you it's a bug country," laughed Birskett, in the act of swallowing his evening dose of quinin. "But anyway it doesn't look as if there are any tsetse here."

Scarcely had he spoken when Kubi sprang up from the fireside swearing and making savage hits with a ladle. The doctor leaped as if he had been stung too, and grabbing his bug net, always kept handy, captured his quarry.

"*Morsitans*," said he after a swift examination.

"As there don't seem any villages about," said Birskett, "probably he's not infected. But he's the more dangerous brute. He's the fellow who follows and infects cattle. How long can he keep the bug going inside him, doc?"

"Several weeks, but we're not quite sure. It's thirty days from the moment his proboscis sucks infected blood until the germ is hatched or sufficiently developed."

"Whew-ew! He can travel some in several weeks! When I was here—I mean Uganda—last, they never reckoned he carried the sleeping sickness bug too, but he does. See what it means, doc, when that fellow's found from pretty nigh Khartoum right down into the Transvaal bushveld?"

"If we don't find a cure, it practically means the depopulation of three-quarters of Africa," returned Kirkton gravely. "And also, I don't know whether you're aware of the fact, Birskett, that there is no valid reason why a mammal may not act as host to this parasite. Already in India has been discovered a form of the same disease in which rats are the hosts and the bite the means of infection."

"Thank God, rats don't often bite a human then!"

"Quite so, but a mouse is a rodent. A mouse nibbles cheese and other food of humans. Should the human by any chance have the slightest abrasion of the mucous membrane of the mouth or throat, he would be as surely infected as by the subcutaneous injection of the fly's hypodermic."

"Good God, it might become a world plague!" exclaimed Birskett.

"Quite so," assented the doctor quietly.

"Queer, how none of you scientific guys can hit it," commented Birskett.

"It isn't queer," said the doctor sharply. "You have no comprehension of the difficulties."

"Thanks, doc! I suppose it's as hard as finding a cure for cancer or tuberculosis, and the latter sure grabs a few millions every year."

"Another point," continued the doctor thoughtfully, "I don't see any scientific reason why a mosquito shouldn't carry the trypanosome, at any rate for several hours or even days. It is the host of the *plasmodium* malaria—the malaria parasite—so why not the other? Infected rodents would form the source of supply and then of course humans."

"Oh, my God, doc, that would wipe out the States if ever it got there!"

"Another curious fact is that apparently these pigmies who live among the tsetse don't seem to suffer from it at all—otherwise they would be exterminated."

"Oh," said Birskett, "maybe they're immune. Like the wild buck and cattle-buffalo which are immune to what is commonly called horse sickness from the bite of the same tsetse fly, the *morsitans*."

"Maybe. H'm. Must make a note of that for investigation."

"How long before we reach the southwestern end—I mean where Stoutt had his camp?" demanded Kirkton, who was writing up his notes.

"Lord knows!"

"Can't you give an estimate? I want to begin serious work. Every day lessens the chance of the preservation of Stoutt's remains."

"I can't," said Birskett. "Recollect, you insisted on coming this road where no white man ever passed before—not lived through it anyway. Ah, doc," as Kirkton, rubbing, like any ordinary, bad patient, his wrists against the table edge, snorted impatiently, "I guess you've no comprehension of the difficulties!"

Next day they plunged again into the recesses of an arm of the forest, but fortunately the river broadened out into a comparatively sluggish stream without the tortuous channels between islands. That night, to the extreme uneasiness of the Wunyamwezi, who insisted upon building enormous fires, they were compelled to camp in the jungle. So for four more days they plugged steadily on, sometimes passing patches of more or less open undulating country, but with no sign of past or present habitation. Birskett supposed that the reason was the native fear of the pigmy, each of the spaces of open country being enclosed by dense forest where lay their lairs.

Since the talk of the possibilities of the spread of sleeping sickness, Birskett had developed a slightly subdued air; for no man with imagination could contemplate the scientific facts unmoved. To famine, war and pestilence and their bloody fellows in arms of known plagues, seemingly was to be added another even more terrible.

Sometimes he caught himself regarding the pallid features and curiously frozen lips of the doctor with a kind of awe—a queer feeling that he as a scientist was a superior being, one of those few who held the future of the race in their hands; a little resembling perhaps the attitude of a savage in dread of the magical powers of a witch doctor.

The following day about noon they came out from a swampy region of forest into grass country where the banks ran up swiftly, rounding what was evidently one of the foothills of the range. Anxious to find out their approximate position they sought the nearest landing place.

"Listen," exclaimed Birskett, as they scrambled up the cliff of the hill. "Hear that?"

A dull murmur floated on the still hot air.

"That explains the sound of water I heard away back! Mighty queer I've never heard it since. Wind in right direction, I suppose. Anyway, that means Old Man Trouble, doc."

"What, a cataract? Well, we can porter round, can't we?"

"Sure," assented Birskett a bit doubtfully.

From the summit, covered in elephant grass, they found that the spur continued inland towards the main range, like a hog's back, but was not of the true mass of foothills. Southeast was a vast ravine, violet in shadow, which seemed to penetrate deeply into the mountains. To the south, the tops of the Ituri forest swept majestically in billows from the western horizon of the Congo hills.

But Birskett noticed uneasily that the jungle seemed somehow on a higher plane to the south, almost as if it were a plateau. Still, it was difficult to judge at that elevation. Upon a conical mountain, which seemed the nearest and a little out of the line of the range, they could distinguish the snow line directly beneath the dense haze.

"Well, there's no sign of man, pigmy or beast here," commented Birskett, "nor does that fellow look like the last of 'em. So I guess we'd better hit the trail again."

As they descended Birskett, who was hunting around for spoor, called to the doctor:

"Look," he said, "that's mighty queer. See that patch there and the peg holes? Some time or other a white man's tent has been pitched here."

"Perhaps Stoutt's?" queried the doctor, peering about.

"Maybe, but I doubt it," demurred the other. "Your pious thief's confession distinctly suggested the extreme southwestern end of the range. More probably those two fellows who disappeared. Possibly they went prospecting into the mountains here and maybe a glacier or something wiped 'em out. But say, didn't that squarehead guy leave a map as a guide?"

"No. But he insisted, as you suggest, that it was the most southwestern mountain. Seemed from what he could tell me that there were no foothills; that the main mountain ran straight down—more or less, I suppose—into swamps where Stoutt used to go to make his investigations and where the villages were already half-depopulated."

"M'm. I should like to know what other things that fellow said before he got a change of heart as he called it—fear of hell, I should call it, the damned cur! Guess it's no use barking up that tree, doc, so let's get a move on."

As the river curved the banks lowered promisingly, then rose again and very swiftly closed in until the current was so strong that they scarcely made any way at all. The sound of gurgling water increased. Twenty minutes later the question of water transport was settled, for after laboring around a bend, they entered a curious wide pool or basin some hundred feet or more in diameter, and saw what looked like a subterranean tunnel, so dark was it, a gorge cut in the rock which seemed to turn the river into a millrace less than thirty yards broad of seething foam-flecked water.

"Gosh!" muttered Birskett back-watering.[5] "We'll sure never make that. Doc," he bawled over his shoulder, "I guess this is where we get off!"

Kirkton's canoe came alongside. The basin formed almost a perfect circle and they noticed that the high banks caved inwards at the top.

"Must have been water erosion," suggested Birskett, "yet it's damned funny, for that looks like lava basalt to me."

"That's right," assented Kirkton. "Most curious. Seems as if the river had somehow forced a way into an extinct crater. Probably extremely deep. I wonder how we could sound—"

---

[5] To reverse the direction of a boat, esp. to push the oars of a rowboat. To retreat from a position; with an opinion.

"Lord! Look out!" exclaimed Birskett. "There's the current carrying us off into a whirlpool. Turn and paddle, man!" And to the men:

"*Mukale, munyweze yani! Mangu!*" (Now paddle hard! Get a move on!)

By strenuous exertions they managed to get out of the grip of what seemed a whirlpool revolving around the caldron before finding an outlet into the river proper. Drifting back with the current, they searched for a likely place to land in the high cliffs, but it was more than half a mile before the banks lowered so that they were able to find a scalable spot.

From the summit they saw at a glance that a short distance from the pool the wall of the forest began again. After a brief discussion they decided that they had better take Bapoko and go along on foot to investigate.

The immediate country around was fairly open with scattered clumps of trees, palms and euphorbia. Some small foothills apparently ran close down to the river. Birskett didn't say anything to the doctor, but he saw that unless they struck a village right close by, or friendly natives, they at all events would have to leave all their gear behind. What the doctor would say to parting with his professional battery he didn't like to think!

As they made their way without much difficulty over ground mostly covered with dense grass, they noticed that they seemed to be ascending a hill which corresponded to the rise in the banks they had noted from the river beneath. When they got to the pool they found that undoubtedly it was the crater of an extinct volcano, as the doctor had surmised, for on either side from the edge of the overhanging cliff the ground fell away equally; moreover they were upon an eminence slightly dominating the surrounding country and looking down upon the forest roof a mile or more away.

"Damned queer," commented Birskett. "How could the river force a passage right into the middle of a hill, for Heaven's sake?"

"Maybe," returned Kirkton, gazing at the swirling pool, "a volcanic upheaval split the crater in two and also forced the river out of its original course, and by coincidence—accident, I suppose you would call it—the water followed the way of least resistance through the middle of what had been a hill. Anyway, the formation of the land beyond will tell us more."

The palms and scrub became denser as they tramped along near the edge of the cañon and the music of falling water increased.

"Damn it, doc," said Birskett, eying the trees ahead and listening to the sound, "I can't see how that's going to be a cataract. 'Fraid's it's a fall. Look at the level of the forest beyond."

"That means, I suppose," said Kirkton frowning, "that we can't get any farther?"

"M'm. Not necessarily. We may have a stroke of luck and find a native village somewhere around. Anyway we could cache the stuff, and I've a hunch that sooner or later we're bound to find 'em. That tribe Stoutt mentioned won't be likely to have shifted anyway."

Kirkton walked silently for a few minutes and then said:

"I can't possibly leave my field stuff. What good could we do without it? No, Birskett, we've just got to go on if we spend a month here getting the canoe up and over."

The ground as they approached was pretty level and full of scored lava with queer outcrops of granite poking through. Suddenly they came to the end of the palm scrub and grass; in front of them began the forest. Breaking through the bush they forged ahead towards the sound of the waterfall, which was marked by a faint column of vapor rainbowed in the sun. Birskett, who was breaking the trail, suddenly backed.

Jutting out from the scrub ran a wall of granite and, over this, the water poured into the gorge some sixty feet below. But what startled them was that right across the edge of the fall grew the forest, like the hirsute growth on a man's lip—the river had no passage, but oozed directly out of the jungle!

"Most astonishing thing I've ever heard of!" exclaimed the doctor. "Look, this gigantic rib of granite juts from the mountain and continues on the other side blocking the passage for no one knows how many miles. Good heavens, in a very dry season I should imagine it would hold up what water there is. If so, the whole of the Semliki Valley would go dry—possibly Lake Albert!"

"I should worry!" retorted Birskett, who was dismally surveying the forest. "Listen, doc, I'm going to tell you something. Look at that, man!" and he pointed disgustedly to the forest. "This means that our goose is pretty well cooked."

"But why?"

"Why, man! Where has the river gone to or rather come from?"

The doctor stared and frowned.

"I see. The forest must be a vast swamp."

"You bet, and some home of the tsetse, believe me!"

"——! Birskett, I believe you're right. But, man, that must be the swamp where Stoutt went to conduct his investigations!"

"Maybe, but if so it's terrifically long, for look at the mountains. This isn't the extreme southwestern end yet by a long way. Well, guess we'd better prospect around the higher land there and see what it's like."

They found by following the forest and swamp edge that the granite wall ran almost as straight as if drawn by a ruler and rose slightly all the time. After an hour's walking they halted. The foothills which had seemed so promising from their last survey were seen to cease, and the forest swamp to sweep on for miles toward what appeared to be the main slopes of the mountains. Kirkton, standing on the edge of the rocky barrier, put down his rifle, remarking—

"There's some of that curious fungus!"

The next moment Birskett heard a startled exclamation and the doctor disappeared. The former ran forward. Evidently, in attempting to gather some of the fungi Kirkton had slipped. The moss-covered rock, descended at an angle of forty five degrees like the sides of a dry dock down some twelve feet into what looked like verdant sward. In this floundered the doctor to his waist, grabbing frantically at the grass and fungi which crumbled in his fingers. The slime was sufficiently heavy to support the precious satchel which floated, together with his binoculars, haversack and fly-net case, like a gigantic lily.

"Keep still, man!" shouted Birskett, seeing that Kirkton's exertions were causing him to sink. He cast about hurriedly for a means to rescue him. His rifle was too short to extend to him from firm ground. He tested a bush but the slender branches broke. Kirkton, who was up to his chest, motionless, said quietly:

"Throw broken bushes to me. Maybe that'll keep me afloat, and send to the camp for a rope. I'll try to loose the satchel. Save that."

But there were no bushes dense and heavy enough, except out of reach in the forest swamp, to help a man to float. Birskett hunted wildly for a solution. Then, tugging at small bushes by the roots, he calculated that they would bear a considerable weight, although the branches wouldn't. But how to reach twelve feet down?

Zapoko was frantically tearing up handfuls of grass with an idea of plaiting a rope, but Birskett saw that there was not enough time.

"Keep still and keep your hands out, doc," he shouted suddenly. "I've got it! *Jangu, mangu, Zapoko! Mangu! Mangu!*"

Wedging the muzzle of the rifle well into the roots and beneath the soil of one bush, he fixed the butt in the same manner into another, and instructed Zapoko to grab the gun in the middle and lower himself down the granite slope. Then, sliding over the body of the Sudanese and hanging on to his feet he could get his own feet within reach of the doctor.

It was touch and go. The doctor was now nearly up to his neck. The suction was so great that he could scarcely drag himself out. By convulsive jerks of his legs Birskett helped him a little. Gradually and painfully he climbed up the human ladder. He had barely gotten on high ground when he collapsed with exhaustion and lay smothered from shoulders to heels in reeking spinach-colored slime. Climbing over Zapoko, Birskett crawled beside him.

"Gosh!" he gasped. "That was a near call, doc! Feel all right?"

"Except for this filthy stench," complained Kirkton. "I— Good God—!"

A native had grown out of the earth twenty yards away. He was fairly tall, bronze of skin and naked save for small skins which fell between the groins. He was armed with a spear, long bladed like the Masai, and arrows. He advanced slowly, stopped uncertainly, and cried out something.

"*Mkulamusiza, Mwami! Otyano munange?*" (Greeting, chief! How are you my friend?) called Birskett and walked forward, grinning largely.

He held out his hand, repeating the greeting. The young savage started to jabber rapidly. Birskett shook his head, still grinning amiably. The man spoke a few broken words in Buganda. For a few minutes the two talked. Then Birskett said to the doctor:

"Seems friendly enough. He says they live not far away and invites us, as far as I get it, to go see their chief."

The doctor rose to his feet, looking like an enormous green frog.

"Great!" cried he, dripping slime. "Now, we'll get really busy!"

VI

The westering sun over the Congo hills superimposed above the summits of the Ruwenzori another and grander range of mountains, mountains clad with pink glaciers and valleys of pale violet against a sky of pallid green studded by an archipelago of crimson islands. The world beneath was a broken line of shimmering blue; and below was another of ultramarine, the bamboo level.

Against one of the foothills, whose tops were haloed in scarlet in contrast to the sepia of the valleys beyond, was a village, the low conical huts like warm topazes, dominating a vast sea of green billows, stretching into the radium glare over which hung a faint iridescent glow.

There were some hundred huts; the ragged eaves touched the dusty garbage-scattered ground where pecked indolently a few tiny fowl. Several mangy goats, whose ribs were countable, dozed in the shade. On the outskirts bordering the tall elephant grass, honeycombed with passages, a woman lay just beyond the shade in the scorching rays. Save for a bunch of old and filthy leaves, worn Eve-like, she was naked, revealing a tautened belly, tiny, shriveled breasts, pipestem thighs and features shrunken to bone and skin. Near her, sprawling in the hot dust, was a male infant, potbellied, with chubby brown limbs, crowing contentedly.

In the center of the clutter of huts was a roofed-in frame, beneath which lounged a company of men. Upon a woven mat squatted an old man. The face was like a wrinkled mass of leather, water-soaked and prematurely dried in the sun; the forehead was partially bald; the dense wool, slightly grayed, was divided by a shaven path that ran right through the center of the skull; the limbs were those of a mummy, the belly clung to the spine; on the scaly chest hung a large bleached bone suspended by a plaited fiber; but the eyes, deep set, and almost hidden by folds of skin, were as bright as an angry bird's. Beside him, a little to the right, was another man even more withered and ancient than he. Upon his wrist was a huge bangle of ivory which was kept on only by the clutching of the clawlike fingers.

A young man among the ruck sat with his back against a pole of the club house, gazing with lackluster eyes at the others. He was not particularly thin for a native, but the glands beneath the jaw were so swollen that his neck appeared to be almost swallowed by his body. Four others among the crowd were like him.

Nobody spoke. The group rested as do cattle on a day of gnats in the shade of an oak tree, as if drunkenly contented with the joy of living. Upon them came Matanzi, seemingly the only being actively alive. On the threshold he squatted and grunted, discarding the air of haste like a cloak for one of bored indifference. Fully three minutes passed, slow minutes, while the sharp eyes of Bafakoki, the ancient wearing the bone, watched him shrewdly.

At length he too grunted. Matanzi murmured and gained another grunt. The other mummy issued a like sound. Whereupon Matanzi said, as if it were of no importance whatever:

"Mine eyes have seen men of white-leaf faces[6] (white men) coming from the country of the wild men (pigmies)."

Several assorted grunts registered a general interest.

---

[6] [Author's note: "Simile taken from a common kind of white African convolvulus, primitives seeing a flower merely as a colored leaf."]

"How many?" inquired the man of the pendant bone.

"As the arms of a man."

"*Aiee!*" exclaimed a young man, wriggling to a squatting posture. "We shall be eaten up!"

"Thy voice is as the bleating of a kid," came the reproof of an older man with gray moss upon his chin, whose opinion was confirmed by a grunt from the two ancients "Let thy elders speak lest the *Ahuu* seize thee!"

At the threat of such a fate the young man subsided like a frightened cat. The group remained silent, but by the nervous movements of limbs proclaimed that the news had stirred them deeply. All eyes were turned upon the withered man with the bone, Bafakoki.

As if very conscious of his importance he posed motionless with closed eyelids. The shadows grew longer. From the lips of Bafakoki began a moan rising into a prolonged howl like a young hyena. A shiver ran through the company. Slowly he opened his deep set eyes and began to speak in a monotone.

"This is the sun of which I have spoken! This is the sun that I have promised ye! Is it not as many wet moons as a man has fingers that you have been eaten by the sleep of the *Ahuu*? Is it not as many wet moons as the fingers of a man's hand that the first white-leaf face dwelt among you? Did he not breathe upon you and your children? Did he not depart whence he came, leaving his spittle upon you? Had you ever before the sleep of the *Ahuu*? Did your young men and maidens wither like leaves in the sun before the time of the white-leaf faces? Where now are your elders? Thou, Zofulo, sleepeth not thy son who was our chief? Where now are the young women that were your wives and your daughters? Where the young men that were begotten of you? Who sleepeth in your huts? Who is stricken by the *Ahuu* when eating or talking? Thou Bufolo, is not the youngest of thy wives a sleeper? Thou, Tanaka, what doth the eldest of thy loins? Thou, Torko, is thy male child fat like unto the buffalo? Were these things before the coming of the white-leaf faces? Answer me, my children?"

Came a deep grunt of assent.

"Ehh! Remember you the coming of the last white-leaf face? What were the words that I said unto you? What were the words of the son of Zofulo? Where is now the son of Zofulo? The *Ahuu* may tell thee! Ehh! And after him? For many moons were not the hands of the *Ahuu* light in their touch? Answer me?"

"*Aghuummm!*"

The last ray of the sun was shot like a searchlight from the tops of the foothills on to the clouds, turning them to crimson peaks.

"If the white-leaf faces are not brothers of the *Ahuu*, wherefore are they not eaten by the wild men? Answer me?"

"*Aghuummm!*"

"If the wild men are not the sons of the *Ahuu*, wherefore are they not devoured by the white-leaf faces?"

"*Aghuummm!*"

"Where dwell the wild men if not in the forest? From whence cometh the white-leaf faces if not through the forest? Are they not brothers and sons of the *Ahuu*?"

"*Aghuummm!*"

"Yet am I wise! Yet have I many wet moons more than you! Yet will I talk with the bones that have healed you! Leave me to speak with the bones!"

As one man they rose. The younger fled with the terror of the unknown upon them; the elders, still conscious of keeping up appearances, strode with hurried dignity to their huts. The scarlet glow upon the peaks of the clouds was turned off as by a hand and out of the east the sepia shadows rushed hungrily from the mountains and swallowed the village.

But Bafakoki did not budge. In the warm darkness, under the stars peeping out through a velvet pall and the hum of grass insects, he squatted quietly until, reckoning that all the others were safely within their huts, he rose and gravely made his way to his own, which was close to the club house.

On one side within squatted his five wives. Four were mothers, but their eyes were bright, and the breasts of the latest shone like inverted saucers of dull bronze in the dim light of the smoky air percolating from dim fire through the roof.

Bafakoki was a serious man and a patriot. His wives were healthy because he was intelligently observant. He had—scarcely consciously—remarked years ago that those who went down into the swamps beneath were touched by the dread hands of the *Ahuu*; therefore had he commanded that those that were his property should not go there.

Had he been more civilized he would probably have told himself that as he had no scientific nor moral justification for this fancy, he had no right whatsoever to persuade his fellows from the benefits of the chase and from the roots and valuable leaves which their women brought them; as a physician of renown he could not afford to risk his reputation. Moreover, had he not discovered a cure which had undoubtedly been of inestimable benefit to them in the matter of the treatment of the last white-leaf? Who could dispute that afterwards the dread disease had nearly ceased for many moons? How could Bafakoki be supposed to know that this was due to an unprecedented drought? Everybody could bear witness that his theory was true.

Bafakoki dined in solitary state, attended by his silent, adoring wives in the smoke behind him, upon boiled wild bananas and a portion of venison gathered and trapped from the swamps, worth several prescriptions in the form of amulets against the evil eye, the breath of *Ahuu* and other tribal complaints. Then Bafakoki, being a prohibitionist and knowing no better, retired to sleep in great satisfaction of mind and heart.

But next morning, when from the forest swamp below came faintly the squawk of the parrot and the hubbub of monkey life, Bafakoki, attentive to his duty to the community, arose, gathered his doctor's bag from a dark corner hidden by a reed mat on the men's side of the hut and departed for the club house.

When the outline of the bare peaks of the Ruwenzori was sketched in crimson and the barubaru bird squealed harshly, Bafakoki was discovered by Zofulo, he of the gray-mossed tuft of beard, squatting in the same position as he had been left on the previous evening. Before him were the contents of his professional bag.

Zofulo, without words, squatted silently in his appointed place as the father of a late chief, for the chiefs of this tribe were as many others of many colors, elected according to their prowess in slaying. Silently regarding the symbols before him, Zofulo grunted solemnly.

Before the crossed shins of the witch doctor were crossed two other shins but bare of meat; in front was a skull.

Those to follow were Bafolo, Tanaka, Bakata, and thirteen others, who read the message there portrayed and grunted sonorously. Then came two more and lastly Matanzi, who was clothed like a prophet in a mantle of golden bronze as the sun shot above the bare peaks. Then each and every one glanced upon Matanzi as a man chosen by divine Providence.

For not once in many moons, when the sun had risen, did the snow clad peaks lack their bridal veil.

Although the carved gargoyle face of Bafakoki showed no tremor of emotion, satisfaction welled within his heart. The choosing of a messenger to the strangers of the white-leaf faces was a delicate matter for the mission was dangerous should anything go wrong. Fortunately Matanzi, whose family had suffered from the dread hands of the *Ahuu*, was a man of little influence.

Yet of the significance nothing was said. Gravely they sat until all the men of the village, some four hundred healthy and those who could walk, were assembled. Then Bafakoki spoke, well aware that none would contradict him.

"O Zofulo, son of him—" for they might not mention the names of the dead—, "is it agreed that Matanzi shall go forth to greet the men of the white leaf, brothers of the wild men, sons of the *Ahuu*?"

"It is agreed!" assented Zofulo, doubting as many a chief before him, yet not daring to differ.

"It is agreed!" echoed the mob.

"O Zofulo, son of him," continued Bafakoki, "is it agreed that the medicine of Bafakoki is all-powerful?"

"It is agreed!" assented Zofulo, knowing that to dissent was a declaration of war.

"O Zofulo, is it agreed that Matanzi shall be thy messenger to the people of the white leaf?"

"It is agreed," responded Zofulo despondently.

And so it was.

VII

The encounter and friendly invitation more than compensated in Kirkton's opinion for his ducking in the slimy swamp, although for days he could not get rid of the stench like sulphuretted hydrogen or rotten eggs splashed into his hair.

Matanzi, eying the four fire sticks, of which he had dread but knew little, the last pale-leaf face having been a missionary, proposed that the white men should go straight with him to the chief. To Birskett's question he implied that the distance was but one sun, but Birskett, knowing the native and seeing the anxiety beneath the wooden exterior, doubled the time.

The doctor at the very suggestion resolutely refused to budge without his beloved instruments; so, conforming to the usual etiquette, they gave him a present of *bafta*[7] for the chief and tried, by piling all the loads in a row, to din into his head the number of porters required to carry them.

"I won't leave the gear and that's all there is to it," stated the doctor firmly. "But don't you think these are the people Stoutt was so friendly with?"

"Maybe, but I've a hunch they ain't. They'd surely send a man speaking better Luganda—or Kiswahili perhaps, whichever Stoutt talked—because they reckon whatever lingo Stoutt used to 'em was every white man's lingo. Besides I

---

[7] Here Beadle inserts the note: "Trade cloth." Bafta (variant of baft): a coarse, loosely woven cloth, made from wool or cotton, originally of Indian manufacture. It was mostly used for manufacturing sacks or for wrapping goods. But it could also refer to a type of garment or material used for various practical purposes, such as covering or protection. "Spotted bafta" suggests that it was imbued with a design featuring spots or dots.

reckon Stoutt's mountain is quite a way down the trail yet. Anyway the luck seems setting our way."

However, to Birskett's surprize and their mutual relief some twenty odd men turned up in the afternoon of the following day, over which went professionally the probing eyes of the doctor. But the primary symptoms are difficult to detect, particularly on the heavily pigmented body of a negro, and the doctor was disappointed.

They were all fully armed with long-bladed spears and bows and arrows, and stood in a circle rather like a bunch of shy schoolgirls, staring at the two whites sitting in state at the table before the tent. When greetings had been exchanged they squatted down.

"*Munyampala aluwa?*" (Which is the headman?) began Birskett.

But they could not understand until he had repeated the words several times. Then Bafolo replied. The *shauri* proceeded, but with long exasperating halts when neither side could understand the other. Even when they had finished Birskett wasn't sure whether they really had grasped that they had to carry the loads. They exhibited a certain uneasiness as Matanzi had done and wanted to start immediately; but as the shadows of the foothills were already touching the slopes of the mountains, the whites refused.

Then came a most considerable and unintelligible discussion among them which ended in a demand for more presents for each one, and the information that they would go away and return on the morrow.

Birskett assented to the latter proposition but not to the first, fearing that they might get some idea into their heads to make off with what they had already got. They seemed inclined to dispute and become ugly, but a harangue from Bafolo, into which the names of Bafakoki, Zofulo, and *Ahuu* were frequently employed, quieted them. As they trooped off, the doctor began to protest.

"That's all right, doc, they'll come back, I guess. But what I can't make out is what the scare of stopping here is. Possibly fear of our magic or something like that. Then it's no use trying to force 'em. Kubi!" he called to the boy who was preparing the table. *"Omanyi kino Ahuu?"* (Do you know what *Ahuu* is?)

"E-e! Manyi ko, Sebo. Omubi Omutukuvu." (Yes, sir. I know a little. It's a sacred evil person.)

"Basetani?" (Evil spirits?)

"Eyeh! Neda! Mwami!" (Yes, no, chief!)

"M'm. Bwonokiriza nga?" (D'you believe in it?)

"Simanyi," (I don't know,) returned Kubi shyly, and showed his teeth in response to Birskett's smile.

"Guess he's like a lot of folks at home," said Birskett to Kirkton. "Wants to back coming and going."

"I suppose it's the idea of evil in contradistinction to good. God and the devil."

"They have no conception of a good power. If it's good, they say, that's fine; if it's bad, slip him something to keep him quiet. That's the idea. But I was asking because these fellows were jabbering about that *Ahuu* guy. I think that's the reason they won't stop here. I had thought that maybe *Ahuu* was the pigmies. It's useful to know when dealing with these people what particular kind of bug they fancy."

However they made preparation. Birskett, on the principle that they couldn't tell when or how soon they might need the canoes, had them paddled down the stream a bit, dragged up the banks and cached in the elephant grass.

Before the sun had surmounted the mountain cloud the men were filing down into the camp. The tent was struck and they were presented to the loads. As Birskett had foreseen there was some confusion. But the first man, Matanzi, jabbered at them until some light seemed to dawn; they consented and began feeling the weights.

Finally, after much more discussion a black raised a load on to his head; then the others followed. After that there was no hitch.

The village was, they estimated, about fifteen miles away, set at the base of the lesser foothills. About three miles farther began the barrier of the swamp which, they saw through the glasses, ran straight for quite another day's march towards the lower slope of the true mountain, where they could make out the smoke of other habitations. Optimistically as usual, because he wished it so keenly, the doctor would insist that they must be the people referred to by Stoutt, but Birskett was as equally certain that they could not be.

They arrived scarcely half an hour before sunset. Women, children, and men (far more than the village could house, Birskett noted) waited silently to stare upon the whites. They had not passed the first group before the doctor's keen eyes had spotted three indisputable cases.

"You see," he said joyfully, "the sickness is here! And yet I haven't seen a single sign of a fly."

"Maybe they hang around the swamps down below where these fellows go hunting or something; again, you may only have them here when the wind or season is favorable. But for Heaven's sake, doc, go slow and don't rush 'em or we'll be having some damned tabu wished on us."

They, with the two Sudanese escorting, were led at the head of the caravan straight to the men's club where sat solemnly

Bafakoki, and Zofulo who, until another was chosen, acted as chief. The strangers were bidden to sit before them. Warriors swarmed around, and without were men, women and children. The doctor was more interested in the crowd than in the chiefs.

As befitted the chief physician, Bafakoki could speak no other language than his own; so Bafolo and Matanzi were summoned as interpreters. After the formal greetings Birskett gathered with difficulty that the ancient with the bone pendant was politely thanking them for the lavish gifts.

He translated to the doctor, who replied—

"Good, but work that up for all it's worth and promise him more if he gives us porters to take us on to the next tribe," adding, with his eyes on the man with the gorilla-like neck, "after I've investigated these fellows."

"In a day or two, doc. You can't rush 'em, I tell you."

He went on to try to give the usual blarney about how glad the whites were to see so great a chief, taking Bafakoki for that exalted personage; but evidently neither of the two interpreters could get his meaning. Then again came a repetition of the appreciation of his gifts.

"Funny," thought Birskett, "they usually play the other game. However, if the old bird, feels like that about it, so much the better."

The rays of the sun shot beneath the awning right on the breast of Bafakoki, attracting the doctor's roving eyes.

"Note that bone on the chest?" he whispered to Birskett.

"Sure."

"Know what it is?"

"Monkey, isn't it?"

"No. Human shin. Cannibals?"

"Perhaps. Now what's old father Noah saying? Right, I get you, son. He means the show's over and we're to be shown up in the elevator to our rooms. Come on."

The whites rose, followed by the two Sudanese, and went with Bafolo, escorted by the entire village except those whose dignity or sickness forbade, to a hut on the outskirts in a more ruinous condition than the others.

"Bright-looking guesthouse!" commented Birskett. "But why haven't those damn fool boys pitched the tent?"

"And where are the goods?" inquired the doctor tetchily.

"Inside, I suppose," he returned as he doubled up to look through the door. "Damn it, I can't see a thing, and it stinks like Hades. Kubi! Matana!" he called. "*Kubi alwwa?*" (Where is he?) he demanded of the Sudanese.

"*Simanyi, Mwami,*" (I don't know, chief,) responded Zapoko.

"Damned funny!"

Birskett straightened up and gazed around at the mass of the crowd whose spear blades glittered in the dying rays of the sun. "*Ku-ubi! Heh, Matana-a!*"

"*Mwami-i!*" came a voice from the far side of the village.

"*Okolaki! Janguwako! Mukalimwetiki?*" (What the —— are you doing there? Come here quickly and bring the loads.)

The reply came soaring in the native tenor used to carry over distance. Birskett swore.

"They've taken the things to the chief's house. I was scared the damn fools hadn't got what we said. I don't believe they've ever seen a white before and they think we've given 'em all the loads as a present! Come on, we'll go across and fix things."

Followed by the doctor and the Sudanese, he turned to walk through the village, but the pressed ranks of the men about him did not open.

"Muvao!" (Get out!) he commanded sharply. *"Mangu!"* (Get a move on!)

But not a man budged. Thinking that they did not comprehend he gestured to make room to pass, tapping one man smartly on the chest. The fellow scowled and grasped his spear. Birskett's instinct was to hit, but looking down on the faces about him, he saw a ferocity that made him realize that something serious was afoot.

"Get your gun, doc," he said sharply, and drawing his revolver, jabbed the muzzle into a stomach. The man did not advance, but neither did he retire; nor did the expression of his face alter. For a moment they stood like that, the white glaring down into the savage's face.

"Don't fire, doc," Birskett said very quietly. "It's very serious. They don't know what a gun is. We could get one or two, but they're too close. They'd finish us in as many minutes. Put your gun up and smile—damn it, you can't, but put it up!"

Deliberately he grinned into the black man's face, lowering the revolver at the same time. For several moments he continued the grin, then slowly the man smiled slightly. The tension relaxed. He looked to see whether Matanzi or Bafolo was there. He could not see either.

"Mwami aluwa?" (Where is the chief?) he demanded, but the fellow stared blankly.

"He can't or won't understand. Don't get up in the air, doc. There's something gone wrong, but I don't know what the game is yet. Let's see whether they'll let the boys come to us. Five guns are better argument than three."

He called to Kubi and Matana to come to them and waited. Presently they arrived.

"You see, doc, they haven't any idea of a gun. Don't look so damn mad, man," he added and laughed for his own benefit as well as the savages'.

At that moment the last sun ray glowed on the mountain cloud, and night came like the drawing of a curtain. There was the sound of movement of many apparently going away, but between the pinnacles of the surrounding huts and against the stars snapping out were the gleams of bayonet-like blades.

Birskett rapidly cross examined the two Wunyamwezi. They had followed with the loads into a compound which they had imagined to be the one allotted to the white men's use by the chief; hence they had not, lacking instructions, pitched the tent; also it was usual for the chief to supply food for his guests. But when they had attempted to set out their camp beds and what not, the natives had interfered and had tried to hustle them off. They had refused to leave the loads.

Birskett asked them their own opinion. Of the local dialect they scarcely understood two words, but they were convinced that the people were "bad."

"And I guess they are right," assented Birskett, turning to the doctor. "This seems a pretty mess, doc. Apparently we've walked right into a trap, but what the game is I can't guess yet. Never in all my experience have I known natives to play a dirty trick like this. But there's something unusual behind it."

"But the loads, man, my instruments—" began the doctor angrily.

"Now listen right here, doc," said Birskett, laying a hand on his shoulder. "These devils are more than usually dangerous, for they haven't yet had the fear of God put into 'em by guns, and right in the middle of the night is no time to start in teaching 'em. They'd rush, and wipe us out before they'd time to know where they'd been hurt or where it had come from. Get that, don't you, old man?"

"Sure," assented Kirkton, still with impatience in his voice, "but the loads—"

"That's all right. We'll argue about that tomorrow. If ever you want to see the loads again, sit right down and look as if you were damned tickled to death with yourself, and we'll have an illumination, just to show 'em. That'll give us some time to think up stunts."

When Birskett told the boys to make a fire and they began to hunt for firewood, the savages got the idea, and two of them brought faggots and glowing embers.

"Now what d'you know about that, brother?" said Birskett as they sat down with their backs against the hut. "Ain't they the friendly guys? Say, doc, it's an awful shame you can't operate on that mouth of yours and carve a grin on it!"

But Kirkton was vexedly regarding the fire lighting operations, oblivious even of the skirling mosquitoes, and clutching his precious satchel as if he feared he'd lose that as well. As the fire flared up the light caught on the sheen of blades. But presently came some women bearing gourds of stewed goat and boiled wild bananas.

Birskett and their four men tucked in as if it were a bridal feast, but Kirkton, who managed a little of the stewed goat, couldn't stomach the banana, which resembles tasteless potato. Afterwards, the doctor took out his waterproof cigar case, but as he extracted one, Birskett ejaculated—

"No, no, for Heaven's sake not that, doc!"

"Good — —, why not?" expostulated Kirkton a bit querulously.

"Might scare 'em too much," said Birskett. "How many have you?"

"Six. Why?"

"Nothing. Keep 'em for later."

The doctor obeyed, but he didn't seem to like it.

"He's a great man, the doc," mused Birskett to himself, "but oh, Lordy, I wonder what would have to happen to him to make him smile!"

They passed the night there, half-lying against the hut in preference to the heat and stench within. The savages seemed to have disappeared later, but muttering voices now and again showed that they were somewhere around, and when a half-moon arose above the cold bare peaks in the east she cast dull star echoes on spear points.

Dawn came at last. During the queer twilight, while the sun climbed the mountains and spread her daily veil of clouds, there was a stir in the village, but none approached them save the scattered guards.

Birskett rose, and after stretching himself, crawled into the hut saying—

"I've a fancy to see what they've got here."

Kirkton heard him striking matches and muttering. Then came a sharp summons—

"Doc, come here!"

Kirkton crawled within, "phewin' " at the stench.

"Lucky I came in," said Birskett. "Now we know what we're up against. Look at that quickly."

He held up a newly lighted match. The doctor saw a broken side of a packing case stuck between the grass of the thatched wall like a picture and what looked like some hieroglyphics upon it. They were letters crudely and apparently hurriedly carved with a knife and filled with clay, presumedly to block them, and in the light of a second match he spelled out in French.

"Sacrificed to cannibals," followed by an indecipherable name.

The match went out in his fingers as he tried to read the signature.

"*On mange bien ici!*" (Good eats here!) came Birskett's voice in the gloom with a sardonic laugh.

Then flowed in the doctor's accents a torrent of oaths almost with tears of exasperation in them.

"Gosh, that's fine, doc!" gasped Birskett, in admiration as he finished. "I never guessed you knew all those words!"

" — — you, you confounded idiot," snarled the doctor. "Can't you understand? Haven't I done all in my power, spent all I have, suffered all sorts of silly — — things, to try to bring some good to humanity, to carry on the really great work that Stoutt began, to benefit all mankind — these insufferable idiots as well — and then this parcel of benighted, impossible fool heathens want to upset all my plans just when I'm almost in sight of my goal — and, my God, then they want to *eat* me!"

"Gosh, doc, that sounds awful human!" There was a peculiar noise in the dark and Birskett added —

"Come outside, doc, and then you'll feel better."

VIII

Some one has remarked that there's only a breadth of a spider web between comedy and tragedy. Birskett saw the humor in the doctor's attitude. The doctor certainly didn't. Yet they both had the object of the expedition just as much at heart; merely the difference in the point of view. True, the doctor lacked what is called a sense of humor, but he lacked another thing—which was fear. It simply never occurred to him to be scared by the idea of being slaughtered and eaten; he could only see that his precious plans were upset. He would have sworn just as deeply and sincerely had an eagle flown away with his satchel.

Yet Birskett perceived in reality more than the scientist; he realized the extreme danger. As far as things looked they probably would be eaten; but if so, well, perhaps it wouldn't matter very much after all; maybe somebody else would find the cure for the relief of humanity, and if so, what did it matter as long as the patient got his medicine? Give in? No, sir. That never occurred to him any more than the funny side of it to the doctor. But sometimes in this world you've got to abandon temporarily looking at the star to avoid the sewer.

When the boys came up he proceeded to investigate the contents of their haversacks; mostly chocolate, tobacco, matches, cartridges and odds and ends for the road. He found a pocket torch and paused, holding it in his hand.

"Pity we didn't start magic with that last night," he commented. "Might have done for the eyes of a devil. H'm. May be useful yet."

He continued to overhaul Matana's bag. At the bottom, among some loose cartridges, his hand closed upon a long cylindrical object. He took it out and regarded a rocket, one of a dozen such as are usually carried on exploring expeditions mainly used for signaling in case anybody gets bushed, which, falling out of a case, the boy had shoved in his haversack.

"H'm. That's useful. Guess it'll have to be a night getaway. Yep. They won't likely start anything today. Now I've got to keep doc quiet. Some job!"

He sat still thinking out things.

"Say, doc," said he at length. "I've scared up a chance to get out of the pot with a bit of luck, but I can't for the life of me figure out how we're going to get the loads away without porters, and I reckon Mister Mesmer couldn't hypnotize these guys into doing that. We'll have to call back for 'em. That's all there is to it."

"We made a mistake," said the doctor sententiously, "in bringing the loads here."

Birskett gave a yowl and literally rocked against the hut thatch with laughter, startling even a savage into backing away several feet, which was more than a revolver in his stomach had done.

"Lord! Lord!" moaned Birskett. "You'll be the death of me, doc, before they get me into the pot!"

"Hysterical!" muttered the doctor, which fortunately was not heard by his companion, and relapsed into a broody contemplation, feeling an unwonted sensation of being lost in his search for a plan to preserve his precious loads.

He had, as he phrased it, no data to work upon. Birskett also was occupied upon the same subject, but in spite of his data, no feasible possibility could he find of getting the loads away unless some one would be good enough to send along an automobile truck. They would be doing quite well, he thought, if his schemes already hatched succeeded, to get away with their hides and what was upon them.

After the sun had resumed his daily broil, a woman came along and placed a gourd of tepid and smelly water at their feet. Armed savages still squatted unostentatiously among the huts. Birskett weighed the chances of each picking a man and making a bolt for it. But they would have to run the gantlet of the village.

"Fire it?" thought he. "No. They would be accustomed to fire. But they were not used to guns and queerly enough that fact was the chief difficulty. No, they must adopt some strategy to get at a distance; then they would have time to drive into the savage minds, which as many others are fairly obtuse, that their weapons were lethal, dealing instant death; thus putting fear into them before they were overwhelmed by numbers."

If only he could get at those loads! In them were more cartridges, rockets, and some dynamite. A deal might be done with that combination. Yet he was acquainted with quite a lot of the workings of the savage mind. That there had been no innocent misunderstanding about the presents, he now realized; but he knew, too, that those loads would now be looked upon as having priceless magical powers merely because they had belonged to a white man, on the principle that what is of a god or devil, a being of supernatural power, partakes of that power. Any attempt to recover or approach these now holy articles would be most fiercely resisted, perhaps more even than their own escape.

Yet never had he known in twenty years wandering, a purely savage tribe act as they had done. What was the bug in their head? Did they take the white man for a god or a devil? Usually the former—hence their delight to honor and flatter him. Yet if the latter, they usually feared and therefore tried to appease him. Something was wrong with their cosmogony. But what?

Squatting there in the hot shade with wary eyes and his rifle across his knees, Birskett tried hard to solve the problem. He started systematically to recall all the systems of superstition that he had encountered or read of.

The nearest he got was to wonder whether, as was quite possible, they attributed the sleeping sickness to the white man? Yes, but, if that were the case, they should therefore endeavor to appease these givers of death. Maybe the secret, he mused, lay with the other white, the man who had written the message in the guest hut. At that moment the doctor, browsing in the next field, butted in.

"Birskett, who d'you suppose this man may have been?"

"The man who went to the pot? God knows. As they obviously don't know anything about a gun he must have been a missionary."

"French?"

"Dunno. If he was a Continental he'd surely write such a message in French. Only an Anglo-Saxon would in English. He must have drifted up here through the Belgian Congo. Yet he might have been a trader, explorer, anything, for they may have caught him without a gun. A dozen possibilities. We'll never know, I guess. Evidently he knew where he was going, so probably he understood something of their lingo. Anyway he did his best, poor — —."

"I wonder," said the doctor, "whether he had trypanosomiasis?"

"Hope he did!" ejaculated Birskett. "So maybe he gave them a dose. Say, doc; could that happen?"

The doctor considered.

"M'm, rather difficult to say. Never studied the subject. Yet—one may contract tuberculosis from infected cattle and milk, so I suppose that the same would apply to trypanosomiasis. M'm, extremely interesting. I must experiment. M'm. It's very annoying about those loads," he added, pulling out his notebook.

The shadows dwindled until they were driven to squat within the hut for protection from the heat. Throughout the morning continued a low murmur from the center of the village where evidently a big *shauri* was going on. Flies buzzed irritatingly, but the eyes of the doctor, now almost mechanically on the lookout, failed to detect the cross wings of the tsetse.

The Wunyamwezi and the Sudanese, to whom he had not imparted the news concerning their probable destination, squatted patiently, occasionally discussing the situation in low tones, Zapoko improving the time by cleaning his rifle.

Both whites, unaccustomed to the native manner of feeding once a day, began to feel hungry. Several times racial disinclination to brook a black man's whims nearly brought Birskett to his feet; but long experience and anxiety, not for himself, but for the object of their expedition, restrained him.

The doctor indeed showed fewer symptoms of impatience than did Birskett. But sitting there quietly, captives, and conscious of eyes watching all the time to see how they were taking it, made hard going.

The shadows began to crawl again, but still the hum of the *shauri* continued. Birskett amused himself by speculating what the subject could be, trying to see whether he could gather any idea that might suggest the advisability of instant action. Once he said casually to the doctor—

"I guess we'd better beat it before supper."

The doctor gazed at him inquiringly and said:

"How about a cigar now? Those creatures can't matter."

"No. But tonight you can smoke your head off."

The doctor made a slight noise of irritable disgust, but deferred to Birskett as the boss of the outfit as he always did. Later Birskett set Kubi to plaiting grass torn from the roof into a cord. Within the hut, out of sight of the curious eyes of men or women, Birskett began binding the rocket on to a bamboo. Kirkton eyed him but made no remark.

"They're squabbling over the dainty bits," commented Birskett, as a sudden altercation broke out from the men's club.

After he had tested the binding on the rocket he leaned it against the wall; selected a slender bamboo on which the thatch was bound, cut it so that a knot blocked one end and the other was left open, and began to whittle holes after the fashion of a flute. Then he took stock of their porters' ammunition. They all four had full bandoliers. The loose cartridges in the haversacks were express cartridges and in addition both whites had their belts full, besides a supply for the revolvers.

Still slower the violet shadows crept on. It was the longest day either man could recollect, yet neither grumbled. When the sun began to peer under the cloud of the mountain Birskett woke up. The long *shauri* had ceased; many more men had joined the cluster of women, who never tired of watching the whites, or their dinner, as you like.

"Now, doc, time to stick on the war paint." He explained at length. Then, addressing their men, instructed them in their parts.

Sitting well within the hut he began to blow on the primitive flute. The result was scarcely soothing to white ears, but seemed sufficiently interesting to the crowd, for they began, the women particularly, to press forward curiously. The weird squealing and squawking carried on the still, hot air.

The sun's rays turned the pinnacles of the hut to golden pagodas and bloodied the cloud tops. Still came the magical squealing and wailing from within the hut. At last night came. The twilight glimmered and was gone.

"Now, doc, get busy!" whispered Birskett. "*Tooooo—loooooo—ooooooo!* That's it! Shove on my veil. *Ooooooow—looooooo!* Stick your finger through so's I can blow! *Meeeeee—ooooow! looooo—loooooo—toooooo! Now* give 'em a shot with the limelight. *Looooo!*"

The sweeping torch revealed bronze face after face, flashing on teeth and spears and charms. Came a perceptible grunt.

"Fine! that's getting 'em! *Toooooo! looooooo! Toooo!* Light up behind my back! *Tooooooo!* Give the boys theirs! *Meeeee—ooooow!*"

There was a glow of a match within the hut and five red hot points moved in the gloom while the flute screamed angrily. Smothered squeals echoed. A blinding light struck out and showed five men with fire in their mouths and two whose masked faces resembled vast white stones. The torch shifted. Fires glowed and moved. Came a chorus of deep grunts.

"That's got 'em going! Touch off the rocket, doc!"

A red fire moved and more fire began spitting like an angry wild cat. Simultaneously with the explosion burst a shrill hiss and a whirling scream as the fire shot into the stars.

Sounded the scampering of bare feet. In the light of the bursting rocket above them came the clank of dropping weapons and of coughs forced from contracted bellies.

"Now let the band play!"

Six glowing red embers began to move silently through the village: a white glare darted, showing here the pop eyes of a woman; there, disappearing feet; beyond, flying shoulders.

"Matana! *Mwiti! Jangu!*" (Loads! Come!) said the voice of the doctor in the darkness.

Puffing heartily at his cigar Matana turned off to the left.

"You're crazy, doc!" snapped Birskett. "We can't take the loads."

"I'm only going to get a few necessary things," said the doctor and marched on, holding Matana by the arm.

Swearing beneath his breath Birskett followed. Suddenly in the darting ring of white appeared a wrinkled chest with the shin bone of a man. The circle flashed upwards revealing an ancient face contorted with anger or fright and yelling, but it was advancing. Cries answered him. A red flame and a crash doubled him up like breaking a gun.

"Ask this idiot where the loads are?" came the unruffled voice of the doctor.

"*Aluwa? Aluwa?*" (Where is it?) he repeated.

"Quick, doc," said Birskett, "as soon as they get over the shock they'll be on us!"

Matana, a bit rattled, turned into a compound. The torch revealed the loads scattered around the hut. The doctor selected one of several special cases made of steel, dampproof and white-ant proof.

Swiftly opening it he expertly snatched this and that package, thrusting each into the boys' haversacks while they and Birskett stood smoking cigars with their rifles ready, facing the yowls, cries and commotion without. A piercing squeal rose and dropped to a moaning howl.

"They've found Noah," said Birskett. "Get a hustle on, doc."

Calmly the doctor opened another box and selected more packages. Then he sighed heavily.

"Right. Go on!"

"Switch that torch around," said Birskett as he came up.

The light revealed a medley of bronze figures and faces. Some were skulking behind huts; others were mouthing like lunatics, spears in hand. Yet they flinched at the electric beam and scuffled back as the six advanced.

As they went through the gate a spear sang between Birskett and Zapoko.

"Volley!" commanded Birskett, and five rifles crashed into the village followed by a belated crack from the doctor's express.

Howls and screeches arose.

They hastened on through the grass. Ninety yards away they stopped to place another broadside into the village, the tops of which they could see against the stars.

"That'll discourage 'em some as well as the evil spirits for tonight," said Birskett. "Now, for the mountains! Gosh, you've sure got some nerve, doc!"

"Oh!" said Kirkton apologetically. "You see I really needed those things. I told you that."

IX

The hereditary terror of an unknown phenomenon is slowly being eradicated from the civilized animal. A telephone, which would have been attributed to magic by our own forefathers, to the modern man is no more astonishing than his penknife. To see any given act as another person sees it is extremely difficult; but for a white man with a mind which has been molded by generations of civilization, it is nigh impossible to understand the terror of a savage.

So it was that the effect upon the natives had been far more than Birskett had imagined or dared to hope. The ground had been well manured previously. Ever since the death of the chief from sleeping sickness there had been jealousy and strife between a faction led by Zofulo, the father, and that under the sway of Bafakoki, the witch doctor.

According to the custom of this tribe a chief should have been elected from among the most renowned warriors and hunters, but since the killing and eating of the white man the power of Bafakoki had grown enormously. Had the dread disease not stricken, as he had prophesied, a man, woman or child, for many moons afterwards? No one could deny it. Now he aspired to be chief as well as witch doctor and had by his newly acquired reputation staved off the selection of a chief.

Then had appeared more whites. Bafakoki rejoiced and sought eagerly to repeat his last culinary triumph and thus to clinch his power for good. But a new factor came, on which he had not counted—greed for the loads represented wealth such as no savage among them dreamed existed in the world.

He was ancient and withered; had more native wealth than he could eat or drink and four wives too many for his management; yet just as with many whites, the older he became the more wealth he desired. He was not sophisticated enough to say that he wanted it for his children.

What was in the loads and what they could do with them never occurred to any of the savages. Everything appertaining to a white man was rare and desirable—therefore exchangeable, therefore wealth.

Thus greed heartened the opposition faction. Bafakoki, as they knew well, would take nine-tenths for himself. Each warrior saw in himself, in his own esteem of his prowess in war and the chase, an indisputable reason why he should be chief and grab the wealth.

Even Zofulo developed a strong sense of injustice, claiming that as no new chief had been elected, the wealth was his as the father of the dead chief. So all day they had argued with each other and with Bafakoki who, to his rising alarm, saw his authority slipping away, and strove to use his prestige as a most mighty and murderous witch doctor to frighten into them some respect for the constitutional law.

He threatened and cajoled, but to no purpose. Greed for the moment was stronger than superstitious fears. Then desperation gave him a brain wave, an obvious argument which he wondered himself why he hadn't thought of before. The loads, as everybody knew, were tabu until the devils pertaining to every stranger's person or goods were exorcised by a witch doctor. Although there were other witch doctors, they were merely, so to speak, small-town practitioners. Then had occurred the uproar that the whites had heard.

That move was an ace; he withdrew the compromises made and secured two-thirds of the loads. Then, very self-satisfied, he retired to his hut to prepare incantations and magical brews as a dressing for the white victims of the feast.

In the hut he heard the first squall of the flute. He listened. He could not recognize it as beast or man. An uneasy squirmy feeling began to grow in his withered paunch. He struggled to retain his dignity. His wives were watching and trembling. He heard the grunts.

"*Ahuu!*" came in a terrified whisper through the hut wall.

He went. After all, *Ahuu* and spirits generally were his job. But when he saw men breathing fire and smoke, and something noiseless and without touch smote him in the face—the arc of the torch—he quit.

Possibly, knowing more about devils, he intended to abandon these foolish creatures to their fate which, if mortal, might mean a bigger share of the loads for him. In his hut he cowered and literally squawked incantations, the primitive form of prayer. The hiss and the squeal of the rocket nearly killed him with fright.

Grunts, whispers, and the scuffle of feet and the dread voices of the devils speaking sounded; then a muffled cry.

So strange is human nature that that cry galvanized him into action, wrenched him to his wabbly feet, and propelled him out; for a man had said the devils were going to take the loads.

He never had time to be scared any more.

At first his fellows could not understand that he had been killed; one kills with a spear or poison. Some gathered around him in the dark, bawling idiotic questions; others ran and hid. Zofulo and some of the bravest, drawn by the same magnet, rushed after the whites, each wildly urging his brother to attack. When the torch ray came again they flinched, half-expecting to fall as Bafakoki had done. They hadn't yet realized that he was dead.

When the whites marched to the gate some of the savages were relieved that they hadn't whisked the loads into the air.

The volley paralyzed them, the noise and the flame stabs were veritable demons. The stricken bawled and howled with fright and pain. A man cried that he was dead. Then the idea of the striking death hit them; they grasped what had happened in some mysterious way to Bafakoki. A dying man in his agony clutched at the legs of another. Crazy with fright the man stabbed at his neighbor. At that moment came the second volley. They went mad, screaming and hacking each at his fellow.

The dim moon rose on maimed, dying and dead and others cowering in huts and corners. When the mountain twilight came bronze figures, writhing and stiff, sprawled all over the village in pools of blood, and from the huts came the moans of the women, the whimpering of children and the bass mutter of men. The sounds died gradually. Men began to peep out of, to emerge from, their huts. But the sun was plowing the usual way through the peak clouds. Women followed, seeking their men.

Those alive and not mortally hurt went by habit, yet fearfully, to the club house. Zofulo was there. The white devils were gone. That was the first topic. Some ventured to scout. They began to discuss the previous evening. Perhaps they had been bewitched. Why else had they fought one with the other? Ehh! And perhaps after all they had been really white men. Perhaps Bafakoki's magic had been weak? Who knows? Ehh!

Talk is often like what is miscalled Dutch courage. They continued busily. But something was already in a convalescent state and was beginning to pluck at their minds, firmly but gently. Presently the lead came. Another witch doctor suggested that perhaps it was just as well that Bafakoki had gone—he had been no good as a sorcerer anyway, otherwise the whites would not have escaped.

Others immediately recalled cases where the departed had sadly lacked virtue. The rival witch doctor was rather surprized and tickled by the success of the suggestion. He enlarged upon it. By the time the shadows were appreciably beginning to dwindle it was unanimously decided that the loss of the whites and the slaughter of their brothers was Bafakoki's fault.

Then burst out the subject which was eating them all—the loads!

They grew bolder as they talked. The bright young medico saw himself as the successful candidate for Bafakoki's place. He boasted that his magic was stronger than Bafakoki's. Ehh! Even than the whites! He would exorcise the devils from the loads.

Amid a crowd without the compound, momentarily expecting him to vanish or to be blown sky high, he sprinkled a magical brew. His was strong medicine! Ehh!

They crowded in then, but respectfully left the powerful wizard to handle the loads. In one of the cases, carelessly left open by the doctor, he found a pot, and in the pot a curious looking substance; long like strips of slender white bamboo.

The stuff broke easily in his hand. With an eye to future constituents he generously handed it around like a child with some candy, and actuated by the same infantile instinct, they each and all put some in their mouths to see if it was food. It was cyanide of potassium, carried by the doctor for his bug-killing bottle—

In a deserted village lie skeletons scattered about; here and there, among what once were huts, pokes up an edge of a rusty case.

Years after, when an expedition of the British Museum passed through that country, the natives fled on sight; not one could be coaxed out of the grass or jungle. The whites wondered why.

X

Nearly forty miles away the two Americans were sleeping in a thicket of jungle grass, unwitting that their precious loads had been abandoned by the savages in their panic stricken hegira; although little advantage would have been theirs even had they known, lacking any hope of finding porters.

At the opening of a primitive shelter made by knotting the tall grass at the ends, squatted Zapoko on guard with eyes and ears. From the look of the land when morning had dawned they had discovered that the distance to the mountain slopes was very much farther than they had estimated; also, that an arm of the swamp circled right around between them and the high ground. As yet they had not been able to determine how far. About three o'clock Birskett awoke and sat up, scratching his half-grown beard.

"Gosh, I've got an almighty thirst!" he muttered.

"*Leta Chai,*" (Bring some tea,) he began and stopped.

For a moment he had forgotten. He looked at Kirkton's naturally pallid face smeared with a dark growth of two days, for he had always shaved punctiliously. The doctor lay curled up, sleeping peacefully.

"Poor old doc," he mused with a grin, "guess he'll have to get used to face moss now. Lord, won't he swear! Wonder how he'll take it all around?"

He stared thoughtfully at the mountain peaks above the grass.

"A fellow will want a whopping big sense of humor to stick it out for the next few weeks or months if I can read any Injun signs when he ain't even got enough to keep a toy boat afloat," he thought. "Still, he'll make it all right once he gets the big idea. Well, I guess my belly says I'd better take a chance and try to scare up some perambulating dinner.

"*Jangu, Kubi!*" he said, shaking the boy awake. "*Tugende tuige.* (Let's go hunting.) *Mangu! Leta mundu. Aluwa*? (Quickly. Bring the shotgun. Where is it?) *Kuma muliro*, (Light a fire,)" he added to Matana.

In future there would be no white man's grub or drink. They'd have to shoot to fill their bellies—at any rate until they found Stoutt's folk, as he called them in his mind.

They had not remarked any village or signs of natives, and even if there were any about they needed food badly; for as they had refused to stop for supper the previous day, they hadn't had a bite since the day before, and the doctor had not eaten much then. But before starting Birskett mounted the hillock and cautiously reconnoitered.

"Damned queer," he commented, "that those fellows don't get on our trail! They must be madder than scalded cats!"

The country, which was a jumble of broken hills ending toward the mountains in swamp, didn't look very promising for buck; but they might flush a bird of some sort. In the long grass the buck would hear or smell them long before they could see him.

They made down hill. Once a bird got up from a clump of bushes, but Birskett saw that it was a carrion eater.

"Damn it," he muttered to himself, as he lowered the gun, "sha'n't get anything, or if we do it'll be too late to cook before dark," for he didn't wish to advertise their presence by night for miles around. A touch on his arm and the black finger of Kubi showed him that something was moving some hundred yards away through a patch of long grass. He grabbed the rifle and waited.

A black tip appeared and sent both of them to earth. Followed, with the pompous majesty of an alderman, a rhinoceros whose hide was a dirty gray color.

"Now," cried Birskett, "if that isn't all the damned luck! And by — — he's white too! Oh, you prize beauty!" he muttered wrathfully. "And to think I can't spare a bullet for you without scaring any buck there may be to Kingdom Come!"

Fortunately, or unfortunately, Birskett was almost in doubt which, what air there was stirring was moving from the beast toward them; a rhino, shortsighted and suspicious, will, nine times out of ten, charge blindly at any smell from a campfire to his own dung. However, he moved on slowly and disappeared. They made back tracks and continued their hunt.

An hour later they were rewarded by bagging a young *pookoo* which, although not very delicate eating, is quite good with hunger sauce. They cut him up and divided the hind quarters and the liver and kidneys between them, for without pepper and salt they had no means of curing the meat to carry with them as biltong.

Well content, they set out for camp, reckoning on half an hour at least after they got there to cook before sunset. Paying more attention to possible roving natives or their friend the rhino, they missed the right hill, and failed to see the camp which was well hidden, until they were upon it.

As they were striding up the incline came a bright flash. In a few paces Birskett grinned. Squatting before a small mirror which had reflected the western sun was the doctor calmly shaving.

Just then Kubi's keen eyes spotted grass tops moving. He stopped and pointed. As they looked, a huge form appeared, moving rapidly. He saw Matana crouched over the fire and the two Sudanese rise and heard their yells. The next instant the bulk seemed to pass right over the doctor as he scraped meticulously at his chin, and vanished in the long grass.

"My God!" groaned Birskett, dropping the hind leg of buck. "He's got him!"

But as he ran, the doctor's voice was raised loud in execration, and he saw his form rise, grab a rifle and, flapping haversacks, disappear in the wake of the rhino.

"Doc! doc!" bawled Birskett. "Come back, you idiot!"

"Good Lord!" he thought. "The beast'll get him as sure as death in this grass," and sprinted to cut him off.

He came round the hillock in time to see the furious doctor standing with his rifle, and the rhino, who had heard as well as smelt him, coming down on him like a runaway Ford truck.

Birskett dared not risk a shot because if he missed he might hit Kirkton. He stopped, holding his breath. When the form of the rhino seemed to intermingle with that of the doctor, came the report. The next instant the doctor reappeared as the brute seemed to curtsy before him and lie down at his feet.

"My heavenly forefathers!" gasped Birskett as he ran up. "Where did you learn to shoot?"

"Eh? Oh, bear," said the doctor calmly. "Vacations. But the — — brute's broken my mirror."

"Good Lord, man, but I thought you were gone for sure! How on earth did he miss you?"

"I was so mad, I don't quite know," confessed the doctor, bending over the dead rhino. "I didn't see him until he was almost touching me and threw myself aside. I suppose. But what a peculiar color he is!"

"Sure, he's a white rhino—rarer than honest folk in Broadway. We saw him away back and didn't dare shoot for fear of scaring the game. Anyway it's a shame to bag a beast you can't eat or collect. Still he surely asked for it! But we've got some meat anyway. Hungry?"

"Hungry? Man, I could eat this fellow all by myself."

By the swarming of the stars the cooking was done. They stamped out the fire and dined well, hunter fashion. Birskett half-expected that the doctor would grouch at having no salt or bread, but never a word was said. Birskett began to lose his fears.

"After all," he reflected, watching the doctor skillfully carving a lump of meat with his hunting knife, "I guess I've let my contempt for town guys carry me a bit too far—thank the good Lord!"

Striking over the hills directly for the mountains they hit the swamp about midnight and holding to the firmer ground struck back along the edge. But presently, as they could not make a hazard as to how far the arm of the forest extended nor of the breadth and crossing possibilities, they camped—that is, they sat down in the long grass in the middle of a skirmishing party of ants. They removed hurriedly and eloquently—and again sat down in the long grass.

"Seems to me," remarked Birskett, "that this damned country of our late friends is a kind of an island surrounded by river and swamp, which probably they're scared to death to cross on account of the pigmies. Recollect how jumpy they were down by the river? Maybe it's the *Ahuu*, as they call 'em, but more probably a combination of both. That would account for their knowing little of white men. I'm for tackling the swamp. In our condition we can't afford to fool walking around like a circus hack."

"If you think so, I'm game," said the doctor. "Probably we shall find the swamp full of flies, and possibly pigmies."

"Possibly pigmies," agreed Birskett, "and also probably flies! Oh sure!"

In the twilight they ascended the highest summit around. From the general lie of the land, Birskett's theory of the island seemed about correct. On the far mountain slope Abdul, the Sudanese, sighted a wisp of smoke.

"Stoutt's people!" exclaimed the doctor jubilantly.

"Maybe, and again maybe it ain't," said Birskett. "But you're sure a hog on optimism, ain't you, doc? Now let's see how far you can swim!"

From the look of the edge of the swamp Birskett's joke seemed true. The grass land ran into the same spinach green of treacherous slime and water as at the granite river barrier, some fifty yards or more. Beyond the snakelike roots of the forest began, rose against the sun like a vast cavern of dense violet shadows out of which gnarled limbs, dripping humid festoons, beckoned in sinister welcome.

"There he is!" exclaimed the doctor, and there seemed to be an exultant note in the voice as a fly about the size of a common horsefly flew past.

"*Mangu! Matana, Mutego!*" (Quick! Matana, my trap—fly net!) But it was too late.

As they stood regarding the dank barrier of swamp, seeking a method to cross, came a shriek followed by a wild and angry chattering. Something caught their eyes near the uprising roots and a vague body like a moving strip of the swamp slowly vanished into the gloom.

"Water python, I guess," said Birskett, in answer to the doctor. "Everybody seems at home and in good health anyway!"

Any attempt to wade they knew would be fatal; to swim was equally impossible; and there was no timber sufficiently solid within reach to make a corduroy passage. They began to walk along, hoping for luck. Several odd flies hovered about. As they put on their net masks, neither made remark; but Birskett was seeing the last inhabitants of those villages, and the doctor found himself recalling the symptoms.

A little after noon a tiny cape of land seemed to run out almost to the forest. And so it proved. At the extremity there was but a gap of twenty feet to the nearest of the forest roots. As they sat in the hot sun studying the problem, the doctor pointed towards the fringe of the forest, remarking:

"See that, Birskett? Some more of that extraordinary fungus we saw in the forest away back."

But Birskett swore and clapped his hand to his neck.

"Fly?" said the doctor.

"Yes," said Birskett. "I think I've got a hunch," he continued, and rose. "Here; give me a hand in case I slip."

Cautiously he waded up to his knees in the swamp edge and then began groping beneath the foul slime.

"Thought so!" he exclaimed and brought up a handful of long fibrous stuff which looked like water lily roots. "Plait 'em. Rope one of those branches. Drag ourselves over."

"But clothes and guns?"

"Make a raft of grass and tow 'em over. Some bath but—coming?"

The doctor sniffed disgustedly at the stench from the disturbed slime, his eyes wandered to the mountains, and he nodded. When they had dragged up a quantity of roots they retired to the grass hillocks behind to avoid the stench and the flies.

With a knife Birskett made slits in the tough fiber stuff and turned in each end several times, a crude splicing, and tested each link by making the boys haul on it. But it was a long job and the daylight had gone before it was finished.

Next morning, after completing the clumsy lariat, Birskett prepared for the attempt. The primitive rope was stiff and greasy in the hand, even after drying in the sun. The first throw fell short, and the second; the third struck the huge forest limb he was aiming for, but failed to grip. Twenty-seven times he tried.

"I'll get you yet, you son-of-a-gun!" he cried and, dripping sweat, sat down. "I've got it, but how the — — am I going to get stones?"

"Stones?"

"Yep. Bolas. Greaser stunt. Only thing that'll do it."

But there seemed to be no stones within a hundred miles. It took him exactly thirty minutes to surmount that obstacle by filling his two boots with earth.

"The Lord grant one doesn't slip off," he muttered as he swung the substitute balls over his head, "or I'll have to hop for the rest of the road!"

At the third cast the weighted boots caught, wrapping even the stiff fiber around the limb and jamming themselves in the branches. They tested it by hanging on and pulling all together. In the mean time the boys had made a thick raft of long grass bound together with the fibrous roots.

Birskett stripped and grimaced at the doctor.

"Fly or no we'll have to take a chance," said he, as he slung his revolver holster around his bare neck. "I'll be some sweet smelling violet by the time I get there!"

"Are there crocs?" said the doctor.

"Perhaps."

"Snakes?"

"Shouldn't be surprized. Ough! — — the beast!" A tsetse had dug its proboscis into the flesh of his hip. "Now for the interstate, twenty yards championship!"

Holding the flap of the holster between his teeth and letting the lariat coil between his legs he plunged, and went hand over hand so swiftly that his body scarcely sank in the dense slime deeper than his thighs.

He looked in the glow of the sun, with green limbs and front, like some strange half-human creature of the forest as he began to clamber on to the great protruding root. He halted for a moment to adjust his revolver and disappeared into a mass of foliage seeking a better platform.

Suddenly his gun whipped out and almost following the report a part of the very limb on which the lariat was attached seemed to detach itself and fell writhing into the swamp. Four more shots followed swiftly.

The doctor stark, with the root lariat in his hands, paused on the brink, watching the commotion in the slime.

"Gang's all here!" Birskett shouted. "Come on, doc. It's all right! This fellow's as dead as cold pork. It's only his emotions!"

XI

On a rump of land jutting out from a sheer cliff of the mountain was a village of some five hundred huts, like brown men squatting with their backs against a wall. From a knoll some hundred yards away was a view of the Ituri forest rolling a thousand miles to the western horizon. There, beneath a great Bombax tree, nigh a hundred feet high, and a great mass of scarlet flowers, was the green tent of a white man's camp.

By the time the sun had escaped the veil of the mountain peaks, the shadows were so small that the people called themselves the Tiny Children of the Mountain, although in stature they were by no means short. The idea was derived partly from the dim sense of insignificance in the presence of colossal nature, and partly from the fact that their souls—their shadows—began their lives—days—in so diminutive a size.

Squatted on his hams upon a leopard skin in the shelter of the club house in the center of the village was the chief of the Tiny Children of the Mountains, a powerfully built man of middle age, dark bronze of skin, with a tuft of black wool on his chin and a safety razor suspended by a circlet of beads upon his carven chest. Over his thighs was a greasy shirt, which had once been white, tied by the arms around his waist like a wrestler's embrace.

Near him, but a little to one side, was an ancient, withered and bony of body and limbs. Worked into the scanty wool of his skull were withered bits of brownish purple specked with dull red like streaks of arterial blood. His skinny legs and hips were enveloped in a ragged pair of lavender silk drawers, and on one foot was a gray sock with green clocks, carefully tied up with fiber.

Facing them was a group of some twenty-five younger men, mostly clad in monkey skins over the loins.

Boko, the chief, was talking to a young man, carrying a short stabbing spear.

"And thou hast spoken with these whites, O Zako?"

"*Mwami!*" (Chief!)

"Thinkest thou they are brothers of the Giver of Life?"

"*Simanyi, Mwami,* (I don't know, chief,) for never have mine eyes seen nor mine ears heard him."

"True. What manner of men be they?"

"One is bald of face with eyes like unto a bird's, and the other is a great man, bearded, who laughs. Their speech is soft and their words are gentle. With them are three men who come they say from where the sun rises, many moons from here. Lubo and I, hunting in the mountain, first saw them coming from the forest. We went to greet them and led them to the village of my father. Their limbs were like reeds and their bellies stuck to their bones, so that we fed them."

"You did well, O Zako," returned the chief, "for maybe they are indeed brothers of the Giver of Life. Who may know? Of what spake they?"

"They spoke of the road and the wild men and craved permission to come to visit the great chief, Boko. Ehh!"

"Have they great wealth, O Zako?" spoke up a man sitting in the front rank.

"Nay, nought have they except that which they carry. They tell of the savages beyond the forest who sought to eat them and stole their goods, but they overcame them with their magic."

"Enough! When they shall come, bring them to me."

The chief turned to the general group.

"What think you then, O my children, of this other white man?"

"His smell is not good, O my father," returned a lusty man in the van. "He comes with a double tongue seeking that which is forbidden."

"Ehh!" added Zano, a young man wearing a broken gunmetal wristwatch. "And he is not of the same tribe as the Giver of Life. This I know, for did not the Sacred One teach me His Tongue? He spoke as a bird speaketh, but this man speaks like to a great bleating, even as the bald one of four eyes, of whom He said, 'Beware, for this man is no brother of mine.' This is a brother of the one of no hair and four eyes. Ehh! This I know."

He held up his hand. "Gave He not me this powerful charm the day I slew the mountain leopard? Ehh! Was I not of His family?"

"Ough! Ough!" grunted others, and even the chief paid attention to his words.

"Let us slay him!" cried out another young man from the rear, followed by savage "Oughs!" of approval.

"Nay," responded Boko gravely, "for that is against the laws of the Giver of Life. Thou, Zano, what said He concerning the matter?"

"He said," returned Zano with the air of a child proudly repeating a lesson by rote, "that never must we turn our spears against the race of the whites; that we must have straight tongues and white hearts in our dealings with them; that the thief shall be punished by us and the goods be returned to the white man; that food and drink shall be for the white man as for our brothers; that we shall listen to the words and the ways of the white man for therein is much profit and wisdom."

"Ough! Ough!" grunted some of his fellows in approval, but there were others that murmured, saying: "Slay him! Slay him!"

"Cease thy idle cries!" suddenly shrilled the ancient. "Do you dare to know the words of the Giver of Life, you sons of wild men? Do you dare to vomit the wisdom of Him? His tongue shall rot between his teeth! His guts shall be spilled as water! His women shall shrivel as thatch grass beneath him! His spears shall be reeds! His chest shall grow hag's breasts! His soul shall be torn by the claws of *Ahuu!* I have spoken!"

A sonorous murmur of horror rose from the recalcitrants at the threat of the witch doctor who relapsed into immobility almost as startlingly as he had broken it. After a pause, as it to allow the fumes of the curse to evaporate, said the chief—

"Let the white man be brought!"

Three youths sitting on the outskirts of the throng rose and loped down the hill. While they were gone all sat motionless. Save for the pounding of corn in many mortars and the occasional whimper of a baby or the laugh of a child, there was silence.

Twenty minutes later appeared a white man with a short, blond beard clad in white, wearing a great solar *topi* with a green puggaree, a revolver strapped around a full waist, and carrying a cane of hippopotamus hide. Behind him marched stiffly a tall native of charcoal hue carrying a green camp chair.

The white man walked through the narrow lane left for him and directed the servant to put the chair before the chief. As he sat he wrinkled his nose with a disgusted "Phoo" at the heat and the smell of the natives. Sharp eyes watched him and keen ears heard him. Boko and Yarazoo, the ancient witch doctor, regarded him mutely and as expressionlessly as tree trunks.

The white man stared back at the chief arrogantly, as if trying to compel him to shift his gaze. The white man's eyelids were forced to blink, but the chief's seemed of metal.

The duel continued for perhaps three minutes, which is a long time to hold a gaze. Then the white man frowned and irritably slapped his leg with his *kiboko*; but the chief had won and all knew it.

"*Otyano!*" said the white, and he spoke as a bad-tempered boss nodding "Howdy" to a floor scrubber and he omitted the courtesy of "*Mwami.*"

"*Nkalamusiza, sebo,*" (I am glad to see you, sir,) returned the chief, tonelessly neglecting the usual superlative.

A few more of the polite sentences which native etiquette demands were stated rather than spoken. Then came another silence.

"*Kirabo?*" (The present?) queried the white, as one sharply reminding another of a breach of manners.

"*Nkirabye. Webale, sebo.*" (I have seen it. Thanks, sir.)

Came another silence. The white man shifted his eyes to the graven image of the old witch doctor and vaguely wondered what he wore in his wool; then he regarded the group of young men, each one a cast bronze statue of wide-eyed indifference.

Having, as he considered, wasted sufficient time in native fashion, he bent one knee across the other and leaning slightly forward, addressed the chief:

"Mazana, thy brother, O Boko, sent thee good tidings of me?"

"*Wao.*" (Yes.)

"His words have told thee that which I seek for?"

"*Wao.*"

"Thou hast not seen aught of the magic leaves which the white man had?"

"*Neda.*" (No.)

"Yet wast thou not a friend of the white chief?"

"*Wao.*"

"Were not these charms upon thy breast and upon those of thy men given by him?"

"*Wao.*"

"How comes it then that thou hast no knowledge of these other things that were his?"

"*Simanyi.*" (I don't know.)

"Were not these magic leaves (books) kept with most powerful charms?"

"*Simanyi.*"

"Have you got them?"

"*Neda.*"

The white man made a sucking sound of impatience, but he continued stolidly.

"*Okirabye?*" (Have you seen them?)

"*Kwerabira.*" (I have forgotten.)

"*Kulimba,*" (Don't lie to me,) snapped the white.

The chief neither deigned to reply nor did the muscles of his face budge, but the eyelids narrowed slightly. A murmurous grunt from the body of the men warned the white, who swore under his breath, uncrossed his leg and straightened up. He began again.

"How was this white man called?"

"The Giver of Life."

The white man stared hard and seemed agitated.

"Why did you give him that name?"

"Who shall know?"

Another "*thith*" of irritation escaped the white.

"But did you not know two white men?"

"*Wao.*"

"Of which speak you?"

"Not of the bald one of four eyes."

"Lörtzer!" muttered the white. Then, aloud—

"But of the other, the Giver of Life, he is dead?"

"*Ezikidi.*"

The white man was puzzled by the word which may mean "put out" or "evaporated in thin air."

"But he died here among you?" he insisted.

"*Neda! Neda!*" (Certainly not!)

"He is not dead?"

"*Simanyi, sebo.*" (I don't know, sir.)

The white paused, frowning angrily and plucked at his beard. It began to dawn upon him that he would never get any information out of them, as he had failed to do with another branch of the Tiny Children of the Mountain who had merely passed him on. He tried another tack.

"Do you know of the sleeping death?"

"*Wao, sebo!*"

"Do many of thy people die from it?"

"None, sir."

The reply seemed to excite the white out of his careful efforts to preserve a native-like restraint. He leaned forward.

"Wherefore none? Are not your neighbors eaten up in their hundreds?"

"*Simanyi, sebo.*"

An exasperated oath escaped the bearded lips and he gripped the *kiboko* as if longing to thrash the chief for his obstinacy. He glared at the immobile features of the witch doctor. The sun caught a red streak of the headdress, which seemed to irritate the white man the more. He restrained himself by an effort and seemed to consider. Finally he said—

"Have you heard naught of two white men who come from the river?"

"*Simanyi, sebo.*"

"Hear my words. They are white. White men shall come and they have black hearts. They are the whites who eat up the blacks in the land of *Mtesa* (Uganda). *Wulidi?*" (Thou hast heard?)

"*Pulidi, sebo.*" (I have heard, sir.)

"Know also, O chief Boko, that he who shall bring to me the magic leaves of the Giver of Life, as you call him, shall have what price he may ask—guns he may have, with ten men's loads of bullets—*bafta* he shall have for twenty porters—I have spoken. Take my words and talk with thy head men and warriors."

The white rose.

"*Emshi,*" (Go,) he said to his servant. The latter picked up the chair, and to the chief:

"*Werabi. Mwami.*" (Goodbye—see yourself—chief.)

"*Kale, weraba, sebo,*" responded Boko politely.

The eyes and heads followed the white man's progress, but no man spoke until he was out of sight.

Then broke out a hubbub of chatter among them.

"Ehh!" exclaimed Zako. "Have I not told you that he is a brother of the Bald One with Four Eyes? Is not his walk even as his like to a crane? Ehh!"

"He knoweth not gentle words," said the chief quietly, "and thou sayest, Zako, these new white men speak. Ehh!"

"Eeh!" shrilled the witch doctor, and silence was instantly given. "The stranger hath blood and greed in his heart! Let no man bite his words. I have spoken."

"Let us slay him!" came a ferocious murmur from the body of men. "Let us slay him before evil befall us!"

"Is not the Giver of Life our father that you would disobey him?" reproved Boko gravely. "Be silent, my children!"

As he rose to dismiss the meeting a long quavering cry reached them on the warm air.

"They come! The white men come!" cried the men and rushed like school children to the gate of the village overlooking the valley. Issuing at that moment out of a clump of trees was a party of natives and with them two white men.

Twenty minutes later these two were ascending the knoll; Kirkton and Birskett, their clothes green-slimed and torn, nearly as haggard as skeletons, their faces so swollen from insect bites that they could scarcely see.

The doctor limped, and Birskett had his left arm stuck in his shirt in lieu of a sling. Breasting the hill they saw the white man's camp beneath the great scarlet Bombax tree.

"Whites, by — —," exclaimed Birskett as they both stopped.

Beneath the tent fly was a white man lounging in a chair writing.

"Say, doc, I've got a hunch who that fellow is," added Birskett quickly. "If I'm right, keep a tight mouth. Get me? Come along, let's see him."

As the man raised his head, Birskett laughed silently.

"Now what d'you know about that!" he whispered. "Your damned jackal-eared Chinaman on the boat, doc, as sure as I'm half-eaten!"

XII

Birskett turned to the head man of the escorting Tiny Children of the Mountains and said in a low voice:

"Excuse us, my friends, we would speak with this white man."

"As the chief shall wish," replied the man politely. "We shall await him in the village?"

"*Neda, Neda, munange.*" (Certainly not, my friend, wait for us.)

For a moment the stranger stared uncertainly. Then his beard split in a smile and he rose, saying in stilted English but without accent:

"Ah, good morning, gentlemen! Most unexpected to find white men in these districts! Sit down if you please! One moment—yes!"

He called sharply to his servant to bring chairs. The boy came at a run with two camp stools.

"Will you, sir?" he said to Kirkton, offering the chair.

"Thanks!" said Kirkton, who was extremely tired and very glad to sit once more in a chair. Birskett straddled a stool, so that his foot was almost in contact with the doctor's.

"Yes, don't look for a bunch of whites around these parts, eh?" said Birskett, eying the host with a slight smile.

"No, certainly not," said he. "Very unusual, is it not so? You will drink, sir?" as the well trained servant placed a bottle of whiskey on the table.

"Oh, boy!" ejaculated Birskett with a laugh, and the doctor sighed.

As they tasted what seemed nectar of the gods and what they both badly needed, the man was, Birskett noted, taking stock of them minutely.

"Ah," he went on, "you have had some very bad traveling, sir? Do you come from the Congo, yes?"

"No," said Kirkton, "round from Uganda. Mighty rough going. Oh, my name's Kirkton—Dr. Kirkton—and this is Mr. Birskett."

"Oh, yes. I am Mr. van der Byl, Cornelius van der Byl of Amsterdam. I intend to explore the Ruwenzori. I believe it has never yet been explored, is it not so?"

Birskett's foot touched the doctor's toes.

"Mighty interesting!" said the former. "Guess we'll be kind of rivals. We're bound on the same track, but anyway we'll come to terms and divide the honors, Mr. van der Byl." He laughed. "Say, did you come around by Muanza and German territory or up along the lakes from the south?"

"I came, as you say, sir, by the lakes from the south—through Nyassa, is it not?"

While Birskett was holding him in conversation, the doctor's bright eyes were watching him keenly, of which he seemed to be aware. Suddenly in a pause the doctor jerked in—

"Did you ever know Dr. Lörtzer, Mr. van der Byl?"

"Lörtzer?"

Mr. van der Byl stared at the canvas ceiling in the effort to recall the name.

"No, I do not recollect that gentleman. He was a Hollander, is it not?"

"No." Birskett, watching the doctor, almost thought he was going to smile. "No. He was a well-known German scientist."

"Very interesting, yes. But why do you ask, sir, in this far country?"

"Oh," said Kirkton, "because he was around here. I thought perhaps he was a friend of yours."

"I am so very sorry, but I do not know him." Mr. van der Byl smiled. "You will please stop to lunch, is it not?"

"Sure, thanks!" cut in Birskett swiftly as he saw the doctor was in doubt whether to refuse. "But we'll have to go right up and fix our camp."

"Ah, but will you not camp beside me? I shall be most happy."

"Guess that depends on the chief," evaded Birskett, as they both rose.

"Gosh!" he murmured to the doctor, as they joined the waiting natives. "He's a bum liar, doc!"

"Are you sure he's the man you saw on the boat?"

"Sure! I wish to God you were as sure of finding the cure, doc!" said Birskett soberly. "I'd swear on fifty different kind of oaths that's he's the fellow whom I caught peeking in the porthole that time you were cutting loose about Stoutt. As soon as he tumbled to who you were—and what you were after—he tried to frame that Uganda stunt to hold you up. Don't you get that? Now he's madder'n Hades. We've got to watch out. Van der Byl! Hollander! Doesn't the damned squarehead know they call themselves Nederlanders? Amsterdam? Guess he was born on the other side of the Rhine!"

"What was his name?" inquired the doctor. "You looked it up on board."

"Sure. And you got so damned mad with me for it! Herr Doktor Hermanus Friedlander." Birskett laughed.

"M'm," muttered the doctor. "Leipzig and Hamburg."

"You know of him then?"

"Heard of him. Never paid attention to your chatter on the boat, Birskett. I apologize. He's a well-known man of the tropical school."

"Then what I thought at first was right!" exclaimed Birskett. "Now his damned lying, like a tenderfoot trying to rope a steer, shows what he's after."

"I wonder he had the nerve, knowing we were on the same boat."

"Oh, a fool always reckons everybody else is a fool. I guess he figured we hadn't noticed him and anyway he'd grown a bit of a beard. But he's clean forgotten those Mongol eyes!"

"Yes, but what *is* he after? That's the point."

"What he's after wouldn't puzzle a kid with the cradle marks on him! The point is, how much and what does he know? And where'd he get it? I guess that pious thug Lörtzer talked some before you ever struck him."

"Yes, but if he did he wouldn't confess to murdering the man—even in Germany."

"Sure, but talk he did, I'll swear. Say, doc, I was that scared you'd refuse the lunch! Man but I'd nigh do red murder for a decent feed. Haven't got a rag of conscience left! Anyway he won't poison us the first round and we may get some more out of him—news I mean. Hullo, here's the chief, I guess. Wonder which one is he? The guy in the shirt or the image in the B.V.D.'s? Lord, they might have been Stoutt's! Sounds near, doc. We'll put up with the chief if we can and not let this Friedlander-Byl fellow know we've got no outfit for just as long as possible."

"*Otyano munange, mwami.*" (Greeting, chief and friend.)

They had been led by Tamangala, the head man of the village, where they had spent two days of needed rest, to the compound of the chief, Boko, who was squatting, together with

Yarazoo, beneath a small awning of palm leaves. Tamangala, murmuring greetings to his chief, remained at the gate with his men. Boko keenly scrutinized the faces of the white men as he bade them sit beside him. Yarazoo, the witch doctor, seemed less image-like than in the club house.

After the usual preliminary domestic and political inquiries the chief—for this was an informal audience—launched a series of questions regarding their journey, apparently not out of a mere native politeness but incited by the story of Zako regarding the cannibals and the loss of the white men's goods. Birskett was a little surprized by the evidence of a prejudice in their favor evinced by the manner and phrasing of the sentences.

Naturally no serious topic was touched upon by either party. When Birskett suggested that they would be glad to avail themselves, as they had no equipment, of their hosts' hospitality, he watched the chief's face. He was well-satisfied, not only by the courtesy with which Boko assured him that a hut and all that they should wish would be placed at their disposal, but by the expression of the eyes which may so often reveal the emotions of a native.

To a question whether they would like to have food and drink immediately—as the native dines only in the evening—he asked to be excused, saying they had already accepted an invitation from the strange white man, whom, he took care to emphasize he did not know, by inquiring from whence he had come and what he sought. To that Boko replied that he knew him not nor his business.

Accompanied by their men they left to taste of the spoil of the enemy, as the doctor put it gravely.

"Damned decent folk!" commented Birskett, as they walked out of the village. "Did you get what he said?"

"Oh, I can follow pretty well now," said Kirkton.

"Sure, but you didn't get exactly the way he said it. That's what counts. Maybe that's something to do with Stoutt. Isn't the game to talk about him yet. But all the same we mustn't forget that this Hamburg guy got here first. Knowing we might turn up, he'd sure try to put us in the wrong somehow. Say, doc, play the same game. You sit quiet, and I'll kid him along. When a hunch strikes you, put it across. That one about Lörtzer got him going. I could see by his eyes that for a moment he wasn't sure whether we'd recognized him or not."

Friedlander they found awaiting them with the promise of a veritable feast laid upon a green table under the tent fly.

"Lordy!" murmured Birskett, licking his swollen lips. "Cocktails! And the son-of-a-gun pretends to think we're just English!"

If he hadn't been so nervously intent upon trying to play a part, Dr. Friedlander would have made quite an excellent host. By the time the lunch was finished and they were taking a liqueur brandy, even Birskett caught himself swearing that after all Friedlander was a damned good fellow. Yet they had had but two drinks.

"Sure," he muttered to himself, "any mutt would play for a sucker that way," and kicked, by way of good measure, the doctor, who looked at him in a mildly aggrieved manner.

Birskett sat bolt upright and scowled in the effort to force himself to pay attention to the conversation. He caught a peculiar glint in the green slit eyes as he heard Friedlander saying:

"I assure you, doctor, that it is most interesting. I have had great fear of catching that terrible disease, but the natives tell me that here there is no danger, is it not? Do you think that you will discover a cure, yes?"

"What's that half-witted idiot been saying?" muttered Birskett indignantly, referring to Kirkton.

"I could not possibly prophesy," the doctor said solemnly, with an unusual drawl, "but, Dr. van der Byl, if you should fall a victim, I should be very glad to experiment upon you in the sacred cause of science."

"I should be very glad, too," answered Friedlander, when a sudden choking on the part of Birskett interrupted him. He glanced sharply at Birskett, but as he seemed to be just comfortably hilarious, he continued his *tête-à-tête* with the doctor. "I suppose, doctor, that you will wish also to experiment upon the natives here, those that have the sickness."

"That's what I've come for," assented Kirkton.

"Ah, yes. But, doctor, let me warn you. These natives are not to be trusted. I have already found to my expense that they are great liars."

"Like all mankind," said the doctor sententiously.

"Of course. Ha! ha!" agreed Friedlander. "But you were speaking philosophically, is it not? I speak as a practical man, yes. The chief here is very cunning and sly. He will promise you, but he will never do. He needs some discipline, yes, but what would you—this is not yet—um—under the supervision of the white man, is it not?"

"Sure!" burst in Birskett a bit heatedly. "Send 'em a bunch of missionaries to teach 'em to wear pants and steal, and an old hat and lie good and hard; teach their women to wear skirts and teach 'em all to get more vices than a monkey has fleas. Sure! I know civilization! Then they're all primed to sell their land for a bottle of hooch. *In vino veritas!* Get that, Mister Ban der Vyl?"

Friedlander stared slightly.

"The sun is exceedingly powerful here," commented the doctor gravely.

"Perhaps Mr. Birskett would prefer another whiskey," said Friedlander with a touch of a sneer.

"Sure, you bet!" assented Birskett. "But don't forget what I said, boy: *In vino veritas!*"

He watched Friedlander pour out his glass, a whacking dose and noticed that he gave the doctor, whom he hadn't asked, fuller measure still. He made a pretense of filling his own glass, in which still remained liquor from his first drink.

By an effort of will Birskett pulled himself together, but decided to keep quiet and watch. He clinked his glass and laughed uproariously and pretended to drink and choke. Then pushing his coffee cup from him, he held his head as if nigh overcome. A covert glance showed him that the doctor's eyelids were unusually heavy.

"Dope!" he muttered. "Right, son, I get you!"

After a few more casual remarks Friedlander reverted to the subject of sleeping sickness again.

"Did you stay a long time in Uganda, doctor?"

"No. Pashed right through."

"Ah, they tell me that there is a great mortality there by the Lake Victoria, is it not?"

"Yes, they told me zo," a trifle thickly. "Birskett's seen it. Ashk him."

"Ah yes," returned Friedlander, glancing at the bowed head of Birskett, whom he didn't seem particularly—and apparently excusably—anxious to question. "I wonder if they'll ever find a cure. Do you, doctor, think that they will, yes?"

"P'raps," said Kirkton, putting his hand to his eyes.

"It is dreadful, yes, ah, yes. Doctor, perhaps you can tell me something?"

"Sure."

"It is not my business, doctor, because I do not know these things, but you will excuse me, is it not?"

"Sure!" Kirkton's hand came down from his eyes; he frowned as a man would with a violent headache.

"I once heard a story of a—these natives told me that a countryman of yours came here some time ago. He was, too, a doctor, and he died here. I wonder if you have heard about him?"

"Wash his name?"

"Stoutt. D'you know him, yes?"

"Heard o' him."

Friedlander glanced at the figure resting on the table which had moved restlessly.

"Was that true, that he died, yes?"

"I dunno. Said sho."

Friedlander bent over Kirkton.

"Tell me, doctor," he said insistently, boring into his eyes, "you must know whether any of his books and papers came back to America?"

"Never heard—never heard—anyzing about it."

Friedlander sat up, lighted a cigaret, looked at the top of Birskett's head and back to the doctor sprawling in the one chair.

"Doctor," he continued, bending over him and persuasively patting his shoulder, "did you ever meet Doctor Lörtzer in America?"

"Lörtzer? Pörtzer?" began the doctor foggily. "Sheem to know name."

"Yes, you told me he was a scientist whom you'd met."

"And when I die don't bury me a-tall!" suddenly interrupted the prostrate head on the table. "But pickle ma bones in alki-alkiho-ol! Put a bot— U-gggh!"

Birskett stirred and sank back again. Friedlander regarded him. He remained quiet.

"You were saying, doctor," he continued, stooping confidingly.

"Dunno. What was I saying?"

He wriggled higher in his chair and blinked his eyes, and then catching sight of Birskett, frowned.

"We were talking about Dr. Lörtzer," reminded Friedlander quickly.

"Dr. Lörtzen?" He blinked at Friedlander. "Dunno. Whosh Dr. Börtzen?"

Friedlander straightened up, darted a look at Birskett and eyed Kirkton doubtfully. Suddenly a new idea seemed to startle him for he clutched Kirkton's shoulder and said dictatorially:

"Have you found those notebooks already, doctor, yes? Do you hear? Answer me!"

He shook the shoulder imperatively.

"You have found those books?"

"I beg your pardon, Misther Van der Byl," said Kirkton, sitting up dazedly, "but I'm afraid your hospitality and the hot shun too mush."

A convulsive heave of the shoulders attracted attention to the head on the table which rose, trying to suppress a yawn, blinked at the doctor, and laughed.

"Gosh, you're sure drunk, doc!" He stood up, swayed and clutched at the table. "Lord, I'm drunk too!" he wailed in an astonished tone. "Gosh, I've never been drunk like zish shince I stole dad's whishky. Shay, doc, what about gettin' home?"

"Yesh," agreed Kirkton, "better go home."

"But, gentlemen," said Friedlander on his feet, "please to stay with me until—until your camp has arrived, I beg you, please!"

"Zanks, Misther Bylander, no place like home, sure zing. Zanks, very mush! Hey, Kubi, M'tana! *Jangu mangu!*" he bawled. "C'mon, doc. Zanks, Bylman, f'r hoshpitality! Guess too mush for us! Nozzer time, huh?"

The doctor attempting to rise from his chair nearly fell. Birskett stood back swaying and regarded him.

"Gosh, ain't he drunk!" he commented and hoo'd with laughter.

"But no, gentlemen," insisted Friedlander, anxiously aiding the doctor by the shoulder. "Please to stop until the heat is finished, yes? You must—"

"No, mush get home," affirmed Birskett. "Shee you t'morrow, ol' boy. *M'tana, wetike mwami yangu!* (Help your chief along!) T'morrow, ol' sport. C'mon, doc!"

In truth the doctor could scarcely walk and Birskett was erratic; yet he had eyes to catch an expression on Friedlander's face as, tenderly helped by their boys, they marched unsteadily in the hot, westering sun to the village.

"Damned shame," said Birskett wrathfully. "C'ming home drunk'n owls and these fell'rs never seen a drunk before. Putting us in wrong, the son of a swine. Have t'tell 'em we were shick, huh? I'm drunk, doc! Never shought o' dope."

"Wasn't dope," stuttered the doctor.

"Wasn't dope, man? What was it for the love o' Heaven?"

The doctor, leaning on Matana's sympathetic arm, halted swaying in front of the compound of their allotted hut, and said solemnly:

"Wasn't dope. Not susha fool. Ninety shix pershent alcohol! Shaw bottle inshide tent."

XIII

That arm of forest swamp had taken them nine days to cross, nine days of continual fight to overcome obstacles, aqueous, vegetable, animal and reptilian. Their food was raw monkey or parrot, for in that weeping jungle where there was not a patch of dry land, nothing would burn. Without hatchets they had been forced to make their way ape-fashion, creeping and dragging their guns and haversacks over tangled undergrowth of vines, and clambering from bough to bough with hands that were not simian.

Kubi fell off a gnarled root, which served as a bridge, and was nearly suffocated in the slime. Hastily retiring from what he had mistaken in the perpetual twilight for a moss-covered branch, Birskett was caught by the hips between the fork of two boughs, and the doctor, sprawling on another, blew off a snake's head within a foot of him. Abdul, one of the two Sudanese, made a similar error in judgment and died in ten minutes. They divided his precious haversacks among them.

The nights had been spent clinging in upper branches, where their ears became attuned to the dread nocturnal anthem: ominous slithers, awful shrieks smothered in muttering weeping darkness; flurries of wings and angry chatterings, mysterious dull splashes, squashing sounds of a heavy body moving, the lugubrious howling of some monkey at the moon barely discernible through the plaited roof. Snatches of nightmare sleep were stolen between spells of pawing hopelessly to drive away the myriads of mosquitoes; for the nets were soon in shreds. Poisonous spiders and huge centipedes swarmed.

"Ain't you ashamed of yourself, doc?" said Birskett that evening as they sat over their fire in the compound suffering from acute headaches.

"A small quantity of liquor would have a powerful reaction upon any man who had gone through the experiences of the last fortnight," replied Kirkton. "Do you realize that we must have taken about three ounces of pure alcohol?"

"But why didn't you shout when you tumbled?"

"Too late. That was when he went inside to get some more cigarets. His medicine case was on his bed and on the floor was the bottle. He dared not use a drug knowing that I, as a medical man, would have detected it. No—merely alcohol!"

"We got drunk and that's all there is to it. Anyway, I'm damned glad we did, for he's sure given his game away now. He evidently is after those notes of Stoutt's which Lörtzer stole, where he hopes, as Lörtzer did, to find the secret of the cure. I guess that's about how the land lies."

"One thing," said Kirkton, "he doesn't know what we're after, except of course the cure, and doesn't know where and how Stoutt died. He's been here a few days. I wonder these natives haven't put him right on that."

"Sounds funny," admitted Birskett. "We're due for a formal *shauri* tomorrow, so maybe we'll get wise to something else. But these are Stoutt's people all right. The old guy with the B.V.D.'s and the chief with the shirt and another fellow with a wristwatch, pretty well prove that. Now all we've to do is to trot right up the mountain and get hold of poor Stoutt's remains, and then it's up to you, doc."

"M'm," muttered the doctor, staring moodily at the fire. "If only I had those leads here. I can't do much with this portable equipment."

"Cheer up, doc. Maybe we can get those fellows to go back for 'em. Um-mum, though, that'll mean a fight, I guess, and we haven't got any dough to stir these boys up with, and anyway the outfit may have been mussed up by now, although I don't think those man-eating guys would dare touch 'em. Magic and that stuff. As for this slit-eyed son-of-a-gun I vote we leave him alone, see what he'll do next until we get a chance to hand him one in return. Shouldn't be surprized if he gets really ugly if he can't get what he wants. If Lörtzer didn't stick at murder I don't see why his twin brother should."

The following morning Birskett was watching the doctor painfully trying to scrape his face.

"Looks mighty bad, the doc," he commented to himself. "Hangover I guess, but I hope he ain't going to get sick now when he's right in touch almost."

When the first rays of the sun were striking the far distant Congo hills a native came to summon them to the audience. He was Zano, the young man wearing the wristwatch, of which he was inordinately proud. Birskett, who was certain that it had been a present from Stoutt, asked him from whom he had got it.

"From the Giver of Life," answered Zano.

"Who was the Giver of Life, my friend?"

"He who dwelt among us. He who has *zikide* (gone out)."

Birskett did not push the matter, waiting to get the sense from conversation.

"Sure he was Stoutt," he told Kirkton, "but the phrase puzzles me. Doesn't usually mean 'dead,' and I've never heard it applied to a man."

Taking Kubi and Matana with them, although they had no stools to carry, they made their way to the chief, whom they found squatting in the club shelter; beside him was the witch doctor, Yarazoo. After the usual little set speeches Birskett merely talked again about the journey and the cannibals, which seemed to interest them. From Boko they learned that that tribe was a branch of the Muamba who lived on the other side of the river farther to the west, and were addicted to cannibalism, which the Children of the Mountain despised intensely.

Later Birskett brought up the subject of ways and means, asking the chief if he would send a messenger for them to Uganda and whether he would trust them until the man could return with a safari of goods.

"Whatever my brothers wish shall be done," returned Boko, and from the body of the natives rose grunts of approval. "What my brothers shall want for food let them but speak."

"Get that, doc?" whispered Birskett. "I'll bet that's poor old Stoutt's doing!"

He continued vague conversation for some time and then gently approached the subject of sleeping death.

"No, our people did not suffer from that sickness," said Boko, "but other tribes were nearly eaten up with it."

"My God!" murmured the doctor. "That practically proves Stoutt *did* find a cure! Ask him about it, Birskett."

"Do my brothers make magic against it?" he inquired.

"It is the magic of the Giver of Life," answered Yarazoo in his squeaking treble.

"Did he give you magical medicine, my friend?"

The doctor was leaning tensely forward, straining to understand every word. But there was no reply.

"Were you in the time of your fathers eaten by this plague?" put in Birskett quickly, knowing that he had struck a tabu of some sort.

"*Wao*. We were devoured as the lizard eats flies."

"The medicine of the white man is all-powerful if he be of our tribe," said Birskett.

"Wao! Wao!" came an emphatic affirmative.

Birskett then dropped the topic and shifted to hunting.

"Do your women and warriors still go even into the swamp?"

"Why not?"

"We ask," said Birskett mendaciously, "that we may know if it be safe to go hence hunting."

"This man, Zano," said Boko, "shall go with you whenever you shall so will it."

"These are Stoutt's people all right," said Birskett as they walked back to their hut at the other end of the village. "The shooting bluff was to find out whether they connect the fly with the disease, but apparently they don't."

"Oh my God!" said the doctor. "Just to think that it's right here under our noses! Couldn't you ask 'em where he's buried or left or whatever they would do with his remains?"

"No, that's why I shut up. They've got some sort of a tabu about him now. Probably promoted him into a god or something. That's why they wouldn't reply to the direct question whether he had given 'em some medicine. I've got a hunch we'd best say nothing about it. Scout around along the hills up there for his shack. They wouldn't have any reason to destroy it—and by ——! If they have deified him they've probably not dared to touch the bodies of any of 'em. Gosh! that's the great idea! But we'll rest up for a few days to get fit again."

"Why didn't you put in something," said the doctor wearily, "about that Friedlander fellow?"

"Because I suddenly guessed that he's been busy knocking us as he was knocking them, so we'd better play the other game. If he comes nosing around—as he will—we'll bump him off."

Outside the entrance to the compound, which was fairly large, was the remaining Sudanese, Zapoko, on his hams. He rose as the whites came up and said:

"*Mwami*, the white man is within. He said he would await you."

Birskett glanced swiftly at the hut and swore. Then he sprinted across the sand on his toes and literally dived through the low door. Kirkton, following, heard a startled exclamation in German and Birskett loudly cursing some one.

"How dare you make such a statement?" came Friedlander's high tones. "I tell you I come to wait for you, yes. You think that a white man will stop in the sun?"

"Stop in — —!" roared Birskett. "What were you doing poking your — — nose into that satchel? And you call yourself a white man!"

"You insult me, sir! You accept my hospitality and—"

"To — — with your damned hospitality! I know all about that, you damned—damned Hollander, and you'll get more than insulted if you don't get out and damned well stop out!"

As the doctor stooped to enter, Friedlander nearly knocked him down as he shot out in a hurry. Birskett came on his heels.

"Caught the damned scut opening your satchel, doc!" he exclaimed.

"I tell you, Doctor Kirkton, that—"

"That'll do! Get out! What I say goes. Understand that?"

"But, Herr Doktor," began Friedlander, "you can not believe that I—"

"I have every confidence in Mr. Birskett." retorted Kirkton coldly, and settled the matter by crawling into the cool of the hut.

"Right, is it not?" snapped Friedlander. "I will make you pay for this! I will—"

"Oh, get out!" roared Birskett, "or I'll throw you over the fence with one arm!"

Friedlander went, muttering to himself.

"Wasn't the boy's fault," said Birskett joining the doctor. "He can't be expected to suspect every white of being a damned thief. Somehow I suspected something right off from what he was trying to dig out of you yesterday. D'you recollect, doc? About your having found Stoutt's notebooks. Sure I was drunk, but my memory ain't so bad. Couldn't see clearly in this gloom, but the son-of-a-gun was surely putting down that satchel there in a — — hurry. Yes, by — —, look! It's been opened! The rat!"

"I suppose," said the doctor slowly, "he will try to buy the natives to turn against us now. M'm. May be very awkward, but anyway we know how we stand."

"I should worry! Say, doc—"

"Goo' mornin' sah!"

"W-who the Sacred Henry—" stuttered Birskett, staring at a head blocking the light.

"Goo' night, sah!" continued the voice, as the body followed into the hut.

"Suffering snakes! It's that fellow—say, d'you speak English?"

"Yes, yes, yes, yes!" asserted Zano, and continued rapidly, showing his teeth. "Goo' boy! Goo' night! Goo' morning! Thatz fine! Thatz fine!"

"Sure, it's fine!" replied Birskett. "I get you, son. How're you feeling, huh?"

"Thatz fine! Thatz fine!" repeated Zano delightedly. Birskett laughed uproariously. Then leaning forward he touched the broken watch on the man's wrist.

"That's fine, huh?"

In the glare from the door he saw Zano's face sober instantly.

Birskett began to speak in Luganda. Zano immediately warmed up again and stated very proudly that the chief had placed the two whites in his especial charge and he had come to know whether there was anything his dear friends desired. Birskett talked for a little and dismissed him by merely remarking that they were still weak and tired and would like to rest for a few days.

"That's Stoutt's boy all right, doc!" said Birskett when Zano had gone. "That's where he learned that parrot stunt."

"Possibly," assented the doctor, "but the best evidence is probably, 'That's fine!' That must have been Stoutt's pet phrase. I wonder whether we could persuade him to help us?"

"M'm. M'm. That'll maybe be a tough proposition, for if there's some damned tabu to do with it they're as obstinate as a Louisiana mule. Anyway he'll keep Mister damned van der Friedlander away."

During the three days that they remained quietly enjoying the rest which they so badly needed they neither saw nor heard from Friedlander. The food was, for native fare, astonishingly good; another proof probably of Zano's knowledge of white men's tastes was the profusion of eggs and chickens and goat's milk supplied them, for the native usually doesn't seem to care for eggs, keeping them rather to produce chicks; even chickens are usually only eaten on feast days.

The young man liked to come and talk with the white men. He would have a dozen or more warriors and women squatting in the compound and by his frequent chattering, Goo' night. Thatz fine! Goo' mornin' was evidently gaining much prestige as speaking the white man's language.

Birskett tried on these occasions to get an inkling of their attitude to Stoutt and information of the use of the cure he had evidently given them; but the subject was always met by a polite—

"*Simanyi, sebo,*" (I don't know, sir,) and if persisted in, by complete silence.

Birskett tried to point out that whatever stock of medicine had been given them could not last forever.

Silence.

Would they not want the white brothers of the same tribe as the Giver of Life—the reason of the name was plain now—to make more for them?

Silence.

"We'll never get anything out of 'em!" said Birskett confidently to the doctor. "It's that damned tabu business. They'd all die out again for want of the injection—"

"Couldn't be an injection," objected the doctor. "Who would administer the needle?"

"Well, whatever it is, rather than break the rules of the tabu by mentioning his sacred name or revealing the cure to any living being."

Kirkton broodingly regarded the glare of the door.

"Maybe this man doesn't know, nor any of the others. Stoutt may—for political reasons or something to keep well in with them—have only told the witch doctor fellow. Maybe he's got the secret or the supply—same thing. Why not tackle him?"

Birskett laughed.

"Last person on earth, man! If your hunch is right it's worse than ever. He's in the profession, he'd rather be cut to pieces than give up the secret and lose his prestige!"

"Obstinate idiot!" grumbled Kirkton. "Can't he be made to see that it's for the benefit of mankind?"

"Nothing doing with any of 'em," insisted Birskett; "it's tabu—their religion—and any boob knows there's no arguing about a religious conviction. That's all there is to it."

"Good Lord, I only want to rediscover it for the benefit of us all and Stoutt? It's Stoutt's honor, if he ever cared for such empty stuff, although I don't think he did. Anyway his people need the cash. Can't you work these wretched people on these lines?"

"That's good stuff, doc, but nothing doing with these guys. They're too mighty human for that. You'd have as tough a job trying to convince this Friedlander guy!"

"Good God!" groaned the doctor. "I'd give my life to get it."

He paused and added solemnly—

"Say, Birskett, has it occurred to you that probably we're both infected by now?"

"Sure!" said Birskett cheerfully. "Guess we're as full of bugs as a dog's full of fleas! More reason to find that cure."

The next day they told Zano they'd like to go around with their guns a bit. He was delighted, and with some half a dozen of his cronies they set out. Birskett noted that the green tent was still under the crimson Bombax.

Zano wanted to steer for the swamps. Purposely they let him for a while, but gradually veered towards the hillside. The cliff at the back of the village seemed to have been caused by a volcanic split. Half a mile beyond was a passably easy escarpment on to what looked like a small plateau. Still higher they could see a belt of bamboo.

When Birskett suggested to Zano that there might be leopards or some interesting game that way, he swore that never was game known to be there, no, not of any sort.

"Looks bad," reported Birskett, but persisted in walking parallel. They managed to edge around until they were walking along the beginning of the steep slope. Birskett suddenly pretended to see some game moving above and calling—purposely in Luganda—to the doctor to follow, made to mount the escarpment.

Instantly Zano and the six warriors, who were all armed, leaped ahead and formed around him. Zano, his face obstinately sulky but determined, said:

"*Neda mwami*, there is no living beast there."

"*Wewao! Wewao!*" asserted Birskett, simulating excitement. "I saw him!" and feigning not to notice the lowering looks of the men, attempted to push past them. Instantly they raised their spears and Zano, clutching at his arm, cried out as if really distressed:

"*Neda! Neda! munange! Nkwegairide! Nsonyiwe!* (No, no, my dear friend, I implore you. Forgive me! There are devils there! The chief forbids you to risk your life.) *Nkwegairide, munange!*"

In spite of the polite words native fashion, there was menace in the features of all of them. Birskett reflected swiftly. Should they force their way they would have to kill, which might mean putting the whole pack of savages on their trail? On the other hand the tabu might keep them off the sacred ground.

But they had no provision; if the mountains should yield neither rabbits, foxes nor birds, they would surely be chased should they come down for food. True, Stoutt might have left canned stuff.

He turned to Kirkton close behind him.

"We can fight our way through, I guess, but—how about it, doc?"

"Hadn't we better try other means first? And besides I haven't got my instruments with us."

"That settles it!" and turning back to Zano he smiled, saying:

"*Muyombera ki, munange*? (What are we quarrelling about, my friend? I didn't understand.) *Onsekererako ki*? (Why do you laugh at me?) *Mangu wansi we!* (Come, let's go down then.)"

"*Thatz* fine! Goo' night! Thatz fine! Goo' mornin'!" retorted Zano, showing his teeth.

XIV

"Stoutt's shack lies somewhere up there above our heads," affirmed Birskett, "and probably his remains are still there. Whether they know or not how he died, they've kind of deified him. That ground's tabu probably to them as well as to any stranger. Now we know what we're at, but that don't amount to much."

They were sitting in the low door of their hut trying to discover some method of circumventing the native superstition. It seemed that the usual stupidity of the human race, as is frequently the case, was to be the means of depriving them and their fellows of a remedy for a plague worse than any plague of old Egypt.

To the doctor's trained mind there was something maddeningly irritating in the fact that reasoning could not drive the truth into the heads of the natives that they were acting against their own interests. Moreover the value of time had risen, for they had both come to realize that they were doomed; if the disease overcame them before they could solve the problem, the cure would be lost for ever; even if Friedlander or any one else succeeded afterwards in discovering the shack, he wouldn't find the notebooks which had been stolen by Lörtzer, and they would not have given any clue anyway.

To fight their way up with but three men to aid them seemed highly impracticable. The doctor had thought of escaping by night. As a test they had sent Zapoko out at night, but he soon reported that they were watched. Evidently courtesy and food and anything else they required that the natives possessed were theirs, except permission to enter the tabu ground.

The messenger had already been sent by the way of Mbarara, going round the south of the mountains, to Entebbe for goods, but they must reckon three months at least before the safari could return, and then there was a good chance that Friedlander would see to it that the goods were held up in German territory. And besides, by that time—

Already Birskett had developed the slight rash on the body which is one of the primary symptoms. However the cortex of the brain was not yet attacked, producing the soporific signs, from which the malady is named.

The knowledge didn't depress either man, inasfar as a lingering death seemed sure, but it angered both; the doctor raged at the thought of the many scientific ambitions he wished to pursue. Birskett swore at the idea of being slowly poisoned before he could carry out the job he had undertaken. He again considered fighting his way up recklessly, but in such a fight they could not win through, burdened as they would be with the heavy haversacks containing the doctor's field outfit. He threshed his mind to find a way out.

"Thank Heaven that Friedlander fellow doesn't know anything about Stoutt's shack being here," the doctor was saying.

"Probably not. Whatever that thug Lörtzer said, he would lie. He wouldn't have let it appear that he knew too much about it. Probably he denied all knowledge of the manner of Stoutt's death or the place."

"Possibly," said the doctor, "the better plan would be to continue on around to the south and endeavor to reach the shack *over* the mountains."

"Good enough, doc, but, there's two things against that. We'll have to pass through German ground and I guess Friedlander would follow and have the power to hold us up somehow as he tried to in Uganda. Recollect that the German Government supports and subsidizes its men of trade and science—which is more than ours does. Also there's the question of time, and we haven't got a long suit on that!"

"True," assented Kirkton. "It's most irritating. To have a thing almost within one's grasp and to be held up by ordinary human stupidity! My God!"

"I guess that's what's the matter with what they call progress. Say, I've a hunch the best thing to do is to try to fool 'em. But first of all look over the ground. Tomorrow, we'll say we're going hunting, but *singly!* Get me? You go one way and I the other. You might with a bit of luck spot the shack if you get on a hill or something. Lörtzer said he did."

"But what's the good of that?" complained the doctor. "How are we going to get away from these jailers?"

"M'm. Take a chance and fight, I guess and— Sacred suffering snakes!" Birskett almost shouted. "I've got it! Makes me think of the tenderloin, man!"

"Well, well, what?" demanded the doctor testily.

"Dope, man! Can't you give 'em a shot of something to put 'em to sleep with the needle?"

"M'm, yes. I have some veronal."

"That's the great idea! We'll both go along tomorrow, take all the gear and camp as near the escarpment as possible. Put 'em to bed that night and be away out of sight long before dawn. There's a good moon, too. Even if Friedlander comes nosing around he won't think of watching us all night."

"Thanks, Birskett," said Kirkton gravely. "I believe you've solved the problem."

"Lord, man, that's my end of the job, isn't it? What a pity we haven't a drink to celebrate! Hullo, here's Stoutt's man. He's a good boy according to his lights and I guess I'd rather dope him than shoot him."

That night they felt and slept better with the dawn of hope, but in the morning Birskett awoke with a splitting headache and a high fever. He crawled off his native pallet of grass, but when he stood up he swayed and nearly fell.

"What's wrong?" demanded Kirkton, who couldn't see distinctly what had happened in the gloom of the hut.

"Nothing," asserted Birskett, sitting suddenly on his haunches, holding his dry burning head.

He essayed again to carry on, but his legs refused duty. This time the doctor saw and came over.

"H'm, temperature," said he, with his hand upon Birskett's wrist. "Lie down and I'll get the thermometer."

"Oh, it's nothing, doc. Just—"

"Do as I tell you!"

Birskett obeyed reluctantly and slightly incoherently. But he lay quiet with the thermometer in his mouth.

"What is it, doc?" he asked, as the doctor went to the door to read the instrument.

"Malaria. I'll give you a shot of quinin and Warburg's and phenacetin. No, no, nothing to do with the other thing," he insisted mendaciously as Birskett's eyes questioned mutely. "*That* doesn't give a high temperature. Hundred and two point two. Nothing. Sweat it out of you and you'll be all right in a day or two."

Birskett swore feelingly and at length. But he was too light-headed to think clearly. He raved slightly and when he had swallowed the medicine and had had a dose of quinin he dropped off to sleep. It was dark when he awoke. But he sensed immediately that he was better; he had been sweating profusely and his skin felt moist and cool. He could hear his companion's regular breathing and in the stillness the cry of a night owl.

"Gosh, I'll be all right in the morning," he thought, and after tossing about for a bit fell asleep again. The doctor was squatting by him in the morning taking the thermometer from his arm pit.

"What is it?" he asked.

"Hundred point one. Doing fine, Birskett. Feel weak?"

"Yep, a bit, but I'll be all right by tomorrow."

He drank some broth Kubi had made from goat stew and lay quiet for a while. Outside in the bright twilight before the sun rose he could hear the regular nervous tread of the doctor pacing up and down. He was irritated and annoyed by Birskett's inopportune illness although he would never have admitted it—probably not even to himself. But Birskett could understand perfectly; he, too, was none the less exasperated that he should be struck down just at this moment when time was so precious.

Sleeping sickness varies considerably in the time taken to develop; with some cases, days or weeks; others, months. Cases had been known to break out after years. Possibly it depended upon how the victim had been inoculated—whether in the flesh, a vein or an artery. The dread disease had marked him already and it wasn't reasonable to suppose, or to act upon the assumption, that the doctor had escaped, considering the number of times both had been bitten. Presently he said:

"Say, doc, holding things up like this worries me a whole heap. Now don't get up in the air, but listen to me. Pack up the things, take Zapoko and Matana and with Zano get along as we arranged. Strike a good place and camp. I'll be O.K. by tomorrow and I'll come along on easy marches to join you. By doing that you'll put 'em off any suspicion at all. No!" as the doctor began to protest. "I'll go plumb crazy lying here and watching you. Leave me a stock of quinin and I'll be all right. And, doc, if anything should go wrong, you put 'em to sleep as we worked it out and get up above."

"But if I do that," objected Kirkton, "they might take it out of you."

"Oh, they won't—and what does it matter if they do! Anyway, don't get cantankerous, doc, there's only one object to the trip ain't there?"

"Yes, but—but there's no need for me to go on ahead. I'll wait a few days."

"No, you *won't!*" Birskett sat up excitedly. "See here, doc, I'm set on it, and you just can't upset a sick man now! No, joking aside, it's a good stunt for you to go ahead alone. Put any idea of trying to double-cross 'em out of their heads and Friedlander's, too."

They went on arguing about it for a while, but finally, being of the opinion that Birskett was in no danger from malaria, the doctor consented to start out the following day.

Birskett sought to make matters comprehensible to the native mind by a long conversation with Zano in which he impressed upon him the fact that the doctor was bored—or, as the natives say, an ant was eating his soul—and wished to be amused, so that he would go hunting alone.

After discussing final arrangements, the doctor departed with Matana and Zapoko and all the gear except enough medicine for Birskett.

Sadness settled upon him like the clouds in the peaks, and a queer feeling, probably produced, he thought, by the reaction of the fever, that he would never see the doctor again. Yet he was glad, for at any rate something was doing. The doctor by now knew enough Luganda to make himself understood and understand. And as long as the boys were with him they had enough bush lore to keep the party fed more or less.

In the late afternoon, after squatting in the shade in the rear of the hut, he took a walk to try his strength and also to see whether the green tent was still under the scarlet Bombax. It was; a fact which relieved his anxiety somewhat.

Although he had spent most of his life by solitary camp fires and trailed many thousands of miles on lonely trails, he never recollected feeling as lonesome as he did that first night after the doctor's departure. He felt indeed as if he were being abandoned to die and foolishly put his hand apprehensively to his jaw. Yes, the glands were already beginning to swell.

"Sudden death in the heat of a fight, yes," he reflected "but sitting down watching yourself go to sleep for keeps— Ugh!"

However there was a little consolation in the fact that the victim of trypanosomiasis, after the microbe has eaten well into the cortex of the brain, doesn't give a —— what happens as long as he can be left alone to sleep. However, he hadn't got as far as that yet!

He called in Kubi—who, poor ——, had just as surely the same fate awaiting him, of which happily he was unconscious— to keep him company by the smoldering fire in the gloomy hut.

He held Kubi talking quite a while. He feared to be left. Fear, in the sense of fear not momentary but prolonged and swelling every moment, was a new experience for him; all the more terrible because in all his life, save for mere touches of malaria and such like sickness, he had never been ill; a touch of cold in an inclement climate would make him rave and curse with impatience.

This fear was like the constricting folds of a python about him; crushing, cold, and remorseless; a something against which he could not use his strength of mind or body.

He thought of Stoutt who knowingly had inoculated himself, and sought to excuse his own terrors by arguing that at any rate Stoutt had been morally certain he had found the cure. Yet the deed was none the less. And there was the cure right close to him! He wanted to rush out and tear his way by main force up the hill. Absurd! The hope of any of them lay in the hands of that queer man with a fixed idea and no sense of humor, whose bright bird eyes seemed always to burn with zeal.

Birskett writhed under the whiplash of self-reproach. Many a poor — — doomed by tuberculosis or cancer or other incurable disease, who has grimly fought a losing battle for years, would have laughed at the agony of that big, strong man that sweaty night in the first grip of fear. But he was unaccustomed to such an emotion; habit, after all, is four-fifths of life.

Worn out with fever and his emotional calisthenics he sank asleep near dawn. When he awakened the rays of the sun were already high overhead. He felt pretty fit and taking his temperature found it ninety-nine—very nearly normal.

He decided to strike the trail that afternoon. Anyway he would be doing something. Some eggs and a little of the everlasting goat made him still more optimistic. He told Kubi to make ready for the trail and suddenly thinking of Friedlander, walked through the village to see whether he was still there.

Just as he thought, the fellow had gone, following the doctor no doubt. He stood talking to one of the natives by the gate of the village. A long quavering cry interrupted them.

"*Bulamatadi!*" repeated the man and ran echoing the cry towards the club house.

Away down the valley to the southeast Birskett made out first the glint of bayonets in the afternoon sun and then a regular column of disciplined troops marching.

"Belgians!" he exclaimed and stared. "Thank God! This may save the whole outfit!"

XV

Doctor Kirkton was also haunted by the specter of fear. He too had developed the primary symptoms of the rash, but he had not told Birskett. Although more callous and less imaginative than Birskett, he had observed more. Several times lately Birskett had expressed momentarily slight peevishness, and more significant still, had in conversation had lapses—quite unconsciously—of several seconds; a sudden break in the middle of a sentence.

This, too, the doctor had noticed in himself. This was the fear that drove him into a frenzy. Once the terrible lethargy got a firm hold, he would never have the continuous and requisite energy to struggle forward, and even if there, to persevere with his research. Soon would come the growing emaciation, the decay of the vital will to do, ending in the creeping coma and indifference to all things.

The inopportune sickness of Birskett drove him into an ecstasy of terror; it seemed the last cruel straw that was to break them. Now he regretted that he had not taken the precaution to have his precious instruments and cases with him when on the scouting trip and then to have fought their way up to the upper slopes.

He could no more judge of how long it would take him to reach the shack—thanks to Birskett's resource—than how long before the *trypanosoma gambiense* reached the cortex of his brain and the mental motor started to slow down. Thus, to Birskett's suggestion to go on he made little resistance; indeed, had he remained seriously sick, the doctor would have considered it his duty to abandon him and risk all on the hazard.

That morning, as he started off, accompanied by Zapoko, Matana and Zano and the six warriors forming what really was a guard, carrying everything that they had managed to save of his precious instruments and medicinal supplies, he was conscious of a great relief.

To the south of the village the escarpment continued almost unscalable for some three miles, but farther on the ground began to break up into rough and broken foothills again. Villages became plentiful showing that the country was evidently thickly populated. From the fact that the village of the chief was that of Zano, who had evidently been Stoutt's guide, he concluded that Stoutt must have passed through that village on his way up and down from the swamps to his snow-clad laboratory; hence that the route up the escarpment must be in the vicinity.

Consumed by desperate energy Kirkton found it hard to restrain the desire to rush ahead, action always tending to alleviate anxiety. But reflection reminded him that the better way would be to select a camp near some hillock or hill away from the line of the escarpment.

That day they made a short journey. Among the foothills they came upon a large village from whence he understood Zano to say they would be within reach of good shooting towards the swamps below.

That afternoon, partially to keep himself from brooding and growing too morbid over watching his own state, he overhauled the whole of his gear, checking in his notebook the instruments and exact quantities of drugs. To his dismay he discovered that yet another delicate phial, kept in cotton wool, had been, as many another, smashed by the jolting. It was the last of the trypsin, an absolutely necessary drug, without which he could not carry out certain reactions.

He didn't swear—not even irritably. The case was far too serious for words. He sat there in the shade of the hut, his still bright, birdlike eyes set upon the mist-swept heights of the mountains as if probing to find out whether—and there was just a possibility—he might find another supply in Stoutt's shack. That indeed seemed the only chance of avoiding complete failure; for he knew that neither he nor Birskett, should they not discover the cure, would ever live long enough, or retain their faculties, to reach an outpost of civilization with the material to send on to New York for analysis. Well, there was only one thing that could be done and that was to go on.

Next morning, gloomily despondent, he allowed Zano and his people to lead him out with a bunch of local hunters on an alleged hunt, but no sooner had they cleared the bush around them and were approaching the end of the clutter of foothills than he instructed Matana, who best understood his limping Luganda, to tell them that he was sick and would rest.

They stopped in a grove of wild bananas, and. beneath a great tree with curious horizontal branches laden with globular scarlet flowers, he lay and brooded, fighting the impatience which bade him rush for the heights at any cost without even waiting for Birskett. Later, under the pretext of searching for game, he mounted the highest and most westward foothill and examined the mountain slope with his glasses, in the rays of the western sun.

They were now about 5,000 feet above sea level. Almost at the top of the escarpment, apparently two thousand feet, began the belt of bamboos which seemed to continue for about another three thousand feet. Beyond that he could make out ragged rocks and cliffs covered with some kind of green, probably lichen.

Above, still higher, appeared to be a plateau and in a ravine to the left, through the swirls of mist he could distinguish the glimmer of the edge of a glacier and scattered patches of snow.

Shifting the glasses about to the north, the direction from which he had come, he caught a glimpse of a safari quite close now to the village. For a moment he thought that Birskett must have started a few hours afterwards, but the number of porters and the general size precluded that possibility. He asked Zano's opinion. After some chatter among them he understood that they were sure it was the other white man. He-of-the-Crocodile-Eyes, as they called him.

"Confound his impertinence, camping on my trail," began the doctor vexedly and then stopped, bringing down the glasses with a jerk. "Yes," he asserted solemnly, "the Lord has delivered the enemy into my hands."

He hurriedly returned to the village and instructed Matana to make Zano take them immediately into the fringe of the foothills, which would make a good hunting camp. Although it was doubtful whether he understood exactly what was wanted, Matana harangued the equally puzzled Zano into obeying the white man's orders.

The next morning he left the rough grass shelter which the natives had made for him and mounted the nearest hill. His glasses revealed what he had expected—Friedlander's safari camped upon his trail about a mile away.

He returned to camp, told them that he was still unwell and prepared to pass the day as best he could. When the afternoon shadows were well upon their daily crawl up the mountain slopes, he ascended the hill again and satisfied himself that Friedlander was still there. So intent was he upon his own plan that it scarcely occurred to him to wonder what was Friedlander's game.

With some difficulty he made Zano understand that he had seen Birskett arriving at the village and wished some of the men to return instantly to him with a message. The men demurred, for they could scarcely reach there by sunset; but as the white seemed so anxious, Zano insisted. The following brief message he scribbled on a page torn from his notebook:

> Imperative reasons force my attempt tonight. If successful will wait you four days on top of escarpment; will leave grass trail. Friedlander here. Before starting take double injection.

"That'll buck him up a little for the effort," he muttered.

He waited, impatiently watching the time. When his watch read five-twenty, for the sun sets at six on the equator, he gave himself a shot with the needle and slipped his revolver beneath his ragged shirt. Taking Matana and Zano he then set out directly for Friedlander's camp. That worthy he found as before comfortably seated beneath his tent fly. At the doctor's appearance he seemed slightly astonished. Matana and Zano waited aside and began talking to some of Friedlander's men. Kirkton advanced with nervous swift steps.

"Good evening, Dr. Kirkton," began Friedlander suavely. "I hope—"

"Good evening, Dr. Friedlander," responded Kirkton sharply.

Friedlander's slit eyes narrowed slightly, but he said with perfect equanimity:

"I do not understand you, doctor? You have made a mistake, is it not?"

"I'm not accustomed to making mistakes. You're Dr. Hermanus Friedlander of Hamburg and you traveled on the same boat from Port Said. Your purpose here is as obvious as your object in denying your identity. But I haven't come here to argue with you."

Kirkton shifted slightly, so that his back was to the natives.

"You see this revolver? Don't move! You will supply me with two phials of trypsin, the use of which you perfectly understand. Don't argue. I have already the advanced stages of trypanosomiasis, so you will understand that my time is limited. If you attempt to call for help your death is certain; moreover you have only your own men, for these natives will not attack me without the chief's order. Now quick, get that trypsin from the same case as the one in which you keep the pure alcohol!"

The narrowed slit eyes looked into the hard and very bright birdlike ones. What he saw there seemed to convince him. He moved with some attempt at dignity. Kirkton followed him to the tent door! Covered by the revolver Friedlander handed over the required phials which Kirkton carefully placed in his breast pocket.

"It is a pity, Dr. Kirkton," said Friedlander sneeringly, "that you should have thought it so necessary to threaten me, is it not? I should have been but too much delighted to help a colleague. However, you shall pay for this, yes. You can not escape me. If that is necessary, I shall reckon with you myself."

"Fine!" said Kirkton, as pleased as a child now that he had gotten his precious drug. "Take my compliments and go to the ——! If you attempt to go for your guns before I'm outside your camp, I shall fire. Matana! Zano!"

Holding him covered, and openly, he backed away until a Phoenix palm gave shelter, followed by the eyes of the wondering natives. As he disappeared into the grove he heard the angry shouts of Friedlander.

"Nothing doing," he thought flippantly as they hurried back. "You won't get a single man to attempt an attack before morning—even if you can buy 'em."

The sun was setting fire to the Congo hills when he reached his primitive camp. Here a surprize awaited him. Birskett's personal boy, Kubi, bearing a note, scribbled in pencil in scarcely legible characters:

> Get out instantly at any cost. Mountains. Can not follow. Don't waste a minute or expedition lost. Take Kubi.
>
> BIRSKETT.

XVI

As Birskett returned toward his hut he heard a great hullaballoo in progress in the village. The men, in answer to a summons, were all hurrying to the club house for a *shauri*. Although this territory was part of the Congo Free State, he was sure that never before had any officials visited there.

From his own knowledge of their regime in other parts he well knew that that would be a sad day in the annals of the tribe. For the future they would have to go out into the swamps and forest in order to help provide a sufficient income to support the royal dignity of the King of the Belgians and a few thousand other complacent whites, his concessionaires. From the excitement the very name produced he knew, too, that their reputation had preceded them.

However, his sympathy for them was at this moment overshadowed by the fate of the expedition and the hundreds of thousands—probably of these very whites now approaching—which depended on the successful results of Kirkton's researches.

To his surprize, as he sat in the shade of his hut, as evidence of the extreme perturbation of the native mind, came Yarazoo, the ancient witch doctor, in his dirty mauve pants and strange headdress of dried purple and vermilion fungus.

After the usual polite greetings and meanderings he approached the object of his visit, which was to ask the white man's advice in their attitude to the approaching askaris of whom, said Yarazoo, they had heard.

Was it true, he plaintively inquired, as was said by the report brought by several of their young men who had journeyed hunting into the far west, that the Bulamatadi ate up all the natives with whom they came in contact? Was there no medicine that he, Birskett, could suggest, or make, which would secure them the friendship of these strange whites? Were they brothers of the same tribe?

Although he knew that in substance the most awful rumors that their young men could have reported were in the main true, yet naturally he had a repugnance to confirm them to a native. As he hesitated, the mention of medicine gave him an idea.

Could he not make a bargain with the old man that should he protect, or pretend to protect them, from any unjust demands the new whites might make, that he should reveal to him the secret of the medicine of the Giver of Life?

The prospect of gaining, before it was too late, that which they sought, excited him. That he could in practise do nothing to protect them against whatever the Belgian commandant might choose to do, or inflict, was almost forgotten. Such a promise, even if he could not carry it out, would not do them any harm; and the results of the recovery of the secret cure to humanity at large certainly seemed to justify the deception.

The Bulamatadi, he told the old man, were a people greedy for wealth; for an extract gathered from the trees of the forest, rubber, and of which they then knew nothing, and for ivory. They should, he counseled them, listen to the words of the white chief and endeavor to placate him, for who could argue with unlimited guns that spat death?

Yarazoo acknowledged the wisdom of this advice and evidently fearful for his own prestige, asked for a recipe against the lethal nature of bullets. The repetition of the word for magical medicine decided Birskett.

"Listen, O Yarazoo," said he, "what thinkest thou would have been the words of the Giver of Life?"

"*Simanya, munange,*" responded the old man. "Of these people he never spake."

"Thou believest that indeed we are his brothers (of the same tribe)?"

"Truly. Hath not Zano, he who was always with him, said so even from the first?"

"That is so. Listen and stretch thine ears, O Yarazoo. Thou wouldst have my word in counsel joined to thine? Thou wouldst have my words in the ears of the Bulamatadi. Is it not so?"

"Truly, my friend."

"Then, O Yarazoo, shalt thou make known to me that magical medicine which the Giver of Life gave unto thee against the sleeping death?"

Every wrinkle in the withered face seemed to become petrified. Birskett repeated the question.

"I do not know," came the stereotyped formula.

As once again the mulish obstinacy was thrust upon him, knowing all that it might cost, a sudden passion to strike the old man obsessed Birskett. He realized again that wild devils with red hot pincers would not overcome this inherent terror of the tabu.

They sat staring into each other's eyes, the white and the brown man, and over the white came a feeling of weariness. What did it matter? Why bother to save idiots from their own stupidity? It had always been like that through the ages, you still had forcibly to smash the bottle of a rum hound or the pipe of a dope fiend to prevent him poisoning himself and his family.

"The words of the white men then," he heard Yarazoo saying tonelessly, "are turned against us, his friends?"

"Nay, nay, I will help you with that which I may," he returned half-heartedly. "But the Bulamatadi have many guns."

They, as white men had, at first sight, appeared as saviors; now the suggestion of their attitude to natives gave him pause; perhaps they would prove merely another gang of Lörtzers and Friedlanders. The interview ended, he stretched out in the door of his hut feeling more tired and dispirited than ever he had done. He had as yet no suspicion of the reason.

Later the harsh blaring of a trumpet startled him awake.

"Oh, yes, those damned Bulamatadi," he thought, and got up feeling somewhat more energetic. He would go down and look them over.

Taking Kubi with him, he went out of the village. He found the Belgians on the site of Friedlander's old camp, with the askaris making grass shelters in a circle about them like a laager. The village was very quiet he remarked, save for the continuous murmur of low discussion from the club house.

As he approached he saw three whites in white uniforms and gold lace seated in chairs beneath the scarlet branches of the Bombax, while their two tents were being pitched. He estimated roughly that the number of troops was at least two hundred and that there were almost as many porters.

"Poor brutes!" he muttered, thinking of Boko and his people.

The nearest Belgian station, he reckoned, must be Matanda on the other side of the Semliki among the Congo hills, about a hundred or more miles away.

"I wonder what the damned devils are after," he mused, for as most who knew the early days of the Congo Free State concessionaires he had no love for their officials, when every man was out to clear up a fortune in the shortest time possible as well as serve his royal employer.

As he approached the group he noticed that they did not seem astonished to find a white there.

"Probably heard of Stoutt or Lörtzer from native rumor," he decided, "and come along to pike their dirty noses."

One man, from having more gold lace than the others, he took correctly to be the *chef du poste*, a large-faced man with a blond beard and truculent mustaches. A younger man, who looked like an Italian, had a small military black mustache and goatee. In the center sat the third; quite a different type even at that distance; a small man with a weasel face and similar bright small eyes.

"Mean little runt," Birskett summed him up. "Lucky I can talk the lingo."

They did not rise, but seemed to stare disdainfully at the figure of the big white man with a ragged blond beard and haggard eyes, is his torn and filthy clothes.

"*Bon jour, messieurs!*" he greeted them amiably enough.

"*Bon jour, m'sieu!*" returned the Scandinavian *chef du poste*. "Are you Dr. Kirkton?"

"*Non, m'sieu'*, I hav'n't the honor."

He was aware of a servant with a chair and the weasel-faced man bidding him to be seated. As he accepted, the Italian whispered something in the ear of the middle man who nodded.

"*M'sieu' le capitain Strindhorst, m'sieu' le médecin major Verhaeren*," and touching his scanty gold lace, "*le lieutenant Villino.*"

At the mention of "*médecin major*" Birskett eyed the weasel-faced one. The first statement, taking him for Kirkton, coupled with his presence, seemed to Birskett suspicious; doctors were usually occupied in big stations.

At that moment came another of those lapses when the spark missed. Then he understood that the commandant was inquiring his name. For a few seconds he had difficulty in collecting his wits even sufficiently to summon such a familiar word as his own name. The *chef du poste* noticed the hesitation and querulously repeated the demand. Birskett complied and the mental machinery picked up again.

"I'd better keep mum about the doc," he reflected dubiously, "and see what their game is."

What was he doing there? Hunting and exploring, he replied and added that he had lost his safari at the hands of the cannibals. The lieutenant asked some details, but the *capitain* didn't seem at all interested as to what had been done to him. In a pause the *médecin major* butted in with—

"But *m'sieu'* knows *le Docteur Keerkton?*"

"I have seen him," said Birskett guardedly, and to distract their attention, added, "there is also another white doctor here."

"*Tiens!*" That news seemed to startle the *médecin major* and he exchanged a rapid glance with the *chef du poste*.

"What does he seek here?"

"He is searching for a cure for trypanosomiasis, I believe," said Birskett, watching his man keenly. The bright, small eyes quivered for a second.

"That's got you, my friend," he mused pessimistically. "Another Friedlander bunch or I'm a Hottentot. You'll bear watching."

"You have not heard of him as of Dr. Kirkton?" he added.

"No, no," returned Verhaeren, but he was evidently thinking hard.

"You have heard the rumor of Dr. Kirkton's presence from the natives, no doubt?"

"*Si, si,*" answered Verhaeren, "at Matanda."

"*Ah, c'est vrai? Tiens,* and the natives speak of him as *le Docteur Kirkton, n'est-ce pas?*"

Verhaeren saw that he had made a mistake but he pretended not to have heard and, calling a servant, ordered refreshment. Birskett did not press the question. There were cigarets on the table. After they had drunk of gin—not trade gin though—the two officers, as if by arrangement, made their excuses and departed. Verhaeren seemed very excited.

"Where are the two doctors?"

"*Sais pas,*" retorted Birskett carelessly. "They went off chasing bugs, I believe."

"You are not interested in the study of the terrible malady?"

"Naturally, *m'sieu'*. May not we all get it here?"

"You do not fear to get it?"

Birskett shrugged his big shoulders.

"*M'sieu'* is a brave man. Have you noticed many cases among the natives here?"

"Nothing at all, *m'sieu'*!"

Verhaeren continued a kind of catechism about the district and the natives and Birskett fended the questions off as best he could to the advantage of the native.

"Have you heard from them of another white doctor who died here about twelve months ago—an American doctor?"

"*Oui, m'sieu',*" answered Birskett slowly. "Mr. Stoutt. You have heard of him, no doubt."

Verhaeren "had read" about him; then at a tangent he demanded whether Birskett knew whether either of the two doctors had yet found the cure.

"I am not in the confidence of the doctors," evaded Birskett.

"That is a pity. I have come to see this Dr. Keerkton, and for this other *médecin,* whom I do not know—*m'sieu'* speaks the native language of course?— Has it ever happened that he has heard them speaking of instruments, papers, that Dr. Stoott left when he died?"

"*Non, m'sieu'*, never. Did you know that Dr. Stoutt had found a cure before he died?"

The question shrewdly got him. The weasel eyes glittered.

"Yes, but yes, I had heard of that."

"Possibly the natives spoke about it?" inquired Birskett sarcastically.

Verhaeren laughed sharply, pretending to think it a great joke.

"There is a possibility that this Dr. Kirkton has found these papers which would reveal the formula, you know, which is of course the property of the Congo Free State."

"Oh, is it?"

"Was it not found in our territory, but yes? Without a permit no scientist, hunter, or trader is allowed to exploit our territory. Certainly not. If he has found these papers or not he must be answerable to the administration."

"At Boma is it not?"

"*Parfaitement, m'sieu'.*"

"A very long voyage and dangerous—to prisoners?"

Verhaeren cackled and shrugged.

"Dr. Kirkton no doubt will be anxious to make amicable arrangements with me—that is with his Majesty King Leopold."

"He sure will," muttered Birskett.

"*Pardon, m'sieu'?*"

"I said that he will be delighted to do so!"

"And the other white doctor?"

"He also, naturally."

"But if the doctors resist?"

"And you are going to send a force to bring the two doctors here?"

"Certainly. They can not escape."

He gestured elegantly to the askaris.

"Perhaps it might save you annoyance should I persuade Dr. Kirkton to come here? I'm sure he would be delighted to see you personally?"

"*M'sieu'* will be very obliging and I assure him that perhaps we may arrange to overlook his personal trespass on the domains of His Majesty."

"Sure, any little thing like that just suits me fine," muttered Birskett, stifling a longing to use his hands.

He rose.

"If *m'sieu'* will forgive me for some half an hour I will try to arrange for Dr. Kirkton to present himself to you."

"And the other, *m'sieu'*?"

"I can not answer for him."

"You will dine with me, *m'sieu'*, I entreat you?"

"I guess I sure will whether I like it or not," murmured Birskett and added, "*Pardon, m'sieu'*, I shall be enchanted."

In the hut he scribbled the note to Kirkton and dispatched Kubi with instructions to make his getaway as quietly as possible. Conscious of an ebb in his energy he took an antimony-arsenical injection and sat down to think things out.

For himself—well, what did it matter anyway? Yet he considered whether he should try to stop where he was, if they would let him, and at night make a break after the doctor? No, the main and only point was to give the doctor time to get away to the mountain; the longer he could bluff the Belgians the better.

While packing up his haversack with the medicinal supply the doctor had left him, he stumbled on a dirty card of the doctor's, which had evidently been discarded or fallen out of his case. He grinned and shoved it in his tunic pocket.

On his way down he heard more commotion going on in the village and one of Boko's sons overtook him crying that the Bulamatadi had sent an escort of askaris to bring the chief before them, an unprecedented act in their minds; for always must a stranger present himself to the chief. What would their friend advise them to do? Birskett urged them to submit as they knew the Bulamatadi were powerful.

He found the *médecin major* and the two officers in their chairs imbibing more drinks. He bowed before Dr. Verhaeren, saying ironically—

"I am enchanted to meet my distinguished colleague!"

"*Quoi!*" gasped Verhaeren. "*Le Docteur Keerkton?*"

"At your service!" said Birskett coldly and thrust the doctor's soiled card at him.

XVII

The Belgian glanced at the card and then gazed up at the tall American. The *chef du poste* was staring also bewilderedly. Birskett smiled mockingly.

"But I do not understand, *m'sieu'*," said Verhaeren. "You have said that you were a *m'sieu'* Birskett, *n'est-ce pas*?"

"Naturally, *m'sieu'*! In some situations it is necessary to be circumspect if not diplomatic, *n'est-ce pas*?"

Verhaeren glanced again at the card and seemed a bit unconvinced. The *chef du poste* broke in:

"*Si, si, mon vieux!* Don't you recall how the fellow hesitated when he gave his name? He is undoubtedly the man we want."

"*Alors, messieurs*, I am at your disposition," said Birskett.

He seated himself nonchalantly and took a cigaret.

Verhaeren still seemed nonplused; he paused as if trying to recollect exactly what he had already said. Then he glanced at the Scandinavian, who nodded and departed as before.

"You will drink, *m'sieu'*?"

"Don't mind if I do. I guess I need it," responded Birskett. He helped himself and grinned. "Well, *m'sieu'*, how about it?"

"*Pardon, m'sieu' le docteur*, I do not understand English very well?"

"You stated to me before that you wished to make a proposition to me regarding the—um—the exploitation of Congo Free State territory, which by the way I can not acknowledge."

"Can not acknowledge, *m'sieu'*. Why not?"

"Because the boundary has not yet been settled."

"*Zut!* What is that? Perhaps there will be no necessity to dispute so small a thing, Dr. Keerkton. Why should there between colleagues, if you permit me to say so, for you are a *savant* and I but a poor — — of a *médecin major*. *Que voulez-vous!* I have every respect for your *savants* of the great *États-Unis d'Amérique*. Of *le pauvre Docteur Stoott*—ah, so sad! You have heard no news of him, *docteur*?"

"D'you think I'm a spiritist?" demanded Birskett sweetly, thinking "now comes the sob stuff."

"Ah yes, you have reason, *docteur*. But as you met Dr. Lörtzer in New York I thought perhaps that he would have been able to indicate to you the place of Dr. Stoott's—um—death. That would be the place to look for the effects he left, *n'est-ce pas*? The natives would not destroy them I should imagine."

"Who told you that I knew Dr. Lörtzer?" demanded Birskett.

Verhaeren shrugged and laughed.

"Have I not read in the papers?"

"— — all journalists," muttered Birskett. "Well, he was too ill to recall things like that," he added in French.

Verhaeren watched him calculatingly.

"You will recall, *m'sieu'*, what I said this afternoon? That it was reported that Dr. Stoott had discovered the cure, was it not? I wondered perhaps that you might have recovered his invaluable books or heard from the natives of their whereabouts?"

"And if I have?"

"Ah!" The weasel eyes registered the swallowing of the bait. "Then you *have, m'sieu'*? *Sapristi!*"

"Naturally whether I have or no is a professional secret. You will, *m'sieu' le médecin major*, easily understand."

"Ah yes, of course, there is the enormous reward for the cure of trypanosomiasis, *m'sieu'* would remind me? But in that case we could of course come to terms, *mais, oui!*"

"*Mais, oui*, my hat!" exclaimed Birskett.

"*Écoutez, m'sieu'*," he went on a little more calmly, "has it ever occurred to you that if Dr. Stoutt has found a cure that that discovery belongs to him?"

"*Oh! Zut! Que voulez vous?*"

Verhaeren seemed so tickled at the idea that the secret had been found and was presumably within his grasp that his beady eyes glittered. From what had been said in the morning this American was no fool; he knew well enough what an arrest and dispatch to Boma, more than a thousand miles through the Congo, could be made to entail.

"Also, *m'sieu' le médecin major*, has it occurred to you that his wife and children are entitled to the financial benefits of his work—not to mention such a small thing as the honor to his country?"

"Ah, but that is a small thing, *m'sieu'*. What matter what country shall have the honor as long as humanity benefits?"

"Well, I guess that there's one rank bit of humanity that's not going to benefit—anyway not in either of those two lines."

"*Pardon, m'sieu'*, I do not understand you?"

"Sure you don't, and you never will. *Enfin, m'sieu'*, I am unable to disclose a professional secret."

"Ah, but you *have* it?"

"Again I am unable to reply. I am sure," he added sarcastically, "that you will respect my motive."

"Motive!" suddenly exploded Verhaeren, as the truth that he was being mocked dawned upon him. "The money is the motive! *Ah oui!* But have you counted how much it may cost you, *m'sieu'*? You are trespassing on the territory of the Congo Free State."

"That I can not admit, *m'sieu'*."

"I shall have no recourse but to hand you over to the military authorities! You will reflect?"

"Oh damn you, go to it!" said Birskett, the effect of the injection beginning to diminish.

The *médecin major* was gazing at him fixedly.

"*M'sieu'* is ill?" he said.

"Sure. I have the sickness!"

"*M'sieu'* has the trypanosomiasis! *Tounerre!*"

"Don't you worry. You probably have it too."

"*Moi! Mais, non, m'sieu'*, I have been extremely careful."

"Yes, you would be," assented Birskett.

"But, *m'sieu'*, if that is so you will not let the secret die with you? That is a crime! *Nom de* — —! All the world would reproach you."

"*M'sieu'*, I ask you, would I die from the trypanosomiasis when I have the cure?" asked Birskett with a tired smile.

"*Nom du* — —! *M'sieu'* mocks me!" cried the weasel face with an ill-concealed note of relief in his voice.

"But has *m'sieu'* forgotten the military authorities?" queried Birskett.

"I venture to think," decided Verhaeren, "that *m'sieu'* should consider what I have said. I do not wish to inflict unnecessary suffering. Perhaps *m'sieu'* will be good enough to remain in my tent to reflect in tranquility. Cigarets are at his disposal."

"Enchanted!" returned Birskett flippantly, and striding within was more than glad to stretch out upon the Belgian's camp bed, for he was suffering from a severe headache and pains in the back and loins and a high temperature, of which now he knew well the meaning.

The feeling of lassitude was even more appreciable mentally than physically; he missed his old cheery laugh and was conscious of frowning frequently in the effort to follow a consecutive thought. The glands beneath his jaw were more swollen.

Through the glare of the tent door he could see the porters still busy building the askaris' shelters in regular company streets. Probably half or more of them, he reflected, were already inoculated.

He began to worry about the doctor and whether Kubi would reach him that evening in time to let him get away that night; for he feared that the Belgians would in any case have dispatched a squad to hunt up Friedlander. Why hadn't he put them on the wrong trail by saying that the doctor had gone to the north instead of casually remarking that the two doctors had gone bug hunting? They would get the direction from the natives. Too late now!

Again came dismally the fear that the doctor would collapse, as he himself seemed to be doing so rapidly, before he had time to find the shack and do any work. There were a hundred possibilities that might hinder him. Even if enough of the body of Stoutt had been preserved by the cold climate, wild animals or carrion might have devoured everything except the bones. But Lörtzer had said something. What was it? Oh, about a glacier. Glacier? what glacier? Oh, yes, he had buried the bodies, Stoutt's body, in a glacier. But what did he want to do that for? Preserve them? — — No, that couldn't be— Funny— Why should Lörtzer—

These disjointed reflections, so unlike his normal lucid self slowed down in jerks into an uneasy slumber.

When he partially awoke he was conscious of a thermometer being taken from his armpit and that he had been stripped of his ragged clothes. Two figures were standing over him.

"But, *mon vieux*, you are sure," the *chef du poste* was saying, "that he has not the sickness?"

"Impossible," responded Verhaeren. "He has the cure, I tell you. How then could he have the sickness. It is but malaria!"

"It is for you to say. But look you he doesn't die under your hands and then where is the secret?"

"No, no, leave him to me. I will give him quinin."

"Do your best, otherwise he won't stand his toes being cooked. What do we gain by sending him to die on the road to Boma. *Peste!* Be careful!"

"He shall stop in my own bed. I will care for him like my own child, *mais, oui!*"

"Tough guys!" murmured Birskett, whose very lethargy had kept his eyes closed. "Well, I'll have a good sleep on a real bed before I die anyway!"

A lantern was burning when next he came to. This time he was really awake. Verhaeren was sitting in a chair near him. He smiled cunningly and laid a hand on the patient's forehead, remarking that his temperature had gone down.

"Sharp attack of malaria," he said. "*M'sieu'* shall have a little soup, yes?"

He called to a boy who brought in a large bowl. Birskett sat up quite perkily.

"Ah, that is well!" said the *médecin major* with genuine relief. "The strength returns, yes?"

"Yes," assented Birskett with a grim smile and added as he tasted the broth:

"But oh, boy, real chicken soup! Guess I'm in heaven before my time!"

He asked for some more and had it; also some biscuits and canned butter. Verhaeren watched him with complacent satisfaction.

"Doing mighty well, ain't I?" demanded Birskett in an erratic fit of anger. "Like to look at my toes, you — —! I'd just love to split your face while I've got a bit of he-man left in me. Still got to remember the doc, bless him!"

He passed his hands over his eyes and frowned.

Verhaeren was regarding him with the air of his profession in the presence of delirium. Birskett saw it and grinned.

"Some doctor you are! Mighty lucky you don't understand, eh? *Ca va bien?*" (How goes it?) he inquired flippantly. "How about a cigaret and a drink?"

Those last two names the Belgian understood, smiled and proffered them. The sudden spurt of the racing motor slowed to nearly normal, and recollecting his part Birskett pretended that he was exhausted and wanted to sleep, although the necessity of pretense was not very great.

The blare of a trumpet awoke him. For several moments he stared uncomprehendingly at the green roof of the tent through the mosquito net, unable to realize where he was. Then he grinned with sheer physical satisfaction; for after those weeks of native and simian life, to awake in such luxurious surroundings was indeed a sweet experience. Verhaeren was stretched asleep in two camp chairs.

"Shame to deprive the little runt," he reflected.

He felt better, at any rate in mind; although from the touch of his hot dry skin he still had a temperature. He wondered whether Kubi had reached the doctor the previous night, and whether they had been able to make a getaway according to the plan by the aid of the needle.

However that he could not know or hope to find out—yet anyway. Also whether they had actually sent askaris after him or Friedlander, and what Friedlander was up to.

Summing everything up, he decided that its best plan was to play for time; the longer he could kid along this *médecin major* the better chance the doctor had of escaping. The pains still persisted in his back and head, but as long as he didn't move his head quickly it did not bother him much. He dozed off.

Semidelirious visions floated disconnectedly; the ghastly bald head of Lörtzer lying on a pillow—the lights, chatter and the bray of a jazz band—the sunlight on the withered grass of the Battery.

Verhaeren woke him again by taking his temperature. Birskett actually hoped it was fairly high, which would give him the opportunity to play his game. When asked whether he felt better he groaned dismally and shook his head. He was rewarded with more chicken broth and quinin. When Verhaeren had gone he got up, intending to give himself another injection of antimony and arsenic, but he could not find his haversack, although his belt and revolver were hanging on the back of a chair.

Evidently they thought he was too weak to be dangerous he realized, yet the loss of the medicine depressed him. The drug was not a cure, but it would have helped to stave off the development a little and give strength. He crawled back into the bed thinking:

"Damn it; it doesn't matter much anyway as long as the doc's got away. I've played my part and that's all there is to it."

A little after, trying to imagine what had happened to Kirkton, he was aware that he must have swooned and that the machinery had gone wrong again. Excited voices reached him. He struggled hard to force his brain to comprehend and reason. As from afar, he at length recognized the voice of Friedlander saying in French with a slight accent:

"*Non, non, m'zieu'*, that is not true. I am not a *médecin*. I am Cornelius van der Byl, a naturalist of Amsterdam. This man who tells you that is a liar. He is not Dr. Kirkton. He is Dr. Kirkton's interpreter. He—"

"Menteur!" (Liar!) shouted Birskett feebly. "That man is Herr Doktor Friedlander of Hamburg!"

"Hermanus Friedlander of Hamburg!" he heard Verhaeren exclaim.

"This man is not Dr. Keerkton?" demanded Strindhorst angrily.

"Non, non, m'zieu', it is impossible. I myself saw Dr. Kirkton last night, yes."

Came an explosive sound from Verhaeren and the *chef du poste* saying—

"But where then is Dr. Keerkton?"

An undisguised German oath of exasperation rapped out and was followed by:

"I do not know, *mezzieurs*, on my honor. That bandit came to my camp last night and put a revolver to my head and made me give him certain drugs."

Birskett grinned feebly.

"He goes; it is sunset," the voice went on. "My men fear the dark as all these native pigs. In the morning I don't find him; neither him nor his two men."

"But," expostulated Strindhorst, "they can not go into air!"

"Non, m'zieu'. He has run away. The others of the natives I find lying asleep. They are drugged. *M'zieu' le médecin major* he will understand."

"Thank God," murmured the listener, "the doc fixed that all right! Now let the big noise come!"

The excitement of the news that the doctor had got away gave him momentary strength of mind and body. Now nothing mattered. He was free to strike at these damned thugs.

"He shall be brought back instantly. Bah, he can not escape!" the *chef du poste* was saying, when the "big noise" arrived tumultuously into the tent as Birskett leaped for his revolver hanging to the chair.

Verhaeren comprehended the move instantly and flung himself upon Birskett's back shrieking for help. Birskett tore himself loose and turning, caught him up and flung him bodily into the faces of Strindhorst and Friedlander as they rushed in. Followed a chair amid the confusion. With a laugh Birskett wheeled and grabbed the holster.

But the flap, which he never used, had been left buckled. Oaths, shouts, and yells were echoed outside. Just as his fingers clutched the butt his strength went back on him treacherously. It was the last spurt. He crumpled from the knees downward. Oblivion took him—

When slowly and painfully he recovered his senses he thought at first he was still in the camp bed, but the light of dawn trickling through the clouds above the mountain peaks undeceived him.

He was clad in his rags and lying on grass beneath the giant Bombax tree. A silent figure with a bayonet moved against the dying moon. But before these simple facts had actually penetrated to the brain the morning twilight had fully come, and the blaring of the trumpet at reveille startled him dully.

Something was registered as being in his mouth. Wondering, he put up his hand and removed the substance and saw dimly a half-chewed piece of bread. Vaguely he recalled an askari placing food before him in the light of a fire. He must have gone to sleep in the act of eating. God! Was he as far gone as that?

Yet the reaction to the realization was feeble. He tried to rise. Violent pains shot through his head and spine. He sank back. Oh well, it didn't matter! Some time he'd—

He glided into a coma insensibly.

Motion once more aroused a partial comprehension of reality. He was being lifted into a hammock. There was a bustle about him. An askari with a devilish grin was cursing some one standing at his head.

"*Zut*, you won't have far to go," a faintly familiar voice was saying in French. "*Non, non*, not Matanda. *Pas la peine!* Don't bother! Drop him on the road!"

The hammock swung and jolted—scarlet trees swayed and moved overhead.

XVIII

Dr. Kirkton had little difficulty in drugging the natives. Before pretending to retire to his grass shelter he invited Zano and his tribesmen to drink some white man's beer, which was merely a compound of their own palm wine and water with some veronal.

When they had succumbed he gave them a good dose with the hypodermic syringe and packing their haversacks—the presence of Kubi fortunately enabled them to pack nearly all the food, boiled banana, chickens and half a goat, that they had in the camp, enough to last them until they reached the shack if ever they found it—and struck away through the hills for the loom of the mountains.

Kirkton was not as far advanced in trypanosomiasis as was Birskett. Whether he had been infected sooner or later he could not know, but the method mattered a lot; on whether the insertion of the proboscis of the tsetse fly was intravenous or intramuscular depended the time in taking effect. As yet he had not had the prostrating fever and violent spinal pains, yet he knew by observation of his mental processes that there was no doubt that he had contracted the dread disease. Whether any of the natives had it he could not yet be sure for the rash is harder to discern on a native, and also the mental state more difficult to remark.

Once, threading through a small valley, they came suddenly upon cultivated fields and raised the yapping of village dogs. They had to retreat and make a detour, hoping that they had not been noticed as humans. To lessen the chance that their trail would be easy to follow the doctor walked barefoot, happily for him not a very painful act in this region of soil and grass.

The moon was soaring above the peaks long before they came to the escarpment. At the bottom they stopped for half an hour to rest and readjust their loads for the steep climb. Then, scrambling and slipping, every loosened rock sounding like a thunderstorm, they began the ascent.

In the half-light, to pick a way was difficult. What were taken for dense shadows turned out to be slabs of sheer rock around which they had to hunt for a passage; bushes turned into boulders and boulders into bushes.

His feet torn and bleeding the doctor put on his boots only to find he could scarcely keep a grip on the steep slope. Sweat soaked him, and his load of the more precious instruments and drugs grew to his unaccustomed shoulders heavier than the burden of Atlas. But, panting, he struggled on; for it was of great importance to reach the summit and hide beyond before any sharp eyes in a dawn-stirring village detect them silhouetted against the ridge.

Near the top came a wall of rock which seemed to be impassable and, in the light of the moon now shining directly upon it, to continue far on either side. He sent out Kubi and Matana to the left and with Zapoko searched on the other.

After some desperate climbing with no success he thought of remaining there during the day behind some bushes for shelter, when he could the more easily search the cliff with his binoculars. But without descending halfway down again there was no shelter to be had; there they would have to cling all day like flies to a wall, readily discernible from below.

Hanging on with one hand, he made another effort with the Zeiss to find the shadow of a break to the north, when a low hoot like an owl told Zapoko that the others had found something. It proved to be a crack through which poured icy cold water from the glaciers far above. By humping the lightest of them, Kubi, upon their shoulders, who pulled them one after another through narrow and wet apertures, they gradually worked through, sprawling over the edge of the escarpment as the dawn trickled through the now clouded peaks.

As they took a well-earned rest the doctor had more time to wonder what had happened to Birskett. From Kubi's account—and he could only relate that a quantity of askaris with three white men had arrived—he could not quite decide what had happened; but he made a shrewd guess by supposing that they had proved officious in some way by claiming that they were on Belgian ground and demanding explanations.

However, thought he, now that he had got away—providing that they did not overtake him—perhaps it was for the best as Birskett would at any rate be properly attended to; in the mean time, should he be successful, he might be able to send the cure in time to save him—for the actual time taken from the beginning of the coma stage to death varies exceedingly and can hardly be estimated from observed cases.

Ahead of them rose slowly a wild plateau covered with huge boulders and bits of heath speckled thickly with flowers and scattered tree ferns for several hundred yards to a wall-like line of the bamboo forest. Above, as he had seen from the valley, were jumbled broken cliffs, green covered, and vast ravines, down some of which he could glimpse the fall of water. At this time the morning mists were low, shutting out the glaciers and the new line.

They ate and hastened on to discover a fact the doctor had not before thought of, or the boys had any experience of—the impenetrability of a bamboo forest without the aid of knives. The young shoots are so dense and strong that for less than a great beast such as an elephant or a rhinoceros to force a way is next to impossible.

Depression—lately always lurking in the back of his mind—seized the doctor. He sat down on a damp rock and stared hopelessly. "God, to have gone through all this and to be held up on the very verge! Burn it?" he thought, but that green stuff and humid roots growing in wet moss would never burn.

"There are no people here?" he asked Matana.

"*Neda, sebo.*"

"Good God!" wailed the doctor despairingly. "What are we going to do?"

Then something seemed to clear in his brain.

"What a fool I am!" he added, but he knew stupidity was not the cause. "Why, of course, if Stoutt passed up to his shack he must have had a trail cut! Find it and that'll lead to the shack itself!"

Ten minutes consideration decided him to make the search to the north, striking more or less a little beyond Boko's village, which probably Stoutt had made his base.

Skirting the edge of the bamboo forest they plugged on; yet in spite of having to negotiate ravines and rocks the going was not so tiring as below on account of the cooler temperature. Night came and they had not yet discovered any trail or any passage that could be forced. They squatted down with their backs against a rock and ate.

With the fall of night came a keen wind like a wet blanket, but so close to the escarpment they dared not venture to light a fire. The damp was worse than the cold, soaking the doctor's fragile tropical rags. He dozed for a while and then sat with his hands on his knees, grimly waiting for morning, fighting against the terrible depression that seemed gnawing him.

"The shack tomorrow, or we're done," he told himself, "for the cold will kill us and I'll never come down."

Three hours after sunrise Zapoko found traces of an overgrown trail through the forest. The young perennial shoots had grown so quickly in the eighteen months that it was already nigh impassable without knives. They did not reach the other side, torn and bleeding, until nightfall, but having that barrier between them they dared light a fire.

Before morning Kirkton was seized by a high temperature and violent pains. The track seemed to suggest turning to the north. Half a mile along, the forest was cut by a great ravine. Kirkton decided to follow the edge.

Anxiously he sought the snow line with his glasses during the few minutes after the sunrise on the other side, the eastern, before the daily shroud was drawn, but no sign of the shack could he find. He injected a double dose of antimony and arsenic and staggered on.

The ground ahead was a wild mass of rocks and steep cliffs covered in lichen with ravines full of tree lobelias in flower and many plants like dog roses in blossom.

His head seemed like a balloon full of heated gas; hot knives dissected his spine and shoulders. Two hours later he collapsed. However, the injection had done some good, for his temperature was down a little. He bade Zapoko take his precious load and cache his own, marking the place distinctly; then on he struggled again.

As he climbed with feet and hands, a sweat of agony poured out of him. But he fought on blindly, sometimes scarcely seeing a yard in front of him. Towards noon swirls of icy mist enveloped them refreshingly. Easy going tracts of small plateaus occurred, covered with mossy bog, and huge blue lobelias began to appear.

Rounding a curve, helped by two of the boys, the doctor let out a squawk at the sight of the tip of a glacier and scattered sprinklings of snow on the black rocks above. They wanted him to rest, but he would not, fearing indeed to stop.

"Shack or — —!" he muttered to himself.

The men were almost done, but were inspirited by Kirkton's furious efforts. The sun was hovering over the Congo hills. Lobelias gave into flowered shrubs and homely blackberries—but these the doctor never noticed—and presently petered into tufts of grass clinging hardily on rocks. Flurries of snow pelted them in a gust. Yet there was no sign of a shack.

Ahead, black forbidding rocks stuck out angrily from patches of snow. The ravine they had followed had narrowed to a gorge, down which tumbled a waterfall from the glacier. Kirkton, nearly blinded by exhaustion, cried hoarsely to Kubi.

The boy did not understand the words, but grasped the meaning. Dropping his haversack, he scrambled ahead.

Presently as the doctor crawled on, he heard a wild shout. He peered painfully. Although he could not see Kubi above who was waving his hands, he could distinguish a bright light as in a window of a cottage.

"A light!" he muttered. "A light!" and collapsed.

XIX

Like the broken strands of a spider's web floating in a summer wind, Birskett's streaks of consciousness were as gossamery and uncertain.

A brazen blue surface, against which flitted in black contrast palm and banana fronds, leafy branches, euphorbia tops and spears of tall grass heads appeared to him. Sometimes like a vast shadow loomed a vaguely familiar face with bright liquid eyes and small black mustaches—men chattered by firelight, a few unremembered words were addressed to a white man—food and coffee tasted—

A repetition of the previous day, except that suddenly the blue seemed unaccountably extinguished, never to come back, was exchanged for a canopy of splotches of vivid green shot with giant limbs all reeling in a manner which hurt the eyes; and he was dimly aware of the fact that the swaying was no longer rhythmical but jolted, stopped, and slipped feet foremost and then upwards.

Then these sense impressions ceased altogether. The world beneath and above remained solidly still. Over him a great branch of a tree festooned with ropelike creepers and moss stretched against a dense mass of leafy foliage. A vast yet incurious wonder possessed him. What could it be? Why? How was it that those other sensations had ceased?

His mind seemed to yawn tiredly and not very interestedly after the answer which floated indistinctly just beyond him somewhere.

Around his face was a whirling swarm of mosquitoes and he pondered impersonally why a bare arm was black, but the question seemed as insolvable as the riddle of the Sphinx. A harsh shriek sounded and vivid colors of scarlet and yellow flitted in the gloom—

A branch seemed to become detached and descend toward him in a sinuous body splotched with greens and more yellows and queer black smudges, unwound until one end with bright tiny eyes seemed looking at him in polite inquiry; then coiling over his legs, the apparition melted into the surrounding scenery.

Another moving creature of many hues appeared like a dulled flash, sat on his chest, with queer toes and weeny feet, peered at him with pink eyes like wabbling beads, and was gone.

Then came a face, an old face with two very bright eyes and a funny black nose above curious gray whiskers. It jabbered at him, showing white teeth. What did he want? Who could he be? The doctor? But the doctor hadn't a black nose. Others appeared all about. And why were they angry? He yawned. He couldn't be bothered anyway. He wanted to sleep.

Uncouth small shapes—the last apperceptions were burned into his consciousness—recalled the doctor and a stirring feeble wonder what he wanted and why he was brown and naked.

The gloom had changed to darkness save for a globular patch of vague light which frequently seemed to go out. Sometimes liquids and soft matter entered his mouth. Noises, too, penetrated into this dream world; queer tiny cries, broken gobblings, and a soft booming, accompanied by grunts and rhythmical quivering—

Then Robert Birskett awoke as a Rip Van Winkle from an agelong sleep.

He sighed, stirred and tried to rise. Surprize at the feeble response of his limbs was the very first emotion. He struggled with difficulty on to his right elbow and stared at the luminous globe. Slowly he made out trodden grass and beyond, vivid green foliage. He put out a hand and touched grass and branches and was conscious of a peculiar smell. A hut! And the smell was native. He was in a native hut.

His brain still worked slowly, and it took him perhaps minutes to absorb this information.

"Gosh, where in thunder am I?"

The sound of his own voice startled him; yet he laughed mildly.

A puling cry sounded, followed by a gobbling which was reminiscent.

"Child," he interpreted solemnly interested, "and the mother—but what lingo is that? Sounds like a monkey. Good Lordy, the monkeys can't have—"

He began to laugh again like a child pleased by its own crowing and then ceased.

"My God, the doc!"

The recollection sobered and jerked him into manhood. He stared worriedly at the globe of light and then lay back to think the better by easing his aching elbow.

The last happening he could recall clearly, any act that was definitely linked to reality, was throwing the Belgian doctor across the tent and fumbling for his gun. But since then the vague images and sensations were as tenuous as the fragments of a half-forgotten dream; so fragile that he could not be sure whether they had occurred or were the figments of a nightmare?

But the hut was real. He put out his fingers to verify it, and then clapped his hand to his forehead which was warm but clammy with natural sweat; not in the least feverish. Quite unconsciously, in letting his hand relax, he found that he was naked, and covered in some sticky ointment.

The discovery compelled a similar reaction to that of a sleepwalker caught in Broadway in his nightshirt, checked by the knowledge of his environment.

"Stark naked! And in a native hut!" He summed up his discoveries. "But why? And where? I guess I'd better find out."

Slewing himself up and around on to his hands he crawled on all fours to the tiny globular hole which was the door and poked his head through.

"Man!" he ejaculated and stared at what in the twilight of the forest resembled an assembly of gnomes.

Four dwarfs, as naked as he was, were squatting in front of another small hut whittling, apparently, pieces of stick. Their heads, densely thatched, seemed enormous and on the chocolate brown bodies—even the football-like bellies—was fine black wool. The face of one was puckered and had a dirty grayish smudge on the receding chin. The simian mouth gobbled beneath the flattened nose.

"Pigmies!" whispered the white.

To the left, and apart, were three similar figures, females, on their hams around a small fire with piles of what looked like mushrooms brightly colored, scarlet, yellow, emerald and blue, which their tiny hands were popping into a calabash steaming like a witches' caldron.

Birskett withdrew inside the hut and sat down to try to think the position out. It was evident that they were friendly to him. By recalling the series of disconnected flutterings of consciousness, he could fairly well follow that the Belgians had sent him off in a hammock. Then by association the word "hammock" shot into his mind the words of the *chef du poste!*

"*Pas la peine!* Drop him on the road!"

He growled a muttered oath. But that cleared up the problem of what had happened. Dropped him they had in the forest and these wild creatures must have picked him up and cared for him.

"Mighty strange," he reflected, "for they are known to be the most ferocious and at the same time the most timid, of all the Africans."

Then, as his mind warmed up and ran the more smoothly, an obvious fact leaped at him. Apparently the sickness had left him.

But how could it have? Antimony and arsenic was no cure—not permanent at any rate. That he knew from conversation with the doctor and technical articles he had read on the voyage out and at Entebbe. At one time the doctors had thought that that compound was a remedy; many patients had appeared to be cured, but in every case only to relapse with fatal effects.

Perhaps that was his condition. The natural man in him drooped at the conclusion. But another thought gave him wild hope; he might yet have life and strength enough to join the doctor. The idea quickened every nerve in him.

And again, reflection recalled that the doctor had never examined his blood. The rash? Some mere blood disorder might have been mistaken for the fatal symptom, influenced by suggestion. The fever might have been severe malaria and perhaps spirilum combined. Why, Kirkton had not even definitely said that in his opinion Birskett had trypanosomiasis!

"Good ——, I guess I've never had the damned thing at all!" he exclaimed: "Nearly fooled myself to death with sheer funk! That damned Belgian runt, by Goshormighty! I'll get him yet. I'll get those boys of Boko together and wipe out the son-of-a-gun! And then by Heavens they'll let me do any old thing on the tabu ground and—"

He stopped. The promise of life rushing back upon him had made him drunk. He was weak, naked as Adam, and the Lord only knew where, in the hands of pigmies!

"Of course I'm weak," he grumbled to himself, "after that bout and living native for so long. Lordy, but how am I going to get out of this mess? I ought to get off right away to the doc. Perhaps he's bad too."

Then he stopped chatting to himself. How long had he been there? He had no means whatever of finding out. Even if his watch were on his belt—if he could recover it—it would surely have stopped. Even if he could make himself understood the pigmies would have no sense of time. He sat disheartened for a while. Then life and hope began to flush together. He stuck his head out of the hole and shouted—

"Hey, Father Adam!"

The eldest of the four, the puckered-faced one, scarcely four feet high, seemed to know his name, for immediately he rose and came over, gobbling at the white man as he squatted before him. Birskett shook his head and tried him in Luganda and Kiswahili. But the little fellow gobbled on, and from his ample and eloquent gestures, Birskett gathered that he was very pleased. The other three joined him, and all four talked.

Lacking any other method he fell back on sign language. At first they appeared to think that he was asking them to admire his nude figure!

After much pantomiming in the open they got the idea, but from frequent head shaking accompanied by a persistent kind of *cluck*, pointing to their own bodies, Birskett understood that they had found him naked.

If the Belgian lieutenant had ordered him to be abandoned, the askaris would have taken care that no useful article was left upon him.

"Suppose they thought I was dead pretty nigh," he mused. Had they been left alone they'd surely have eaten me; damned lucky the — —s didn't mutilate me."

After duly cussing out his late hosts he decided that the next effort would be for food. He was easily understood and rewarded with half-singed antelope and a stew of what looked like roots of some sort and those chromatic mushrooms the women had been cooking.

"I wonder what made 'em look after me?" he wondered as he tore off lumps of flesh, native fashion, the whole tribe watching him.

"Guess the old shrimp must be the chief. If he wasn't a pigmy I'd think I'd seen him before. H'm. Gosh, that's good. These vegetables taste fine—a bit bitter like spinach. I'd better eat my head off while I can and try to pantomime these fellows into helping me back to Bokoland. In this confounded forest you can't see where the mountains are, so it's no use pointing. M-mum. The sun is the only chance."

The meat had the effect of wine. He felt as if strength was pouring into his veins and muscles. A reaction after the physical and nervous collapse gripped him. He began to chant:

> "You are old, father Adam, the young man said,
> And you're getting most horribly fat!
> I shouldn't be shocked to hear you are dead!
> Now what d'you know about that?
>
> "You are old, father Adam, the young man said,
> And your beard has become very gray!
> I wonder you'd mind just to stand on your head,
> And please to point out the right way?

"Good Lord, I'm getting childish!" exclaimed Birskett laughing almost hysterically as the audience chattered with much delight. "Well, I guess if you like it—

"Lordy, that's it!" he exclaimed. "Gray! Why, that gray tuft of whiskers! That's where I've seen him before! That's why he's so mighty keen on playing the good Samaritan stunt. He's the little old runt the gorilla was after!"

He rose and touched his own and the old fellow's chest and mimicked the stoop of the gorilla gathering fungus which resembled Indian pipes, the shooting, and the fall of the beast. The chorus of gobbles and clucks confirmed his theory. He came back, took the withered little hand and placed it on his chest as far as the man could reach and placed his own on the pigmy's shoulder. Again the primitive symbolism was understood and accepted.

"Fine! Brothers!" agreed Birskett, grinning, and they all grinned industriously.

After this satisfactory sealing of the alliance, a tiny pipe was produced from a woolly thatch and proffered to him.

How was a man, stark naked, set in the middle of the dense jungle among pigmies, to start a plan of campaign against the Belgians; or even contrive to join the doctor? That was the stiff problem Birskett had to solve.

Clothes he could not make out of leaves sufficiently durable to afford enough protection against the sun in the open. The sanest scheme he could hunt up was to endeavor to find Boko or his tribe who, knowing him, would be inclined to help him as far as lay in their power. In the mean time the first thing was to recover strength.

His constitution aided him. Within four or five days he was fit enough to walk a considerable distance. The following day, as if the chief had noticed the fact, he saw by the preparations that the tiny tribe was about to move. He decided to make every effort now to persuade them to go towards the mountains, the direction of which he had carefully marked by observing the glare of the westering sun through the canopy of the vast trees.

Of course he had no idea what distance the Belgians had had him carried; nor whether they had crossed the Semliki river. However, Kikkik, as he understood the old chief's name to be, as soon as he grasped what the white required, seemed only too pleased to consent.

But they were as solicitous of him as a hen with a brood, marching but the shortest of distances, the tiny women carrying their calabashes, spare bows and arrows, and knives and tobacco, which constituted their only household effects. At night they roosted in swiftly made shelters in the lower limbs of trees. During the day the men disappeared for hunting, usually to return with either buck or bird; flesh and roots, berries and fungus were their daily fare. The poison for their tiny arrows, he learned, was made from crushed ants and decomposing meat and had no deleterious effect upon the rest of the flesh. The sticky ointment, he discovered, was made from a pungent herb and kept off most of the flies and bugs, but not, he noticed, the ferocious tsetse.

Kikkik loved to spend hours trying to teach the white man his language, and in a few days Birskett picked up enough simple words for everyday needs. He was surprized at the intelligence they evidently possessed; perhaps that, he reflected, was the reason that they were so careful to keep from contact with any others save their own kindred!

Indeed they appeared very happy; their needs were little and those supplied by small exertion. Of the gorilla they had evidently more fear than of any other living creature; more apparently than of the white man. Once they encountered another family of nine pigmies who at first seemed very desirous of attacking the strange white giant, but afterwards were as friendly as children.

So Birskett marched on slowly, hoping that soon they would at least come to a break in the forest where he might get his bearings, ever chewing upon the problem to be solved, and undoubtedly gaining strength with an extraordinary rapidity.

XX

Which Roman Emperor said that "All roads led to Rome"? Leopold might well have amended the saying by "Many roads lead to the Congo!"

Were you an official in a Belgian bank suffering from a shortage in the accounts? A corporal hankering after the sweets of Junkerdom? A Dutch *ambtenaar* bewailing the dearth of pickings? A Parisian Apache who had bungled an affair on the slopes of Montmartre? Honor and cash would have awaited you all, gentlemen—in the Congo!

The concessions provided rubber and ivory unlimited. There was but one condition—get it!

In the good old days these things were, but now all such evil is banished.

M'sieu', le médecin major Verhaeren, annoyed by the vigilance of the Brussels police, had accepted that invitation; also Karl Strindhorst had decided to take a cure for an inability to distinguish between his own wife and a superior officer's; Signor Villino had been suffering from the disgraceful refusal of a rival to recover from a stiletto wound in the back.

Although the perquisites attendant on good service, diligence and a strict attention to duty, were capable within a few years, of reinstating black sheep in a respectable position—in a fairer clime—the life and climate were fatiguing to the delicate constitution of a gentleman.

Several articles in a medical review had led to the profound reflection that nearly a million francs would be worth winning even at a little sacrifice; hence the presence of the trio nobly braving the perils of the sleeping sickness and the pigmies in the interest of mankind.

After the disposal of the impostor, Verhaeren and Strindhorst held a council. The first doctor had to be dealt with. The sole question was, what did he know? Already arrested on the formal charge of trespassing on His Majesty's domain—the anomaly of the Free State of the Congo and a Majesty's domains never seemed to strike them—Friedlander was brought before them. Verhaeren once fooled was not now inclined to be diplomatic; but this man was not Dr. Kirkton, the actual interviewer of Lörtzer.

Friedlander now acknowledged frankly that he was a scientist of Hamburg and also admitted that the object of his mission was to discover the lost cure. The whereabouts of Kirkton he swore he did not know, and brought the men who were with him, native and his own servants, to corroborate the statement. His emphatic sentences when speaking on the subject seemed to convince the skeptical Verhaeren.

Could they not, suggested Friedlander suavely, unite in the search for this missing villain? For his part he was a scientist merely, engaged in research, and to whom the material rewards were nothing as long as humanity benefited; whereas this American, as he had proof, had obtained confidential confessions from the sick bed of the illustrious Herr Professor Lörtzer which he sought to make use of for obvious base purposes. Everybody knew that America was the land of the dollar, said he.

They must, he assured them, do their utmost to capture this Dr. Kirkton; for he had reason to believe that the natives had communicated something to him regarding the whereabouts of the missing effects of Dr. Stoutt; indeed he would not be surprized that they had connived at the extraordinary disappearance. There was in reason no other solution to the mystery.

"The chief then will duly communicate the facts to us," stated Strindhorst.

"I don't think so *messieurs!*" said Friedlander. "I beg your pardon, but they are most unusually stupid. I have reason to believe that this Dr. Kirkton convinced them that he was the brother of Dr. Stoutt by showing them some article that he had brought from America—possibly merely a hat or a bangle of Dr. Stoutt's. You know how gullible these natives are. What would you?"

This statement, a purely imaginative conjecture of Friedlander's, impressed the officials.

They consulted apart and decided that, although they did not believe his professions of altruism, he was not dangerous and might be useful. They recalled him, and graciously accepted his offer—in the name of King Leopold!—informing him that they would now deal with the chief in a manner befitting a master.

Friedlander's wily slit eyes narrowed as he turned his head to observe the view. He knew the men he was up against; also he summed up the technical knowledge of the *médecin major*. If he played his game well he might use these clumsy boors.

Let them find the missing notes of the American scientist. Verhaeren would, he was sure, be too ignorant to recognize a formula of the cure when he saw it; he, Friedlander, would merely attract his attention to some other formula and walk off with the prize. The only serious matters that worried him were the whereabouts and the actions of Kirkton.

Immediately, while the sun was still obscured by the mountains and clouds, the *chef du poste* sent for Boko and his notables.

Seated before the three green tents beneath the huge scarlet Bombax tree the *chef du poste* and Verhaeren with Friedlander received the native chief and his councilors. Around them, drawn up in military formation, were the askaris, big ebony-black fellows recruited from a tribe of cannibals notorious for their ferocity.

In spite of the impressive show of the whites in white and gold and the military pomp Boko, the chief, wore the old shirt of Dr. Stoutt's, as he strode before them, with the dignity of a Roman bearing the purple. He was outraged, angry, but not a muscle of the bronze face showed a quiver of emotion. Yarazoo, in his mauve pants sagging down one side of his skinny hip, looked like an ancient Hamite chieftain risen from the grave, the tortoise-like head bearing insignia of his profession held motionless, unseeing.

A giant of a black sergeant with the filed teeth of his tribe stood bold upright beside the noble representative of a distant white king who thought no courteous greeting necessary, a fact which hurt and confused the native mind more than the startling assertions that their country was not their own.

"Tell him," said Strindhorst in a dialect of Kiswahili, "that I wish to know what he means by saying that his people do not know where that white man has gone to."

"*Ezikide!*" (He has vanished!) the phrase seemed a kind of ventriloquism, for the lips scarcely moved.

"*Tonimba, nkima!*" (Don't lie to me, monkey!) snapped the big sergeant.

Neither the bronze face nor the eyes of the chief flickered.

"*Owulide, mbwa?*" (D'you hear, dog?)

"*Pulide.*" (I hear.)

"What does he say?" interrupted Strindhorst irritably.

"The ape refuses to answer, *bwana.*"

"*Pardon, m'zieu',*" interrupted Friedlander, who was anxious to prevent the brute of a sergeant from destroying any valuable information that the parade of force might frighten out of the natives. "*Pardon, m'zieu'*, the chief said he did not know."

"*Diable!*" growled Strindhorst. "Who asked you to interfere?"

"*Non, non, non! Attendez!*" whispered Verhaeren. "He understands this monkey language. Let him interpret."

"*Pense-tu!*" retorted Strindhorst with an ugly laugh, and added to the sergeant. "You interpret exactly what this animal says or I'll flog the black hide off you. Understand?"

"*Bwana! kwell!*" (Truly, master!) asserted the sergeant and grinned at his triumph.

"Don't terrify him yet," whispered Verhaeren "or he'll be so scared he won't answer."

"*Écoute, mon vieux!*" said Strindhorst roughly. "D'you think you know these beasts better than I do? Haven't I lived among the pigs for five years and thou—"

"*Si, si!*" replied Verhaeren soothingly.

"Tell him," continued Strindhorst while Friedlander's eyes smiled at the scarlet Bombax branch, "that if he doesn't tell me the truth I'll flog him."

This the sergeant interpreted literally. There was no response nor movement.

"Now," said the *chef du poste*, "ask him where his men are who were—" he hunted for a word for drugged—"put to sleep by this man."

"Animal," said the sergeant, "where are thy monkeys who were made dead by the white man and brought to life afterwards?"

"They are bewitched and have fled," returned Boko mendaciously.

Then he was informed that he was to have them recalled within one day or—the sergeant interpreted with gesticulations of his own.

"What was the name of the man he talked about before? The name of the white doctor who is dead, fool?" as the sergeant gazed blankly.

"The Giver of Life, *bwana*?" for Boko naively had spoken of him as he had to the Americans.

"*Indio*, ask him again what has become of his body?

"*Ezikide*," replied Boko tonelessly.

"The creature says it has gone out."

"Tell him I'll flog—"

"Wait, wait!" implored Verhaeren. "Ask him about the books first."

"*Nom de* — —, art thou the *chef du poste* or am I?" grumbled Strindhorst, but he repeated the question to the interpreter.

"He says, *bwana*, that he does not know of what you speak."

"Tell him that if he doesn't find his tongue I'll cut his hide off."

"*Indio, bwana*."

The sergeant repeated the threat with gusto. There was no reply.

"That creature there," demanded Strindhorst, suddenly pointing to Yarazoo. "What is it?"

"He is the witch doctor," replied the sergeant.

"What's that fool headdress thing he's got on his head?"

"He says it's great medicine, *bwana*."

"What does it do? What is it?"

"He says it is a weed which makes him always young," returned the sergeant with a contemptuous sneer.

"*Nom de* — —, he looks it!" said Strindhorst in French, laughing at what he considered his own joke. "Superstitious brutes! Pah! Sergeant, ask him where the books and papers of the dead white man are? He'll know if anybody does," he added to Verhaeren. "The fools would think they were great medicine, as he calls it."

"*Nini, nkima?*" (What, monkey?) shouted the sergeant when Yarazoo had mumbled his reply.

"What does he say?"

"He says, *bwana*, that he is deaf and has not heard what—"

"*Lekerawo!*" (Shut up!) interrupted Friedlander, and added:

"*Pardon, m'zieu'*, but the man did not say that. He said that the white men are as foolish as a bird pecking at the shell of a tortoise."

Strindhorst stared at him, angrily tugging at a mustache, doubtful for the moment whether Friedlander or the native was making a fool of him.

"What d'you mean?" he growled.

"He means," said Friedlander with a slight smile, "that you will never get anything out of them by those methods."

"*Quoi!*" shouted Strindhorst enraged. "— — I'll teach 'em who's master. — —, they want a lesson and they'll have it."

"*Mais, écoutez,*" interrupted Verhaeren feebly, "let's try to—"

"*Ta gueule!*" (Shut your jaw!) growled Strindhorst, jumping to his feet in a rage. "Sergeant, lay that animal out and give him thirty—to begin with."

As the sergeant coughed orders in military style the *chef du poste* thumped down in his chair, a berserker rage in his blue eyes.

Verhaeren mumbled—

"Oh, la la!" disgustedly, and Friedlander turned aside to shrug his shoulders.

A corporal marched up six men and surrounded Yarazoo. A keen observer would have remarked that the witch doctor swiftly put his hand to his mouth.

One askari, seizing him, threw him roughly on to his face; another with a whip of hippopotamus hide, stood over him looking with expectancy towards the *chef du poste*, who nodded.

At the first lash the mauve pants were split. At the tenth they were streaked with blood, but the prostrate figure neither flinched nor yelled. The swish of the whip and the impact sounded clearly in the still, hot air.

Boko's face, cast in bronze, was turned as if indifferently contemplating the grass at his feet; and so was every one of his men's! At the thirtieth the askari stopped, peered at the victim, and, disappointed that he had failed to produce a single scream, angrily kicked the skinny body and looked around anxiously.

"The man seems dead," said Friedlander casually.

"Is the animal dead?" demanded Strindhorst.

"*Siwezi, bwana,*" (I don't know, master,) returned the askari and catching an arm jerked the figure on to the back. The ancient head lolled sidewise, and the limbs fell listlessly.

"*Indio Kufa,*" (Yes, dead,) added the askari disgustedly.

"Take it away then!" ordered Strindhorst as indignant as the askari at the lack of sport. "And see what this other animal's made of."

"*Indio, bwana!*" chorused the askaris joyfully.

Disdaining to employ more than one man, an askari caught up the legs and dragged the body of Yarazoo through the ranks into the grass, and with a final disgusted kick left him to be attended to later—in the pot if they had a chance, bony as he was.

"Wait!" roared Strindhorst, as they roughly yanked the chief to the place of execution. "Sergeant, ask the brute whether he will reply or not?"

The sergeant put the question, embroidered with suitable threats. But the features never moved, not even the contemplative eyes regarding the grass in front of him.

"The monkey is sulky, *bwana*," said the sergeant with an anticipatory grin.

Strindhorst swore and nodded to the man with the *kiboko*.

"Give him sixty," he added, and the blacks grinned with delight.

With the first swish of the whip through the air came a muffled grunt from Boko's men squatting in a circle, echoed by the remainder, who had assembled without the square of armed askaris. Strindhorst glanced towards them with the lust of slaughter in his eyes. He, too, grunted but said nothing, and fastened his cold blue eyes on the prostrate chief.

At the thirtieth blow a groan was forced. The back from the shoulders to the thighs was bloodily wealed; for the askari had deliberately chosen a fresh spot each time, returning carefully upon the wounds.

"Enough!" commanded Strindhorst at the fifty-seventh. "Ask the brute again, sergeant."

The corporal roughly jerked the chief on to his bleeding haunches to answer the questions. His features were an ashy greenish color, but the eyes were still bright and deliberately regarded space; the lips did not move.

"Give the sulky swine another sixty," ordered Strindhorst and there was a high note of excitement in the voice.

"*Indio, bwana!*" said the black sergeant exultantly and barked the order.

As the lashes began again Verhaeren leaned towards the *chef du poste* whispering:

"But he can't stand another sixty. You'll kill him. Let me examine him."

"*Ta gueule!*" almost shouted Strindhorst now seemingly in a frenzy. "I'll have the bastard cut to pieces alive if I want to. I'll teach 'em to lie to me! Give him a hundred!" he bawled at the askari.

"Rub some salt in," said Friedlander quietly, whose green eyes were watching the scene like a cat playing with a mouse. "It will revive him, although you've made a mistake *m'zieu'*. A little fire is more effective in extracting secrets and—"

The monotony of the swishes was broken by a loud cry from the crowd of Boko's men, and was echoed immediately by a screaming yell from the bush, a howling war cry. The ringing *kiboko* hung in the air as the natives leaped to their feet.

"*Mon Dieu!*" began timid Verhaeren wriggling from his chair. "They will—"

Simultaneously Strindhorst with an oath sprang up and drawing his revolver, fired into the mass of Boko's men as he shouted an order to the askaris to bayonet them.

Twenty blades flashed eagerly in the sun.

During the massacre Strindhorst stood, revolver in hand tugging ferociously at his mustaches, watching and listening. Friedlander backed against the tree nervously, being unarmed. Verhaeren began to shout hysterically—

"They're attacking us!"

One man, only a knife in his hand with an askari after him leaped forward at the *chef du poste* who coolly shot him, and walking across, blew out the brains of the prostrate chief.

At that moment crashed a volley of shots from the askaris as a handful of villagers charged wildly. Wheeling about, Strindhorst glanced at the slaughter. None of the natives lived. Striding forward, he shouted to the sergeant to advance and burn the village.

And it was done, as thousands of others before!

They took no prisoners, neither man, woman, nor child.

As the smoke swirled in a column in the still hot air of noon Verhaeren danced with rage under the scarlet Bombax tree wailing:

"*Mais, mon Dieu*, the imbecile may have burnt those notes. Oh, la la! Oh, la la!"

And Friedlander, squatting at the base, smiled contemptuously at the crudity of the methods employed.

But neither white man saw fifty yards away a skeleton of a figure with rags of blood and mauve hanging to his ancient limbs crawling painfully through the long grass.

XXI

Among the jumbled foothills to the southwest of the camp from which Kirkton had started for the mountains in one of the denser groves of bananas were gathered some five hundred of the tribe; for fear of the askaris they dared not assemble in any village. Although all were armed they talked in muffled tones, testifying to the effect of the massacre and the burning.

In the centre of the throng sat Yarazoo and three of his brethren of the craft, the chief's ninth son, for the others had been slain, and Zano, he of the wristwatch.

The calamity which had befallen them was the more overwhelming in that their previous dealings with whites had rendered them confident and friendly. True, they had heard of the doings of the Bulamatadi from afar; but then distant disasters are never very convincing; those terrible things had happened to other tribes; whereas, were not they, the Tiny Children of the Mountain, under the protection of the Giver of Life?

The whole affair, the thrashing of Yarazoo, the death of their chief, the massacre of his sons and the elders and the terrible effects of the askaris' Snider rifles was on the level of a miracle; something not understandable to the human mind. Even in their wars with other tribes the sacredness of a *shauri* and the dignity of a chief had never been thus betrayed.

There were many who asserted that they were not white men at all but evil spirits, *Ahuu*, taking the human shape; and in proof, said they, had they not nigh done to death the white man, He-who-laughs, brother of the Giver of Life? And had he not said that they were powerful and wicked? Where was he now, the big man who had dwelt with them as a brother?

"Eh!" said another, "but what of the other, he who has 'vanished'? Was that not more of the magic of these devils?"

"Nay, nay," contradicted others, outraged by this approach to blasphemy, "had he not 'vanished' as had the Giver of Life?"

"Ehh! That was indeed true. Likely that he knew of the coming of these *Ahuu* and had left his big brother to warn them. Yet why had he not aided them, made magic against them?"

"Yet," argued another, "had not the Bulamatadi with all their askaris and white magic beep unable to kill their witch doctor, Yarazoo? Ehh! But his magic was powerful! He would be able to make medicine that should prevail against them!"

So disputed the mob. But in the circles of the elders and witch doctors other opinions prevailed. Yarazoo who for five days had lain in a hut in the bush making magic—apparently by lying on the grass bed covered with ointment made from his own specifics—had bidden his professional brethren and deputations of warriors from all the tribe for a great *shauri*. His own prestige considerably augmented by the judicious use of a herbal drug which produced almost a complete anesthesia of the flesh, he advocated a general attack on the camp which the Belgians were making some five hundred yards to the north of the site of the old village.

Success was insured, he guaranteed, by the assistance of medicine which he was preparing.

But there were two factions which opposed this plan. One, led by the ninth and eldest surviving son of Boko, was terrified by the disaster and claimed that no human beings could expect to survive the flaming fire sticks of the terrible black devils; another band, of a more religious turn of mind, protested that the Giver of Life had solemnly forbidden them to injure any white, referring to the apostle conversant with the sayings of the departed master, the unhappy Zano, who, filled with rage, was strong for the war party, but was confuted out of his own mouth.

Yarazoo after saying his say squatted as silent as a Maori effigy, listening to the disputes around him. Like an old sage he let them talk for two days until, reckoning his time, he suddenly announced that he had arranged to procure such powerful medicine from the Bulamatadi themselves that they would be overcome as easily as plucking bananas. Simultaneously with this calculated statement was heard a low but piercing ululation proclaiming the coming of their own people.

In complete silence presently there stalked through the grove fifty warriors headed by a young chief who bore upon a spear blade a gory head of a white man with black mustaches and imperial. Deep chest grunts applauded this and the heads of askaris borne by the followers.

When they had laid the ghastly trophies before Yarazoo he spoke briefly and to the point. These were the promised powerful medicine! And so were the factions silenced.

Next morning runners sped to the south, where dwelt the bulk of the tribe and allied tribes, for none of these was very big, bearing the war message and bidding them assemble at a rendezvous near the forest to the west.

For five days a great dance was held, and every warrior was smeared with a magical concoction.

Four days later, when the clouds above the mountain peaks were paling, a sentry's shot rang out. Spears glimmered like butterflies in the grass. Howls on the slopes were answered by convulsive but merciless spurts of red flames; and then swiftly by the sputter at each end of the camp of two demons hysterically coughing sudden death.

The witch doctor's extract of the handsome Villino's head prevailed not and the Tiny Children of the Mountain fled.

The defeat was a grave setback to the prestige of Yarazoo. He cursed his men for cowards, but that was their first experience of machine guns and volley firing. They were cowed. Many talked of immediate submission, recalling the words of He-who-laughs advising them to submit; others cried that the Giver of Life had himself forbidden them to attempt to injure a white man. Was not this the terrible penalty?

But boldly Yarazoo called again a big *shauri* and announced that he had made more magic, magic that this time should call to their aid no less than the brother of the Giver of Life himself.

Eh! And behold there limped into the grove before the astonished eyes of the warriors wounded and hale, the tall gaunt figure of a bearded white man having upon his head a plaited cone of wild banana fronds and about his bony body a girdle of woven grass.

"Eh!" grunted the warriors as Birskett squatted beside Yarazoo.

"*Mulabe, mwami! Mulabe, mwami! we-wao! webale—wao! webale—wao!*" (Greeting chief, thanks very much, yes!) they chorused.

"*Agafewamwe, bunange?*" (How are things at home my friends?)

"*Nungi, mwami, webale—wao!*" (Fine, chief, thanks very much!)

"*Erade?*"

"*Erade!* (All well!) *Webale—wao!*"

After this polite greeting, for it is a direct invitation to the spirits ever to admit that things are bad, a deep silence fell, all eyes regarding with reverence and hope the miraculously resurrected white man.

Then after compliments, Yarazoo, who had by silent consent taken the rôle of chief until the necessary formalities of appointing the successor should be made, dismissed the crowd. He was satisfied that once more not only had he retrieved his prestige as a powerful witch doctor, but that, human-like, his past dreadful and costly error was already nigh forgotten in the excitement of the latest miracle. All of them he sent away even Zano and Boko's son. While they were going young girls brought calabashes of goat's milk of which Birskett was known to be fond. Then Yarazoo, dropping a little of the native rigamarole as if between professionals, recounted all that had happened since Birskett had been sent to seeming death.

After Birskett had put a few questions, he told the story, as much as he saw fit, of his sojourn among the pigmies. His tale astonished the ancient, although he said no word, because of the white man's power over these wild men of the forest who are more feared by the native than any living animal, biped or quadruped.

A hut of grass in the temporary camp had already been prepared for him and he was glad to lie down.

Birskett had discovered from the natives that he had been away nearly a month. Heaven knew what had happened to the doctor during that time. His need for clothes was imperative. The tribe certainly could not supply him with a helmet, the most necessary; half an hour of an unprotected head in the rays of the equatorial sun would be swifter death than sleeping sickness. The primitive hat of banana fronds was neither durable nor manageable. Boots too. His feet were almost a bloody mass. Walking slowly in the forest from root to root, on marsh and moss, had been easy compared to the reed and stuff of the swamp which he had had to cross between that and the foothills.

That confounded Yarazoo was just as stubborn about any kind of tabu as ever he had been, he reflected savagely. Yet if he could devise some means of overcoming the Belgians—and he had quite a score to pay himself—they would surely make a chief of him. Then he would be able to handle matters as he would.

That the Tiny Children of the Mountain had been repulsed easily did not surprise Birskett at all. They were not numerous enough, even if they could have stood the shock, to overwhelm the garrison of two hundred askaris and two machine guns. Contemplating the situation, Birskett grew despondent.

He had nothing save his wits and bare hands—and even then he had not yet got back his normal strength. But somehow the problem had to be solved. But how?

They brought him food and he ate wolfishly; in spite of the heat he had always now a sharp hunger. At last the germ of an idea began to develop; hazardous truly, but the only one he could see.

"It's a mighty good job," he mused. "I'm an amateur dacoit and still better that those sentries aren't Gurkhas!"

He could give the natives he believed a chance to win through, but the drawback was that the rest of the plan depended upon them. He sent for Yarazoo.

To him such of his scheme as he thought judicious to communicate he did, naturally wrapped in the native mold of sorcery. An important point was—would Yarazoo, or could he, anoint them with special magic so that they would attack in the night?

Yarazoo with much circumlocution explained that such a thing had never been done. Although his magic was surely proof against the spirits for warriors *en masse* so that they could travel and hide awaiting the usual attack at dawn, when the spirits of the night were actually abroad they could wreak dreadful work upon any single man separated, as during a fight, from his fellows.

Patiently Birskett went over the ground again, emphasizing that he would guarantee the successful delivering of the Belgians into their hands should the natives carry out his instructions.

"To the brethren of the Giver of Life, my friend," returned Yarazoo solemnly, "such things are as a lizard catching flies, but to the weak Children of the Mountain the spirits of the night are powerful. None can withstand them, and they be of malicious mind."

For the first time self-control, strengthened by experience and practise, nearly broke into a loud and hearty curse. He changed the subject native style.

"My friend," said he, "where is he now that was my friend, Eyes-of-a-bird, that went forth with Zano and his men?"

"*Ezikide*," returned Yarazoo as Birskett knew he would.

"Even as the Giver of Life has vanished?"

"*Simanyi, munange,*" (I don't know, friend,) replied Yarazoo, his tortoise features beginning to freeze palpably.

"O Yarazoo, lend me thine ear. Knowest thou well that should the power of the Bulamatadi not be broken that indeed they will eat up thy people until none be left but slaves and concubines?"

"*Wao, munange!*"

"Knowest thou that when they lay hands upon thee that thou shalt be served even as was Boko the chief?"

"*Wao,*" agreed Yarazoo whose dignity had forbidden him to tell the white man of his own beating and escape.

"Hath not thy magic failed utterly against the demons of flaming voices?"

"*Wao*," assented Yarazoo reluctantly as if not yet quite convinced.

"Knowest thou what my magic hath told me?"

"*Simanyi, munange.*" (I don't know, my friend.)

"My magic hath told me that my brother, Eyes-of-a-bird, awaits me not in ghost-land, but among the hills above the village of Boko."

The small eyes of the witch doctor began to grow a veil of mysticism. He did not reply.

"If through my magic these Bulamatadi are delivered into the hands of the Tiny Children of the Mountain wilt thou guide me into the mountain, the abode of my brothers?"

Birskett's steady eyes were drilling compellingly into the witch doctor, but the latter's had become utterly lackluster.

"Doth understand, O Yarazoo?" continued Birskett, his voice nigh trembling with rage, "that if I do not this thing for you the Tiny People of the Mountain and all that is theirs, shall become ghosts and slaves?"

Silence.

Slowly as a man coming out of a trance the small eyes awakened and looked calmly into those of the white man.

"At the hour of the parrot (about half an hour before dawn)," said Yarazoo placidly, "shall the warriors be as my friend hath asked."

"— — damn you, you ugly mutton-brained bonehead!"[8] burst out Birskett gripping his nails into his palm, "you'd sacrifice your own silly —"

---

[8] The original text reads "mutton-<u>branded</u> bonehead," a possible typo. About a dozen pages later, Birskett exclaims: "Of all the blind, mutton-<u>brained</u> boneheads I'm the prize specimen on earth!" According to Green's *Dictionary of Slang*, "mutton" has a long and complex history, comprising

He regained control, blinking in the effort.

"Listen, my friend," he said quietly, "wherefore canst thou not do this thing for me, the brother of the Giver of Life? Am I not about to renew life again to thy tribe by delivering them from the Bulamatadi? Am I not thy friend and brother?"

For several moments Yarazoo retained his fixedly placid gaze; then said he slowly and very softly:

"Those are white words even as thou hast said, white man, my friend and brother. But dost thou not know that were that which thou demandest of me granted that for ever afterwards would the virtue of the Giver of Life be gone out? Thus is it."

"So be it, my friend!" returned Birskett resignedly and added after a moment's reflection:

"But if I do this thing for thee, thou shalt not harm the Bulamatadi, but let them loose to return alone whence they came, or else surely will their brothers return to avenge them, aye, and leave not one of you alive. Thou hast heard?"

"Pulide, munange!"

Birskett growled disgustedly when Yarazoo had gone, throwing himself on to the pallet of grass.

---

multiple meanings and applications. Among other things, it can refer to "a gullible individual, 'a sheep'"; hence, *mutton-brained* and *mutton-headed*.

XXII

The clouds, unusually low over the mountains in the setting sun, seemed to reach out ghostly scarlet fingers plucking at the bamboo forest. The stars overhead struggled out. The clammy air was thick with heat; even the insects fluttered and crawled around the lights as if limp with fatigue.

From the dull circles of yellow, blotched with figures, rose the continuous hum of a camp of men engaged at food, above which sounded at regular intervals the unceasing hoot of an African nightjar, the shrilling of numerous crickets, and from a short distance the rhythmic chorus of frogs.

In the white men's quarters in the center of the camp was a separate mess tent within which, sprawled around a table inside a large mosquito net, were the *chef du poste* and Verhaeren at dinner. The former with a gold-laced tunic and shirt wide open exposing a wet, hairy chest, was slumped forward with an elbow on the table. He ate gloomily.

Verhaeren, primly sitting up, ate mincingly, regarding from time to time the gross table manners of his chief, which never failed to irritate him. A gin bottle stood between them.

"You are sure that little good man has the sickness?" growled Strindhorst between noisy sups.

"*Si, si,*" said the little doctor. "He has a temperature of forty-two point two as well as the rash on his body."

"*Diable!*" complained Strindhorst. "Maybe I've got it myself. *Nom de* ——! Verhaeren!" he added loudly as if he feared the little man had gone suddenly deaf. "D'you think I have?"

"Who knows?" retorted Verhaeren, experiencing much pleasure in the glare of fright in the blue eyes.

"——! If I have then thou hast!"

"*Mais, non,*" expostulated Verhaeren not liking the insinuation. "You have more blood than I, *mon capitan.* These pests love the red blood, but for me I am skinny, yes. No, I will not have it."

"Don't be sure, *mon vieux,* if I have it I don't see why you shouldn't. *Diable!* Why was I so foolish as to listen to your fool's tales? *Peste,* I don't think you know anything about it any more than I do."

He mumbled unintelligibly to himself and pushed his plate away as if the idea had put him off his food.

"How many of the men did you say?"

"Eleven—as yet—but," added Verhaeren "the microbe, you must know, takes days or weeks to develop."

"*Sainte — —,*" muttered Strindhorst. "I tell you, if you can't find these — — books— I don't believe there ever were any—in two days, we go. I strike camp the day after tomorrow. *Morte de — —,* I am not paid to live in a filthy hole like this with death flying at me! And this pig, how long will he last?"

"Oh perhaps six months—perhaps six weeks. Who can tell?" said Verhaeren and continued watching the big man's eyes with cunning pleasure. "You will have frightful headaches— insupportable! Pains in the shoulders—excruciating! Sickness of the stomach—frightful! Then after the fever you will become thin slowly, lose your paunch and forget to eat. Then you—"

"*Sacre — —! Tais-toi, imbécile!*" roared Strindhorst, banging his fist on the table and pushing back his chair so violently that he nearly capsized. "— —, I'd sooner be cut to pieces by these black devils than go through all that."

"You are afraid?" inquired Verhaeren softly.

"*Zut!*" snorted the Chef du Poste. "It is disgusting! *Pouf!* It is no death for a man!"

He grabbed angrily at a box of cheroots on the table and stuck one savagely in his beard.

"But this German ought to tell where the dirty books are now? Surely he'd find the secret if he could to save himself? *Diable!*" he cried. "We never thought of that! But if we could find the American hound couldn't you make him have the filthy disease. Then, *mon vieux,* he'd render all he knew, I'll swear."

He laughed deeply at the bright idea.

"Easily," returned Verhaeren. "I have already thought of that."

"Pah!" Strindhorst scoffed, pouring out a stiff glass of gin. "Why didn't you try it on this other brute then?"

"Because I suspected that he had already got it just as that creature had whom we sent away."

"Again I listened to your idiocy," growled Strindhorst, "and lost my men! Do you think, *mon vieux,* that trained askaris grow on palm trees here?"

He sprawled backwards and mopped his sweating face with a vast handkerchief, and Verhaeren finished his glass.

"*Pouf!*" snapped Verhaeren shrugging his shoulders as he got up. "What is the use to talk to you? Always it is I that am wrong. Always it is you who have the wisdom of *M'sieu'* Solomon."

"*Ta gueule!*" growled Strindhorst. "If your tongue was as long as your cheek you would be a rare fellow!"

"*Zut!*" spat Verhaeren from the curtain edge, looking like a spiteful terrier snapping with bared teeth. "What would you do, my great man, if I were not here to help you? You would have been food for ants long since but for me— *Oui, moi, nom de* — — and my medicines!"

"*Toi!* You lazy little kind of dirt, keep your rat-mouth still or I'll break your face for you one of these days."

He began a commotion in his chair as if to rise.

"I'll teach you to respect your superiors, pig!"

"*Tonnerre!*" screamed Verhaeren from the door. "You, my fine man, you shall die of the sleeping death which has gotten you! *Si, si!* it is the truth I tell you!"

As the big man emitted a cross between a grunt and a groan Verhaeren disappeared into the night, chuckling audibly. Strindhorst sank back into the chair swearing and sweating profusely. He poured out another big swig and gulped it. For several moments his heavy breathing panted above the night sounds.

"Bah!" he said aloud resentfully. "The little rat doesn't know any thing about it — But —!"

With another smothered curse he climbed out of his chair and shouted childish threats at Verhaeren as he walked off to go the rounds of the sentries, which he was compelled to do personally now that Villino had gone. Having vented sane of his spleen on the askaris he returned to his own tent.

Thus it went every night. Deprived of swaggering his authority over the eleven whites in Matanda and worked upon by greed and fear, he was growing more irritable every day; particularly under the perpetual sting of the malicious Verhaeren, whom he dared not injure or send back in case he himself should fall ill!

Kicking off his boots and flinging his belt and clothes into a chair Strindhorst crawled under his mosquito net into bed and bawled for the servant to bring him smokes and drink.

The fever had left Friedlander and he was sitting up in his own tent taking some broth when Verhaeren, whose services he had refused, entered.

"*Ca va mieux?*" (How goes it?) asked Verhaeren suavely.

"No thanks to you!" snapped Friedlander, who was furious at his captivity and angry at the failure of all his menaces of what the Imperial German Government would do.

"I am as you have said not a servant as you are, *m'sieu'*," returned Verhaeren humbly, sitting down, "but could *m'sieu'*, if necessary, inoculate a man with the trypanosomiasis, yes?"

"Certainly, but why? Do you wish to murder your chief or what?"

"*Ah! Non, m'sieu'*," returned Verhaeren raising a horrified hand. "But supposing we can find this Dr. Keerkton and you will be so kind as to give him the disease he will then tell us all he can to find those invaluable notebooks or anything else to save himself. I am so sure that he does know much. Think of it, *m'sieu'*!"

Friedlander's slit eyes narrowed the more.

"Hah, but you have not got him yet, my little man!"

"Yes, yes, but if we do! What d'you think, *m'sieu'*?"

"I think," retorted Friedlander, "that you're a pretty pair of Apaches, and I don't much care what you do, for I believe I've contracted the disease myself. Still it would be some consolation if that cursed thief of an American had it. That would revenge Lörtzer too. That's true."

"But, yes, he certainly deserves it. But you, *m'sieu'*, you can not have it. Ah no!"

"What d'you think! Both of you have it or will before you get out of this — — country."

"May I assist, *m'sieu'*, for anything?" inquired Verhaeren suavely.

"Get out and leave me alone," snarled Friedlander, with a spurt of violent temper.

"*Oui, oui, m'sieu'*," returned Verhaeren.

"But I will tell the *chef* in the morning. *Bonne nuit— Nom de —
—!*" he mumbled to himself as he went to his tent. "If I should
have— *Oh!* —— *non,* not that! I can not have. Yes, it is
impossible. But that pig—"

The noises of the camp faded and the fires grew to embers
gleaming dull red on the stacked Sniders in the street of grass
huts of the askaris. From the porters' quarters came the mutter
of subdued grumbles and an occasional clink of the light chain
which bound them together.

The night grew hotter and more clammy. The mosquitoes
hovered like a cloud around the dim glow of the inverted "Vs"
of the white men's tents. Monotonously the nightjar hooted
against the throb of the distant frogs. The mountain mist blotted
the stars overhead. By the machine guns at each end of the
camp the chained crews sprawled on their bellies on their
blankets the better to protect their faces from the mosquitoes
and crawling bugs.

The four sentries gradually ceased their automatic, stiff-
kneed march up and down. First one and then another sank to
his haunches. Savages, as they called all other blacks save
askaris, never attacked at night; spirits were much better
sentries than they, so why should they bother when the night
was so hot and all human creatures were made to sleep?

The big fellow on the northern end could, from his position
almost on the ground, have seen against the farther stars the
spear points of a clump of elephant grass move ever so slightly,
although there was not a breath of breeze, and then remain
motionless for perhaps five minutes.

Half an hour afterwards across the trodden grass of that
sentry's path glided a curious green beast of no known specie of
animal. Presently between two huts in the farthest glow of the

embers of a fire some thirty feet away, was a mass of wild banana fronds like a refuse pile. Later the pile had grown—or had the firelight increased?

Nearly an hour afterwards the pile was lying half in the glow of the lantern and half in the shadow of one of the tents.

From under that tent wall at the back of Strindhorst's bed rose a tall, bearded, and naked, white man, holding in one hand a native knife.

For a moment he regarded the large recumbent form of the *chef du poste*, one hand thrown out against the net to feed a bevy of mosquitoes, and the whole of a hairy leg lying straight above. Then sticking the blade between his teeth the intruder slipped around the tent and noiselessly let fall the flap. Back he came on bare toes and from behind the head began very slowly to work out the tucked-in net and raise it. Just as he had finished, the sleeper choked in his sleep, turned over on his back and began to snore.

When that job was accomplished he bent over the chair, buckled the revolver belt around his nude waist—in case of urgent flight—and selected a sock and the scabbard cord.

Strindhorst sleepily became aware of the prick of something sharp in the side. He stirred, winced, and moved slightly. Again came the prick. The *chef du poste* awakened, and heard a voice saying in a whisper—

"*Ne bouge pas!*" (Don't move!) and then he saw the bearded face of the man whom his askaris had left for dead in the forest.

The prick increased. The combination deprived him of breath. Then a realization that the prick was a knife right over his heart persuaded him to obey.

His own sock was jammed not too lightly into Strindhorst's mouth and bound with the scabbard cord far from gently. Feet and hands were also trussed, and a low voice offered him the choice of lying motionless and silent or answering for his sins to whatever god he fancied.

Birskett's next move was to take a needed drink, then to get into the full uniform of the *chef du poste*; rather tight around the chest and short in the arms and legs, not forgetting the boots which were usable although a bit large.

The sounds of a subdued military bark reached him and the jingle of accouterments—the guard changing. The time according to the captive's watch was 4 A.M. Sitting in the chair with the revolver on the table beside a drink and many cheroots—he stuffed the box into his pocket too—he prepared to pass the hours in comfort. Several times Strindhorst, who was probably becoming more indignant and more scared, seemed about to choke, but a suggestive prick with the knife cured him rapidly.

At last when the hands of the watch pointed to five-forty Birskett rose, tightened up Strindhorst's gag and lashed him to the bed. Then with a grin he took the pillow, which he buttoned inside the tunic to make a realistic paunch and putting on the helmet well over his face, stepped outside.

He stood listening to the murmurs and after a sharp glance around the camp fixed his eyes upon the mountain tops. A bright star snuggled between two peaks began to lose its glitter. A long way off a jackal was yapping irritably. The nightjar had ceased. He heard the mumble of a sentry speaking to another, they as usual for the sake of their own hides, being most alert at the coming of dawn.

The star had dimmed, and the outline of the peaks was creamy. Loosening the revolver belt which annoyed him by being strapped continental fashion tight to the waist, he peeped inside the tent to see that the prisoner was behaving himself, and then wheeling so that his back was to the lantern and the dawn, bawled gruffly, slurring the words—

"*R-rrrrnt-m-j-orrr!*"

A slight commotion in an adjacent hut answered him. He repeated the noise angrily and elicited a gulped:

"*Bwana! Bwana!*"

The big black, jingling sidearms, stalked up through the gloom.

"Bring the gun crews here, quick! *Upesi!*" Birskett snarled gruffly.

"*Bwana!*" gasped the sergeant major. "I am to unchain them?"

"Do I speak in the wind, dog? *Upesi!*"

For a moment the man stared mystified at the blond beard beneath the helmet, puzzled by the unusual order; but as he dared not disobey the *chef du poste* he departed at a run. Birskett stood watching the adulteration of the night by the slow dawn. As soon as he heard the sergeant major releasing the second machine-gun crew he bawled at a man emerging from his hut:

"You beast! Call the men here instantly. Every man! Don't wait for your guns. *Upesi*, brute, or I'll cut your hide off!"

The black corporal was startled, but, afraid of the temper of the commandant, he rushed wildly from hut to hut ordering the askaris out and driving them towards the tents. The supposed *chef du poste* glanced again at the filtering dawn and gave vent to the prolonged howl of a hyena.

The converging parties of askaris and the gun crews involuntarily stopped at this strange demonstration superstitiously thinking that their chief had been seized by a devil. In the ensuing moment of silence came a slithering ripple like a sweeping rainstorm. A hysterical voice rang out—

"The savages come!"

The askaris stood, frightened now of they knew not what, waiting for orders. None came. The *chef du poste* backed slowly behind the tent.

The next instant a screech accompanied the thunder of feet upon earth and half a thousand spears flashed in the milky light. Most of the men paused, still automatically listening for orders; others ran helter skelter for their arms. The next instant the Tiny Children of the Mountain were upon them, howling like sirens.

Among the foremost of the warriors was one on whose wrist gleamed a broken watch. Birskett attracted his attention. As the black leaped at the uniform of the hated Bulamatadi, spear upraised, Birskett swept off his hat.

Zano recognizing him, pulled up, and was about to swing away into the general massacre. But Birskett sprang, caught him by the arm and literally dragged him into the nearest tall grass; then putting the revolver to his head he bade him march. Stupefied and scared by the revolver, the meaning of which he well knew now, Zano obeyed.

XXIII

The sun was westering deep when Birskett, with Zano in the lead, sullenly frightened, toiled through the region of the tree lobelias. The mist was that afternoon higher than when Doctor Kirkton had passed, and these two had come by a quicker and easier route known to the apostle of the Giver of Life, so that scarcely half an hour later he stopped to point upwards where Birskett saw a red glow as of a window.

"Thank God!" he murmured. "The doc's all right and with a mighty good fire going too!"

Yet as they passed over a boggy plateau, skirted with brambles in flower, the light went out.

"Funny," thought Birskett, "he must have—" Then glancing behind he perceived that the sun had set. The light had been but the reflection of the sun.

"*Mangu! Mangu, Zano!*" he urged on the man. "We shall be eaten by the night."

But Zano, trembling still at the horror of invading the sanctity of the holy ground, needed no encouragement to speed; indeed, unable to turn and bolt for the double dread of revolver and the long way that was troubled with evil spirits, he broke into such a pace that Birskett was soon forced to clutch his arm lest some crazy impulse seize the fellow, or that he might lose sight of him in the swiftly gathering darkness which rolled from the Congo hills like a fog across the Golden Gate.

But Zano, who would rather have been blown to pieces outright than have passed the night upon the mountain, and from fear of the cold, did not miss the trail. So at length they came to a dim form which sent a clutch at Birskett's heart. As

Zano was whimpering and fumbling apparently at the door the white man heard a deep bass grunt of Zapoko, the Sudanese.

With a smothered glad oath and the cry of, "Doc, old boy!" Birskett pushed past Zano and into the hut.

He could distinguish only the dull glow of a fire silhouetting a huddled, shapeless form.

"Doc, man!" he cried again.

But there was no reply from the doctor. The huddled figure by the fire stirred and a bass voice murmured again.

"Zapoko!" exclaimed Birskett sharply, angered, he hardly knew why. "*Mwami yagenda?*" (The master is away?)

"*Neda, mwami,*" drawled the deep voice languidly. "He is here."

"——, where? Why doesn't he answer? *Kufa?*" (He is dead?) Birskett added softly, fears crowding thick upon him.

"*Neda, mwami,*" returned Zapoko indifferently. "*Afude. Alwade mongota.*" (He is nearly dead. He has the sleeping sickness.)

"Oh, my God!"

Birskett stood paralyzed for the moment. Then he burst suddenly into a rage.

"Get up, you lousy brute!" he cried at the Sudanese. "Where is he? Why don't you get a light you idiot son of no parents! *Mangu,* fool!"

But the complacent figure by the fire scarcely moved.

"What is the use, *mwami?*" he muttered indolently. "I am sick, too."

"Where are Matana and Kubi?"

"I don't know. Oh, Matana is dead."

"Good God!" exclaimed Birskett, as shocked as a man emerging from the morgue and seeing a dead sparrow. "Good God!"

He had figuratively to kick himself into action, for the crash of his dearest hopes had half-stunned him. His eye caught a large bundle of faggots, branches of lobelia, in a corner. He snatched a double handful and threw them on the fire. In the blaze he saw a camp bed and on it the gleam of a pallid outline of a face beneath a stubble of fair beard.

"Doc! Doc, man!" He was bending over the still form, shaking it. "Doc, don't you know me?"

The eyes opened in their deep sockets and stared at him blankly.

"Oh my God! Too late!"

He shook Kirkton tentatively once more and then as if crushed, stood back trying to think. A movement of Zano crouching over the warm blaze brought back his sense of action. He strode over to the half-somnolent Sudanese.

"*Mpa candelli!*" (Give me some candles!) he commanded.

"*Neba.*" (There are none)

"— —!"

Birskett swore peevishly in his violent irritation. He was strung up to the point of breaking nerves. Then by an effort, comprehending things more in their proportion to reality he bade Zano make up the fire. In the glare he examined the doctor again. He turned away feeling sick at the glimpse of the sunken features and the terrible emaciation of the doctor's shoulders.

Depressed, forgetful of food, of which he had not tasted since the previous day, he crouched down over the fire.

The wind began to moan and somewhere afar off some animal was howling a deathly dirge. Every sigh in his overstrained imagination hinted at the death of his friend. Twice he got up and tried to look for medicines with a torch, but the whole place was a wild jumble of things. He came across Kubi lying wrapped in blankets in a corner seemingly as far gone as the doctor.

What his thoughts were that night he could scarcely ever recall—flashes of impotent anger at the stupidity of these superstitious savages, violent denunciations of those perfidious Belgians, furious curses at Lörtzer and all his kidney.

If he slept at all he only dozed, waking with anxious starts. But as death comes so at last came the trickle of dawn. Gradually, like a developing negative, the interior of the hut grew out of the darkness.

On the southern wall the morning crept through a talc window taken from a tent, gleaming on a microscope on a rough table littered with other instruments, glass slides and papers. Along another side were several metal uniform cases marked with the initials M.S. evidently Manfred Stoutt's. Kubi was crouched beside these.

On the other side of the hut lay Kirkton and in the cold pallid light he indeed seemed to have the ashen gray color of a corpse. But he stirred slightly when Birskett tried again to arouse him and opened his eyes. This time recognition glimmered, but apparently his mind could not react enough to be surprized.

"D'you know me, doc?" said Birskett.

"Water," whispered Kirkton.

Zano who had recovered a little of his normal state brought a cup at Birskett's command. The doctor half-raised himself, took three or four swallows, and then fell back again.

"Doc," persisted Birskett seeing that he was dropping into a coma again, "did you find anything—the cure?"

But it was too late. The sick man merely stared at him blankly and dozed. Birskett turned abruptly and searched for the hypodermic syringe and the case of ampules. Then after sterilizing the needle he gave the doctor an intravenous injection.

The powerful drug almost immediately began to have an effect. Within a few minutes the doctor was not only fairly awake, but his mind was beginning to run in spurts and starts. He stared bewilderedly at Birskett and said slowly, putting a hand to his head in a puzzled way:

"But you, Birskett? Oh, I recollect. The note. What happened?"

"Oh, never mind that for the moment, doc," said Birskett. "Too long a yarn. But tell me, have you found the cure?"

"Cure? What— Oh yes, of course."

"What! You *have* found it?"

"Yes, I found it."

"Yes. But why don't you—I mean," hastily and fearfully. "What is it?"

"Eh? Oh, I don't know. That is I—" Again he pawed at his eyes and scowled in the effort to keep his brain going. "Oh, yes. They were there—the bodies I mean. Glacier had partially slid over them—almost perfect preservation. But no trypanosomes. Perfect cure. But— How did you get here, Birskett, d'you say?"

"Never mind, doc. What did you find? The cure?"

"No. Yes." He paused and stared fretfully at Birskett as if protesting at being baited.

"Yes, what?"

"Oh, a drug—unknown. Can't possibly find any trace— Unknown I tell you, man."

"What d'you mean exactly. Unknown to the pharmacopoeia!"

"Impossible to recognize any of the properties and—oh, I don't know."

He turned his head wearily. Birskett stood staring, trying to fathom what the doctor had really meant. Zano moving recalled him. He demanded of Zapoko what he had been feeding the doctor with. The Sudanese lethargically pointed out a calabash in which Birskett found some canned meat stew. He warmed it slightly and gave some to Kirkton who was lying sidewise, watching him with a stupidly puzzled look. However he ate some, but not very much. Birskett attempted once more to gather information, but the brain was slowing down again rapidly. Presently he was semicomatose.

Birskett took some food himself, threshing his mind to decide what he should do. He realized that the doctor had found traces in Stoutt's blood of some unknown and unclassified drug. He looked despairingly at the recumbent figure on the bed.

In a frenzy of emotion he got up, went outside and fell to pacing up and down. He felt he couldn't think and he didn't know where to begin if he could. The doctor was doomed! He had to sit and watch him die.

The only thing he could do was to discover what he had done with his experimental blood tests and take them back to New York in the hope that some other scientist might solve the problem. Yet if Kirkton, who was a specialist, could not identify the drug, how should another?

It was terrible that the doctor should pass out now with the cure in his hands and be unable to aid himself. He glanced to the west at the rolling ocean of the Ituri forests and, in a passion of rage, shook his fist.

That cursed idiot of a Yarazoo *must* know the secret. Would nothing overcome his superstitions? Stoutt must have given him a supply. Lord! Why the only chance to save Kirkton was to carry him down. He'd have to frighten Yarazoo into giving him of the medicine Stoutt had given them? But that wouldn't identify the drug though!

He set Zano to work immediately to make a litter with the aid of the bamboo poles of which the hut was constructed. The doctor was still in a coma. Birskett began hunting about the worktable hoping to recognize something. There were many test tubes, ampules, and slides having some dark stains that were evidently the results of the doc's experiments. He would have to take them all.

He turned his attention to searching for a small case to pack them in and opened one of Stoutt's which was full of presses containing botanical specimens. Another, about the size required, he found, was full of the same dried purple and vermilion-streaked fungi that Yarazoo wore on his head.

Funny! What on earth did Stoutt want with such a quantity? Suddenly he shouted to Zano to make up the dying fire, grabbed an empty calabash and flung in a double handful of the herb.

"Of all the blind, mutton-brained boneheads I'm the prize specimen on earth!" he muttered to himself as if it were an incantation as he set the concoction on the fire to stew. "I'll sure have to get the doc to have me put away or find me a nurse!"

The sight of that dried fungus had linked up a sequence of isolated facts: Stoutt would not have collected such a quantity without a reason; the same fungus was the headdress of Yarazoo the witch doctor; he himself *had* been ill with all the symptoms of trypanosomiasis which he had tried strenuously to ignore, and yet had recovered while in the hands of the pigmies who habitually ate that same fungus, and who, although living amid the tsetse fly, never suffered from sleeping sickness.

The unclassified drug? Why the sum was as easy as two and two! And that damned son-of-a-gun Yarazoo had been wearing, as very naturally, a symbol of his witch-doctorship, right under their noses the whole time what all of them had been looking for!

EPILOG

Three weeks later Doctor Kirkton was seated before Stoutt's little table lighted by the talc window, at work upon a specimen of his own blood. Although his shaven face was still emaciated he no longer resembled an animated corpse. In spite of his rapid convalescence, he had, from the beginning, remained skeptical; for there might be other reasons for his recovery than the purple and scarlet fungus; as a scientist he could not accept the theory until he had proven the fact.

As Kubi squatted over the blazing fire, cooking, Zapoko entered, bearing a load of tree-lobelia trunks. Without, Birskett, shaven too, and still clad in his Belgian whites but with the gaudy trimmings torn off, paced in the bracing air and westering sun, smoking.

The doctor on arrival had found plenty of canned goods and blankets as well as a first class scientific equipment. The remains of poor Stoutt were already packed in one of his airtight, steel, uniform cases, the best they could do until Entebbe was reached.

They planned to leave on the morrow. Their safari, long since dispatched to Uganda, they hoped to encounter on the back trail, now that Friedlander's influence was stilled.

Judiciously Birskett had not inquired of the fate of the Belgians, but he could guess; and he regretted nothing save that the tribe would some time perhaps have to pay a bitter price for a just revenge, but then, the ordinary treatment by the Bulamatadi would not be much worse.

As Birskett paused to stare at the sinking sun turning the Ituri forest into a sea of blood, he grinned at the recollection of the pigmy chief, Kikkik.

"Damned if I wouldn't like to shake the little man by the hand," he mused. "By Jingo, he should have a society's gold medal or something! Maybe the doc and I'll come back and look him up one of these days. He's surely got a heap more secrets as well, but he surely hasn't the faintest notion of their effects— eats the stuff just as the gorillas and possibly buffalo and wild buck do—because it tastes good and his people always have! Old man Yarazoo reckons it was Stoutt's magic, not the herb, that cures. He'd think that if he had told us the secret the magic would be ruined and therefore the fungus would be rendered useless. Self-preservation, I guess."

"But the old wizard might have treated us both," he reflected, flinging away the stub of one of the excellent cigars Stoutt had packed, "yet as a matter of fact we never asked him and we were all pretty busy with the Belgian bunch then. Friend Zano's solicitations for our white man's food of goat and eggs probably deprived us of the fungus remedy, which they eat all the time with their banana-mess as the pigmies do. Oh, well, we've got it now I guess if—"

He wheeled eagerly and strode for the cabin in answer to a hail.

"Well?"

The doctor was sitting half-turned at his table, the sunset glow upon his face. The eyes were glistening bright and the rocklike, pale lips were parted in a half smile.

"Not a trace of a trypanosome!" he announced triumphantly. "An absolutely perfect cure!"

The Lost Cure:
The Insect and the Adventure

An Afterword by John Locke

Charles Beadle traveled widely in Africa during the first decade of the twentieth century, making it easy for him to vary the settings for his Africa stories. He employed South Africa, Rhodesia, British East Africa, German East Africa, the Belgian Congo, the French Congo, Sudan, Morocco, and other places.

His 1912 novel, *A Whiteman's Burden*, takes place in Uganda (or, in tribal language, Buganda). The approximate period of 1904-06 corresponds with his visit to the territory. It was a critical time, when a plague of African trypanosomiasis – the sleeping sickness – was at its peak, spread by the tsetse fly which populated the swamps on the periphery of Lake Victoria. Without a cure or effective treatment, the disease was decimating the native African population, and starting to afflict the British colonizers.

The combination of the time, the place, and the disease make for a narrowly tailored setting; thus, it was surprising to discover Beadle tapping into it again in *The Lost Cure*, the lead novel in the 30 January 1923 *Adventure*. From 1918 to 1923, Beadle was one of the magazine's featured writers, its Africa expert. During that span, he made 29 fiction appearances with 24 stories (two were serials). With the exception of two stragglers in late 1924 and early 1925, *The Lost Cure* ended his regular run with *Adventure*, suggesting that he'd perhaps revisited Uganda as a last resort.

The Lost Cure is certainly not a retread, though. While it draws upon some of the same themes of *A Whiteman's Burden*, the stories differ significantly. In fact, with both novels now available from Dominantstar, we have the rare opportunity of seeing how an author utilized a rather specialized setting in two distinct arenas: the literary novel and the adventure story. Note that prior to these two reprints, this comparison would have been challenging. First, the commonality of setting was a revelation to us. Second, *A Whiteman's Burden*, a scarce British hardback, sparsely reviewed in its day, was never previously reprinted; while *The Lost Cure* has only been available in the original *Adventure* issue, making this its first book appearance.

A Whiteman's Burden concerns the strained and complicated relationships among the disparate groups that live in the vicinity of the British administrative capital at Entebbe – an outpost of European civilization within the vastness of Africa. A contained locale, the narrative could be reworked as a stage play.

Primarily a social drama, Beadle uses a handful of characters to illustrate the misunderstandings between disparate groups. The divisions cut across numerous lines. The widest gulf is between Europeans and native Africans. Their respective interpretations of reality are often contradictory and not often subject to reconciliation. Further, Africans argue among themselves and, within the European population, institutionalists, the agents of the empire, contrast with freelancers who pursue private opportunities. Another friction line lies between men and women, regardless of caste or color. With the mingling of disparate groups, relationships across racial boundaries enter ambiguous territory.

The dominating conflict, which none can evade, is between Man and Nature. Entebbe, on the ragged northern shore of Lake Victoria, is only a few miles north of the equator. It's often oppressively hot and humid. During the rainy season, when most of the tale takes place, the omnipresent downpour traps the characters within their habitats, pushing conflicts toward their breaking points. Hovering over events is the sleeping sickness crisis, which slowly depopulates societies. Once vibrant villages become ghost towns. When the deadly plague strikes within the circle of Beadle's characters, relationships are irrevocably altered. Within this hothouse of drama, attitudes and decisions are magnified; time is on nobody's side; and the characters are forced to understand each other better.

A Whiteman's Burden is decidedly not an adventure story. The emphasis is on character and relations; there's little physical action. There is a murder, but we only hear about it secondhand. The process of an investigation ensures that the culprit – and motive – go unsolved for some time. Indeed, when Beadle sets up opportunities to escalate into action, invariably he pulls back. When one character discovers that his wife has rekindled affections for an old suitor, the archetypal British reaction is dignified and restrained. When the old suitor's current paramour detects the new relationship, she is dismayed, but only *attempts* suicide. When she sets her pet leopard loose into her rival's tent, two terriers ward off the danger. Finally, when the lone murder ignites a native uprising (in the background), the authorities quickly round up the rebels.

Ultimately, the novel is less about events and more about relationships. It focuses on the universal quest for private peace.

In *The Lost Cure*, the adventure version, the lines of conflict return, especially Man versus Nature and Europeans versus

Africans. Since the high-adventure motif tends to be a male domain, and because *Adventure* appealed predominantly to male readers, female characters don't play a role. Men and women will not work out their differences here. (Other magazines of the era welcomed female characters in adventure stories, "romances" in the term of the day, e.g., Tarzan and Jane. *Adventure* specialized in the undiluted product.)

The protagonists in Beadle's adventure tales tend to be explorers of different stripes. A special breed, they're not drawn from conventional society. A pair of them carry the action in *The Lost Cure*. The American, Dr. Fraser Kirkton, is determined to travel to the heart of the crisis in search of a sleeping sickness cure. Like other medical researchers in the story, he's a brave man, but not two-fisted, willing to put the mission above his personal safety. Kirkton's guide, hired in New York but knowledgeable about Uganda, is Birskett. The last name alone is apparently good enough for the self-proclaimed "professional adventurer"; his first is never given.

Their journey offers what *Adventure* readers wanted, a trek into the perilous wild. The story must take place well outside the civilized existence found in the homes of most readers, i.e., American towns and cities. The environment must be maximally challenging, from geography to weather. In the Ugandan outback, Kirkton, Birskett, and their porters confront everything from a treacherous river to hostile wildlife.

An important environmental element in much of Beadle's Africa fiction, which made a deep impression on him while he was there, is the "kingdom of bugs." Indeed, the impact of insects is critical to understanding human life in Africa. Insects account for countless debilitating afflictions and diseases. In that time and place, sleeping sickness was the tip of nature's spear, not as immediately fatal as a crocodile bite, but just as deadly in the end. For Beadle, insects were as great a threat as other more action-oriented dangers and, thus, a suitable theme for an African adventure story. In *The Lost Cure*, the tsetse is a near-invisible force of doom.

Another Beadle theme, common to his Africa adventures, are the ambiguous beliefs and intentions of native tribes. In less authentic adventure fiction, the natives of foreign lands are inherently hostile, as "otherly" as they can be. See stranger, kill stranger. The tribes in Beadle's stories often occupy a middle ground. They may be friendly, or understandably guarded. But they're hard to understand. What does their personal ornamentation mean? What do their unfathomable rituals portend? Are they secretly hostile? Are they preparing for attack? What does it mean for one party to have white skin and the other black? Is there common humanity which bridges the divide? Or will superstition and prejudice maintain the gulf? Will fear push one side to genocide or the other to cannibalism? In the adventure story, the ambiguity creates suspense, followed by fighting, escape, or other resolutions.

In *The Lost Cure*, Europeans contribute to the suspense, as well. Their motives may be mysterious, lurking behind deceitful words. One may fear murderous intent behind a friendly face, though cannibalism isn't in the cards. It comes down to a single question: what does everyone want?

Thus, the novel is structured as a quest, a treasure hunt. The prize is the notebook of the deceased Dr. Stoutt. It contains his findings on trypanosomiasis and, as commonly assumed, his discovery of the desperately needed remedy, the "lost cure" of the title. His notebook is more than a MacGuffin, though; the multiplicity of motives among the treasure hunters contributes to Beadle's presentation of the complexity of the situation.

Dr. Kirkton, an American hero for American readers, pursues the treasure for the noblest motive: the inherent benefit to humanity of curing the disease and saving lives. Dr. Adolph Lörtzer, the trypanosomiasis-inflicted explorer who sets the story in motion, had another reason to risk his life: the monetary rewards for a cure, offered separately by England, Germany, and Belgium. Lörtzer also wanted what others sought: prestige for the individual credited with the discovery, and, certainly not least, the glory reflected on the nation whose researcher claims the cure.

Beadle was canny in populating the story with British, German, and Belgian treasure hunters, whose respective territories converged at a point due west of Lake Victoria, roughly the area where the story takes place. The stakes among the competing hunters are so high that deceit and murder complicate the quest, casting direct light on the often-ruthless European impulse to exploit Africa, and, in the logic of Kipling's "white man's burden," the cost of doing so.

There's a circumstance we shouldn't forget, that Beadle wouldn't have overlooked. Though he set the novel a decade before the First World War, he wrote it several years after, when the events were all too fresh in memory. Thus, the novel's future was the author's recent past. The same nations that raced for the cure would soon contribute their prestige to a horrendous conflict fueled by national pride and unrestrained ambition. *The Lost Cure*, then, was not only Beadle's great Man versus Insect adventure epic, but an eerie foreshadowing of the disease to come.

Illustrations

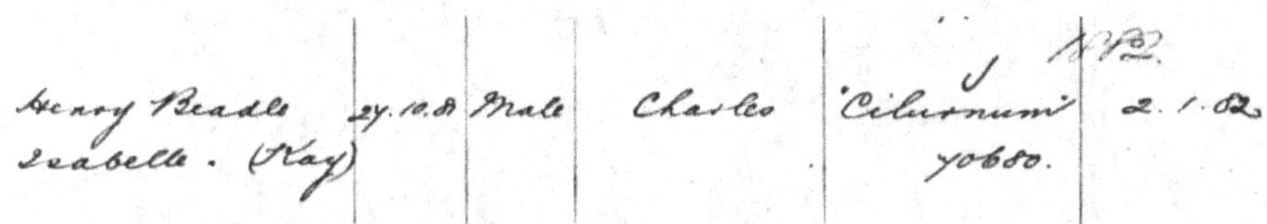

12 July 1873: Marriage of Henry Beadle and Isabella Kay at St. John's, Hackney, London. Both Henry and Isabella's father, Peter Kay, were master mariners. Henry's father, William, is listed as a "gentleman."

27 October 1881: Record of Beadle's birth aboard the SS *Cilurnum*, from "UK Registers of Births, Marriages and Deaths at Sea, 1844-1890." Other documents, such as his draft registration card, indicate he was born the day before, on 26 October 1881.

(Above:) The brothers Henry, Charles, and William Beadle. (Below:) Various portraits of Beadle from a family album. Courtesy of Beadle's great-niece Patricia and her daughter Liz.

Circa fall 1900 or 1901: Beadle in Mashonaland, South Africa. Courtesy archive of Patricia and Liz.

During this period Beadle received various decorations and service awards. The "Roll of individuals entitled to the South Africa Medal and Clasps, April 1901" includes trooper Charles "Marmaduke" Beadle, who served in the National (Waldon's) Scouts and Orange River Colony Volunteers, Nesbitt's Horse, Regiment Number 1014. Beadle may have fictionalized his middle name in order to enlist a second time.

Undated photo of Henry Beadle (1844 – 1906), father of Charles. Courtesy of Patricia and Liz.

Another photo of Henry Beadle, courtesy of Patricia and Liz.

Photo of Charles Beadle featured in *The Wide World Magazine*, May 1907.

Passenger list of the SS *Agadir*, 23 April 1908, with Beadle on his way to Morocco, where he would interview Sultan Mulai-El-Hafid.

Beadle disguised as a dancing girl or, alternately, a holy man, during his June 1908 expedition to Fez, published in the photo essay "A Talk with the New Sultan of Morocco," *The Pall Mall Magazine*, October 1908.

"Your [affectionate] nephew Charlie." Courtesy of Patricia and Liz. "I might have had reason to view some of these encounters with even more miscellaneous feelings, had I known that my guide accounted for my complete disguise by confiding to our assistants that I was a dancing girl bound for the household of a distinguished native official. At other times I was, it seemed, a holy man." ("A Talk with the New Sultan of Morocco.")

(Sideways view:) Rare dust jacket of Beadle's first novel, *The City of Shadows: A Romance of Morocco*, published in the spring of 1911.

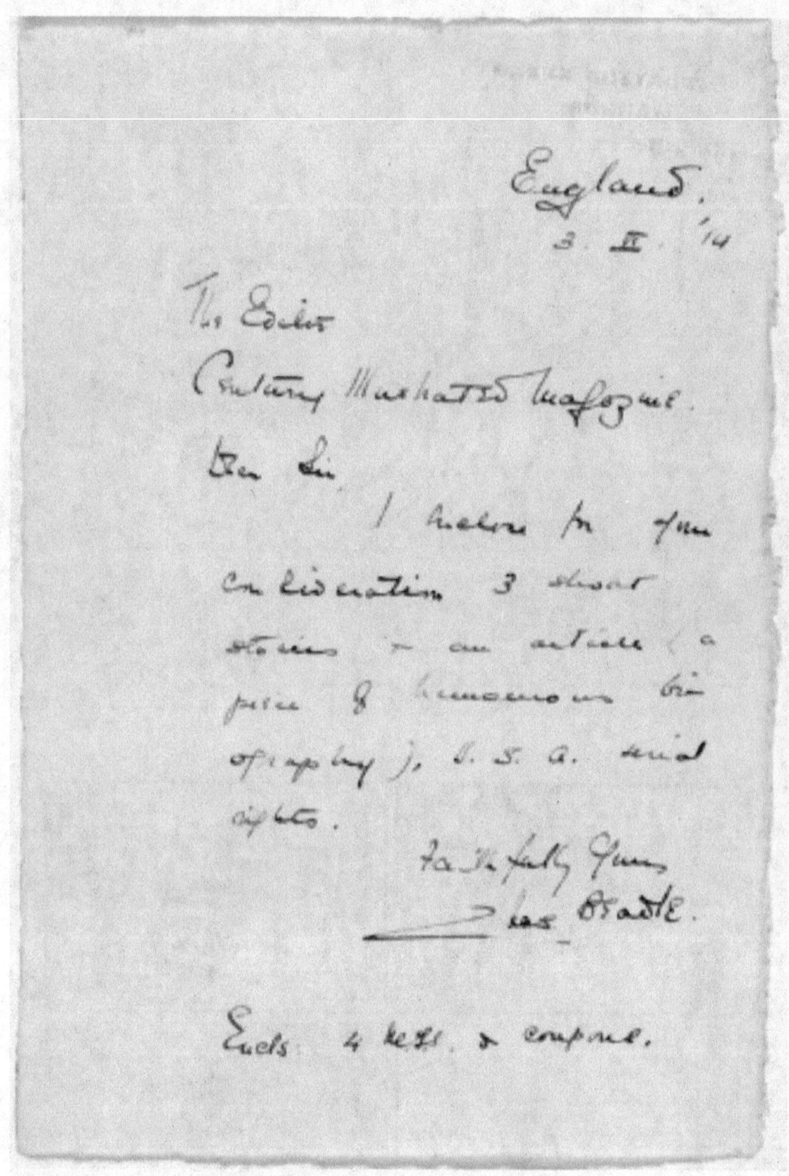

3 June 1914: A letter to the editor of *Century Illustrated*: "England. / 3 VI 1914 / The Editor / Century Magazine / Dear Sir, I enclose for your consideration 3 short stories & an article (a piece of humorous biography) for USA serial rights. Faithfully Yours Charles Beadle Encl. 4 Ms. & coupons." A watermark on top reads: "Creek Cottage, Bosham, Sussex." Courtesy of New York Public Library, Century Company records, Series I.

A PASSIONATE PILGRIMAGE

By CHARLES BEADLE

September 1915: Publication of *A Passionate Pilgrimage*. Hardcover edition, embossed with an image of Beadle's handwriting in red ink.

Early twentieth-century train compartment, South African railway: the setting of Jim's first steamy encounter with Joan in *A Passionate Pilgrimage*. Photo courtesy C. Carlyle-Gall, ed., *Six Thousand Miles Of Sunshine Travel Over The South African Railways* (Johannesburg: South African Railways & Harbours, 1937), p. 13.

Rickshaw driver, Durban, South Africa. Photo courtesy *Six Thousand Miles Of Sunshine Travel Over The South African Railways*, p. 68.

REGISTRATION CARD

SERIAL NUMBER 4661

ORDER NUMBER 13379

Charles Beadle

(First name) (Middle name) (Last name)

2 PERMANENT HOME ADDRESS: 334
King George Hotel Mason St. SAN FRANCISCO CAL
will be 119 Central Av. Sausalito Cal

Age in Years 3 36
Date of Birth 4 Oct 26 1881
(Month) (Day) (Year)

RACE

White	Negro	Oriental	Indian	
			Citizen	Noncitizen
5 ✓	6	7	8	9

U. S. CITIZEN			ALIEN	
Native Born	Naturalized	Citizen by Father's Naturalization Before Registrant's Majority	Declarant	Non-declarant
10	11	12	13	14 ✓

15 If not a citizen of the U. S., of what nation are you a citizen or subject? England

PRESENT OCCUPATION 16 Novelist
EMPLOYER'S NAME 17

18 PLACE OF EMPLOYMENT OR BUSINESS:

(No.) (Street or R. F. D No.) (City or town) (County) (State)

NEAREST RELATIVE 19 (Miss) Jane Beadle
Address 20 22 Gordon Road - Boscomb. England
(No.) (Street or R. F. D. No.) (City or town)

I AFFIRM THAT I HAVE VERIFIED ABOVE ANSWERS AND THAT THEY ARE TRUE

P. M. G. O.
Form No. 1 (ited) (Registrant's signature or mark) (OVER)

ORIGINAL

REGISTRAR'S REPORT 4-1-24. C

DESCRIPTION OF REGISTRANT

HEIGHT			BUILD			COLOR OF EYES	COLOR OF HAIR
Tall	Medium	Short	Slender	Medium	Stout		
21	22 ✓	23	24 ✓	25	26	27 Blue	28 Grey

29 Has person lost arm, leg, hand, eye, or is he obviously physically disqualified? (Specify.)

12 September 1918: A month short of his thirty-eighth birthday, Beadle registers for the military draft in San Francisco, just before relocating to Sausalito. Under the heading "Description of Registrant" it notes that he's of medium height, with a slender build, blue eyes, and gray hair. His occupation is "Novelist." Under "nearest relative" he lists his daughter (then living in Boscombe, Bournemouth, England).

Copie délivrée selon procédé informatisé.
A Cannes, le 28 juin 2022

Pour le Maire,
L'officier de l'état civil par délégation

Copy of Sylvia Hornsby's death certificate, retrieved by Céline Cardon on 30 June 2022. The French vital statistics bureau had misspelled her surname (it appears in their index as "Homsby"), making its retrieval a particularly tricky task. From this document we learn that Sylvia died at the Hotel Beau Rivage (now known as the Hotel Majestic). This was during a period in which the villas and hotels of Cannes were used as hospitals, especially for the soldiers of WWI. So she essentially died "in hospital" on 13 September 1915.

FACING PAGE:

Circa 1915: A Modigliani portrait of Charles Beadle, titled *Le Pèlerin* ("The Pilgrim"), pencil on paper, 42.5 x 24.5 cm., featured in a Sotheby's catalog for Sale 6019, held in New York on 17 May 1990. The estimated value was set at $40,000 – $50,000.

The catalog caption quotes a passage from *Artist Quarter* in which the narrator says that Modi represented him with "the head of a hunting dog protruding between my thighs." The catalog adds: "There are three similar drawings of young pilgrims in private collections, but none include the dog.... [Modigliani biographer Pierre Sichel] "ascribes much of the [*Artist Quarter*] biography ... to Charles Beadle ... He attributes the anecdote concerning *Le Pèlerin* to Beadle rather than Douglas."

The anecdote in *Artist Quarter* includes Beadle's statement that the drawing was stolen: "Some years after Modi's death the drawing was on show at Zborowski's gallery – just before the latter's death – and was stolen." (*Artist Quarter*, page 227.) Léopold Zborowski died in Paris on 24 March 1932. Therefore, the portrait was still in circulation in 1930, the year that *Expatriates at Large* was released.

Sotheby's dates it from 1916 to 1917, but by November 1916 Beadle was in New York. A more likely time frame is 1914 to 1916, when Beadle's friend and neighbor Beatrice Hastings was involved with Modigliani. (Note how the date corresponds to the 1915 publication of *A Passionate Pilgrimage*.) Regarding the related "Pilgrim" drawings mentioned above, the Sotheby's catalog cites the authoritative J. Lanthemann, *Modigliani, Catalogue Raisonné*, Barcelona, 1970, pp. 345-346, illustration nos. 774, 778, 779. One of these drawings, titled *Le jeune Pèlerin* ("The Young Pilgrim"), was sold at a Christie's auction on 18 June 2007 for $55,636.20. On page 209 of Beadle's novel *The Esquimau of Montparnasse* (1928), the Esquimau protagonist remarks: "I'm merely a pilgrim, I seek and never find."

Collectors are searching all over the world for pictures by Modigliani, the artist who died in obscurity, who has now become a sensation in the world of art. A new Modigliani has just come to light, a portrait of the novelist, Charles Beadle (above), whose new book, "Expatriates at Large," is soon to be published by Macaulay.

From the *Omaha World-Herald*, 23 February 1930, p. 57. On 9 November 2024, John Locke discovered a fifth Modigliani "Pilgrim," and one that includes a hunting dog. Note Modigliani's signature at the top left and the words "Le Pèlerin" at bottom left. If this was the portrait that was stolen and never recovered, its disappearance could explain why it doesn't appear in any catalogs and has, until now, been lost to history. As noted above, Lanthemann's *Catalogue Raisonné* includes three other "Pilgrim" portraits "but none include the dog." The newspaper caption unequivocally identifies it as Modigliani's "portrait of the artist Charles Beadle," which we know was still in circulation in 1930, when *Expatriates at Large* was first published. So, it appears that Modigliani made at least *two* portraits of Beadle as the "Pilgrim."

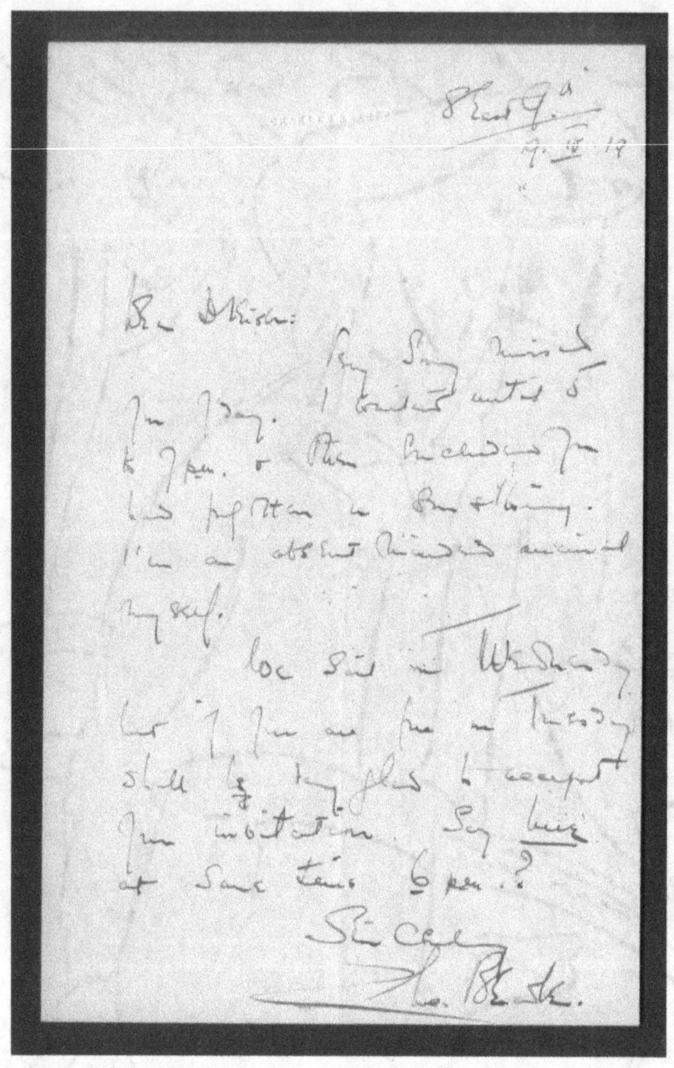

19 October 1919: Letter to author Theodore Dreiser: "8 East 9th / 19.10.19 / Dear Dreiser: Very sorry missed you y'day. I waited until 5 to 7 p.m. and then concluded you had forgotten or something. I'm an absent minded animal myself. We said on Wednesday but if you are free on Tuesday shall be very glad to accept your invitation. Say here at same time 6 p.m.? Sincerely Chas. Beadle." Beadle's flat was located between University Place and Broadway, three blocks north of Washington Square Park. Dreiser lived at 165 West 10th, a half mile west of Beadle. (Courtesy of the University of Pennsylvania, Kislak Center for Special Collections.)

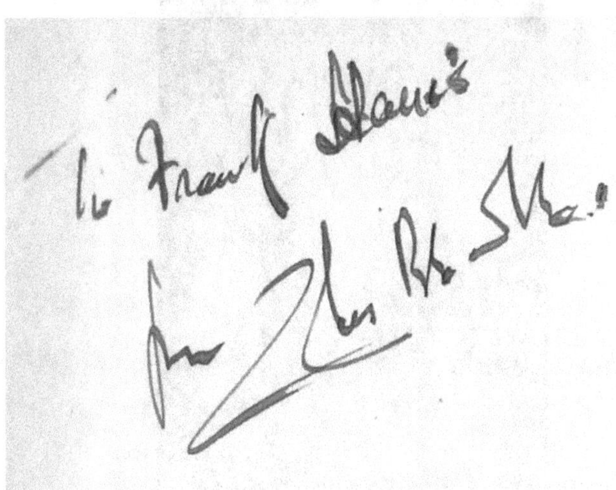

Autographed copy of *Witch-Doctors*, inscribed "To Frank Harris from Charles Beadle." (Obtained in February 2025.) After Harris self-published his banned multivolume memoir (*My Life and Loves*; 1922 – 1927) it was republished by Jack Kahane's Obelisk Press in 1931: the same publisher who later issued Beadle's *Dark Refuge* (1938). Following the outbreak of WWI, both Harris and Beadle expatriated to New York. Harris became editor of the American edition of *Pearson's*, while Beadle published his stories in *Adventure* and occasionally served in an editorial role. They also traveled to London, Paris, and the South of France at roughly the same time and moved in many of the same circles. Harris settled in Nice in 1922, the same year that *Witch-Doctors* and *My Life and Loves* were published; and he died there in 1931, while Beadle was also residing in the Côte d'Azur. It's possible that Harris introduced Beadle to Kahane or suggested that he approach the innovative publisher with his *Dark Refuge* manuscript. *My Life and Loves* was banned in the United States until 1963, when it was republished by Grove Press.

An artistically enhanced photo of Beadle from the 6 April 1930 edition of the *Buffalo Times*, featured in their "Important Books of the Week in Review" column. Reviewer Kate Burr writes: "'Expatriates at Large' is a novel of genuine power. But the power is impaired by a splurge at brilliancy. Too often the cynicism is forced. The dialogue oscillates too sharply between wit and vapidity. Why ignore the intervening gamut?" Thanks to John Locke for uncovering this rare image.

On 18 May 1930 the *Sioux City Journal* published a copy of the same publicity photo but without any enhancement. Writing about *Expatriates at Large*, reviewer Vera Edwards opens her piece ("Paris Quartier Latin Sans Romantic Gloss") with the sentence: "A portrait of Charles Beadle has just come to light, by Modigliani, the artist who died practically unknown and has now become a sensation in the world of art."

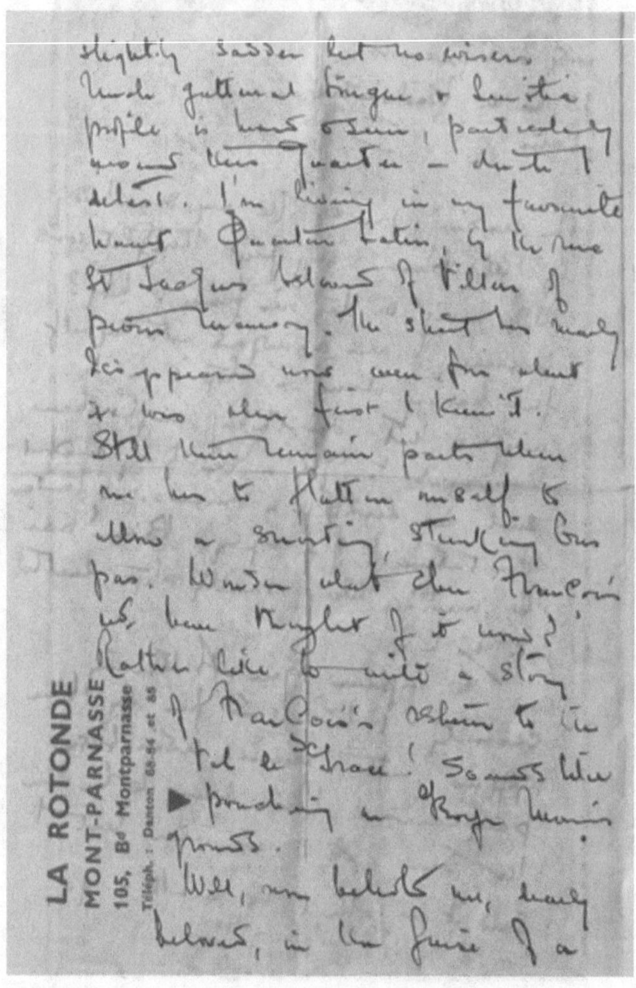

Circa spring 1933: Second page of a letter composed by Beadle and sent to his niece Isabel, with the return address of "Hôtel des Capucines, 13, rue des Feuillantines, Paris." The letter is written on stationery from the Café de la Rotonde, which was located just a few blocks from the Hôtel des Capucines. Courtesy of Patricia and Liz.

Passport-sized snapshot of Isabel Hettie Beadle (1904 – 1999), daughter of Charles' older brother William. If Isabel is thirty years old here, the photo would date from 1934, when she was corresponding with her uncle. Charles severed contact with the rest of his family, but he conducted a lengthy correspondence with his niece, writing from various locations in France. Courtesy of Patricia and Liz.

When and where born	Name, if any	Sex	Name and surname of father	Name, surname and maiden surname of mother	Occupation of father	Signature, description and residence of informant
Seventh August 1946. 9 Saxonbury Road. U.D.	Elizabeth Owen	Girl	Igor Bely	Jane Owen Bely formerly Beadle at 14 Dean Park Road. Bournemouth. U.D.	Chemical Engineer of 29 Rue Assalit. Nice France.	Jane Owen Bely mother 14 Dean Park Road. Bournemouth.

7 August 1946: Birth of Elizabeth Owen Bely, daughter of Jane Beadle and Igor Bely, at 9 Saxonbury Road (about four miles east of Jane's residence at 14 Dean Park Road, Bournemouth, England). Igor is identified as a "Chemical engineer of 29, rue Assalit, Nice, France."

Le *vingt trois août* mil neuf cent soixante deux, *trois* heures *trente minutes* est décédé en son domicile 9 9 avenue *Cyrille Besset* Elisabeth Owen BELY Née à Bournemouth (Grande Bretagne) le sept août mil neuf cent quarante six, sans profession, fille de Igor Bely quarante six ans traducteur et de Jane BEADLE son épouse interprète domiciliée à Nice 20 rue Parmentier. Célibataire Dressé le *vingt cinq août* mil neuf cent soixante deux, *six* heures, sur la déclaration d'el père de la défunte

qui, lecture faite a été invité à prendre directement connaissance de l'acte et à le signer avec Nous
Auguste VEROLA, Chevalier de la Légion d'Honneur
Adjoint au Maire de Nice, Officier de l'État Civil par délégation

Elizabeth Bely died at the age of sixteen on 23 August 1962 at her home at 99, Avenue Cyrille Besset, Nice. Her death certificate identifies her as the daughter of Igor Bely, "translator," and his wife Jane Beadle, "interpreter." Jane's address is listed as 20, rue Parmentier, Nice.

VILLE DE NICE

ACTE DE DECES
COPIE INTEGRALE

N° 005012 / 2002 Jane BEADLE

Le vingt six novembre deux mil deux à une heure treize minutes, est*****
décédée avenue des Roses "Rimiez", Jane BEADLE, née à Saint-Tropez (Var)
le 8 juillet 1915, en retraite, domiciliée à Nice (Alpes-Maritimes) 8,**
avenue Georges Clémenceau; fille de Charles BEADLE, et de Sylvia Grace**
Ellen HOMSBY, décédés ; veuve de Igor BELY.****************************
Dressé le 28 novembre 2002 à 9 heures 28 minutes sur la déclaration de**
COPPOLANI Tony, 39 ans, Chef de Bureau à Nice (06), 3 rue Alexandre*****
Mari, qui, lecture faite et invité à lire l'acte, a signé avec Nous,****
Andrée GUILLAUMIN, fonctionnaire de la Mairie de Nice, Officier de******
l'Etat-Civil par délégation du Maire.*********************************

Nice,
le 7 juin 2022,
Pour copie conforme,
L'Officier de l'Etat Civil délégué,

Aurélie FAREY

Jane Beadle's death record, retrieved by Céline Cardon on 13 June 2022.
(The surname of Jane's mother is misspelled, and it appears as "Homsby"
instead of Hornsby.) Jane lived at 8, Avenue George Clémenceau, but at
the time of her death on 26 November 2002 she was at the Avenue des
Roses, in the Rimiez quarter of Nice. This quarter also hosts the Hôpital
Les Sources, a geriatric institution. The record also includes the name of
Jane's husband, Igor Bely (1916 – 1978).

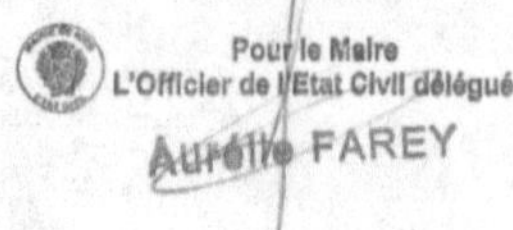

Thanks to her dogged determination while navigating labyrinthian French bureaucracy, my research assistant Céline Cardon finally unearthed the elusive death certificate of Charles Beadle. Though it doesn't reveal where he's buried, it says that he lived at 4, avenue Victoria, in Nice; and that he died on 27 January 1957, at 20, avenue de la voie Romaine, Nice. It also includes the names of his parents and of his wife Sylvia. The Pasteur Hospital is located at 2, avenue de la voie Romaine; so perhaps #20 was part of the Hopital Pasteur Urgences complex. The cert states: "Born London 26 October 1886. Without profession. Son of Henri Beadle and Isabel Kay. Only spouse deceased, widower of Sylvia Honsby." (Note the misspelling of *Hornsby*.)

Timeline

2 January 1844. Birth of Charles' father, Henry Beadle, in Barking, Essex, England.

23 May 1849. Birth of Charles' mother, Isabella Kay, in Liverpool.

12 July 1873. Marriage of Henry Beadle to Isabella Kay at St. John's, the parish church in West Hackney, London. According to the marriage certificate, Henry Beadle and Isabella's father, Peter Kay, were both master mariners. Henry's father, William, was a "gentleman." The newlyweds live on Dunlace Road.

12 July 1876. Birth of poet Max Jacob in Quimper, France. Max will later play a major role in Beadle's novel, *Dark Refuge* (1938), portrayed as the character "Isidore 'Izzy' Ginsberg."

27 January 1879. Birth of Beatrice Hastings (née Emily Haigh) in Hackney. Hastings was romantically involved with Amedeo Modigliani while she was Beadle's neighbor in Montmartre and is portrayed in both Beadle's fiction and nonfiction. She also produced the first English translations of Max Jacob's poetry.

25 October 1881. Birth of Pablo Picasso in Malaga, Spain. Born just days apart, Beadle and Picasso will move in similar circles in both Montmartre and Montparnasse.

26 or 27 October 1881. Birth of Charles Beadle at sea, aboard a Merchant Marine vessel, the SS *Cilurnum*, to Isabella and Henry, the ship's captain. Charles is the youngest of four children. (Henry junior, born in 1874, is the oldest, followed by William, and then Catherine, who died after less than nine months.) The family resides in West Hackney, where Charles is raised.

[Age 2] 2 July 1884. Death of mother from "consumption" (i.e., tuberculosis) at sea, while aboard the SS *Cilurnum*.

[Age 2] 12 July 1884. Birth of Modigliani in Livorno, Italy. In *Dark Refuge*, Modi is portrayed as "Ceccilini" (or "Cecci"), and his biography forms a major part of Beadle's *Artist Quarter* (1941). Modigliani composed a pencil sketch of Beadle circa 1915, a reproduction of which was recently rediscovered by John Locke and included in our new edition of *A Passionate Pilgrimage* (Dominantstar, 2025).

[Age 3] 22 October 1885. Sixteen months after the death of Beadle's mother on the SS *Cilurnum*, the ship is destroyed by fire. A court rules "the explosion and the subsequent loss of the said ship was due to the fire generated by spontaneous combustion in the coal which she had on board, and that the master, officers, and crew used all proper measures ... to save the vessel." Source: Merchant Shipping Acts, 1854 to 1876.

[Age 9] 5 April 1891. English census records that the Beadle family is still residing at 80 Benthal Road, West Hackney.

[Age 9] July 1890. Death of maternal grandmother Catherine Owens, who raised Charles while his father was at sea. Perhaps as a tribute of his enduring affection for her, he will later give his daughter, Jane, the middle name of "Owen." (And Jane will give her daughter, Elizabeth, the same middle name.) On 8 March 2009, Beadle's great-niece Patricia wrote to biographer Neil Pearson and said that Charles "had an odd upbringing." When I spoke with Patricia on 6 October 2022 and asked what she meant by this, she said Beadle's father Henry and his second wife, Sarah Killick, "were frequently away at sea on long voyages, so we think the children were cared for by Henry's sister Sarah Beadle, and by Catherine Owens, Charles' grandmother, who lived with them. Catherine was wealthy and blind."

[Age 17] 6 November 1898. Enlists in the British South African Police (BSAP) as Charles "Marmaduke" Beadle, Regimental No. 1019, Matabeleland Division. (Stationed in southwestern Zimbabwe.) According to Beadle's great-niece Patricia, "Charles and his brother joined the South African Police to fight in the Boer War. London was rife with recruiting posters back then. Henry later went missing. He was possibly killed in the war, although there's no military record of his death. I also heard that Henry may have died in a bicycle accident." Source: Conversation with Beadle's great-niece Patricia on 6 October 2022.

[Age 18-21] Abt. 1899 – 1901. Transvaal, South Africa. Serves in the Second Boer War (BSAP), in Morley's Scouts, Stock and Recovery Department. (Source: autobiographical sketch in "The Camp-Fire" column, *Adventure* magazine, 3 July 1918.) During this period Beadle receives various service awards.

[Age 18] September 1900. At age sixteen, Modigliani contracts pleurisy, which develops into tuberculosis.

[Age 18] Fall 1900. Mashonaland, South Africa. Guest of an Englishman named Mason, who owns a large farm. Beadle is nearly killed by a lioness during a hunt organized there on his behalf. (Source: "My Narrow Escape From a Lioness." *The Brooklyn Daily Eagle*, 7 August 1910.) Historian Geoffrey Pocock informed me that "the only Mason who is listed as a Founder-member of the Legion of Frontiersmen in London is Charles "Chinese" Mason, whom Beadle would have known and have met at early meetings." Source: email from Geoffrey, 18 August 2022.

[Age 19] 18 July 1901. Discharged from British South African Police.

[Age 21] Abt. 1902. Transvaal, South Africa. Employed by Transvaal Customs as Assistant Compound Manager, Witwatersrand Native Labor Association. Source: *Adventure*, 3 July 1918.

[Age 22] August 1904. Travels along the Zambezi River, Chikoti, Zambia. The expedition is chronicled in Beadle's essay, "Our Trip Down the Zambezi," published in the *Wide World Magazine* in 1907.

[Age 23] 1905. Henry Roger Pocock forms the Legion of Frontiersmen; Beadle is a founding member.

[Age 23] December 1905. Government House, Fort Portal, Uganda. "Engaged in recruiting and registering fresh porters" for an expedition into the Congo. (Fort Portal: aka Kabarole, formerly of the Toro Kingdom.) Source: Beadle's essay "Two Close Calls" in *The Captain: A Magazine for Boys and "old Boys,"* June 1910.

[Age 23] 5 January 1906. Beadle's expedition embarks from Fort Portal and enters the Congo, where he's attacked by a buffalo and almost killed by stampeding elephants.

[Age 24] Abt. January 1906. Modigliani expatriates from Italy to Paris.

[Age 24] 19 March 1906. Death of father in Buenos Aires. Charles receives a substantial inheritance, including assets that would normally have gone to his brother Henry, who disappeared in South Africa. This allows Charles to finance future expeditions. Source: conversation with Patricia, 6 November 2022.

[Age 24] Abt. 1906. London. Elected as a Fellow of the Royal Geographical Society (FRGS).

[Age 25] January 1907. Residing at 98 Cazenove Road, Stoke Newington, near the street where he grew up. Source: Masonic registry, listed below.

[Age 25] 11 January 1907. London. Initiated into the Masonic Commemoration Lodge No. 2663. Source: United Grand Lodge of England Freemason Membership Registers, 1751-1921; Folio Number 153.

[Age 25] February 1907. Northumberland Avenue, London. Elected to the Royal Colonial Institute. Source: *Journal of the Royal Colonial Institute*, February 1907, p. 138.

[Age 25] May 1907. Publishes photo-essay, "Our Trip Down the Zambezi," in *The Wide World Magazine*. One photo portrays Beadle with his back to the camera, sporting a pith helmet.

[Age 26] June – July 1907. Picasso paints *Les Demoiselles d'Avignon*. Modigliani visits his studio and sees the painting. In the first volume of *A Life of Picasso* (1991), John Richardson calls it a work that "established a new pictorial syntax" and "the first unequivocally twentieth-century masterpiece, a principal detonator of the modern movement, the cornerstone of twentieth-century art."

[Age 26] September 1907. Resigns from the Masonic Commemoration Lodge.

[Age 26] Abt. February 1908. Travels to Borneo. (Source: diary of Roger Pocock, housed at the Bruce Peel Collection, University of Alberta.) In his autobiographical "Camp-Fire" sketch from 3 July 1918, Beadle notes: "Went to Dutch Borneo, rubber planting. Afterward returned to go to Morocco."

[Age 26] 23 April 1908. Embarks from the Port of London aboard the SS *Agadir*, heading for Morocco.

[Age 26] 4 May 1908. Arrives in El Jadida (originally known as Mazagan), a port city on the Atlantic coast. There he secures the services of William Redman, a British merchant and mercenary versed in the local language and customs. Together they travel seventeen km (about ten miles) north along the coast, to the nearby town of Azemmour.

[Age 26] 19 May 1908. Beadle and Redman embark on a steamer, the *Gibel Kebir*, heading further north to Tangier, where they will join Andrew Belton.

[Age 26] June 1908. A confidential memo penned at the British Foreign Office notes that, after departing from Tangier for a fortnight, Beadle will return around 17 June, to reside at the Hotel Cavilla. Source: letter from Lord Mountmorres to Hubert White, Chargé d'Affaires, Tangier, archived at the British Foreign Office. (Appended to 21 June 1908 memo, as noted in Timeline below.)

[Age 26] 8 June 1908. Prevented from traveling from Tangier to Fes due to civil war. Beadle then boards the *Quetzil*, a steamer headed south, to the coastal city of Larache.

[Age 26] 9 June 1908. Arrives in Larache, where he's joined by Redman and Bolton, who had arrived earlier on another vessel.

[Age 26] 10 June 1908. Redman, Bolton, and Beadle travel inland to Ksar el-Kebir, about thirty km southeast of Larache.

[Age 26] 14 June 1908. After a "wretched journey" during which Beadle is disguised as a dancing girl, the expedition arrives in Fes. Source: Beadle's interview with Moulay Hafid, published in *Pall Mall Magazine*.

[Age 26] 21 June 1908. Following Beadle's successful interview with the Pretender Sultan, Hafid, a memo from the British Foreign Office expresses concern that Beadle, Redman, and a third man (presumably Andrew Belton) "are being treated as if on [a] mission from His Majesty's Government. Steps taken to counteract this impression." The memo adds that Beadle and Redman "arrived from Gibraltar via Larache."

[Age 26] 19 August 1908. According to a contemporaneous newspaper report, Beadle and Redman remain in Fes during the Battle of Marrakech: a decisive encounter between opposing sultans that results in the forces of Moulay Hafid defeating the army of Sultan Aziz. (Source: "Swindon Doctor in Fez," *Swindon Advertiser and North Wilts Chronicle*, 5 May 1911.) Beadle later portrays this conflict in his novel, *The City of Shadows*.

[Age 26] Early October 1908. Publishes photo-essay, "A Talk with the New Sultan of Morocco," in *Pall Mall Magazine*. It includes a picture of Beadle in disguise, his face obscured by veils.

[Age 27] 17 November 1908. Camping in South Africa with fellow members of the Legion of Frontiersmen. Source: Roger Pocock's diary, which notes: "Beadle to camp."

[Age 27] January 1909. Socialite Natalie Barney moves from Neuilly to 20, rue Jacob, Paris, where she hosts a famous salon for the next sixty years. Beadle uses her as the model for his character, "Theodosia" (a wealthy sybarite, poetess, and self-identified "androgyne") in the novel *Dark Refuge*.

[Age 27] Circa early 1909 – June 1909. Morocco. Begins to write fiction. Source: Beadle's contribution to the forum "Contemporary Writers and Their Work," published in *The Editor*, 25 February 1920.

[Age 27] Circa May – June 1909. Repatriates to London from Morocco. Source: "What Has Happened to Muley Hafid," *The Sphere*, 3 July 1909.

[Age 28] 9 December 1909. Henry Roger Pocock's diary notes that Beadle was one of several friends who "visited Pocock the day after an operation on his foot," but their whereabouts are not recorded.

[Age 29] October 1910. The first issue of *Adventure* (dated November 1910) appears on newsstands. Beadle will become one of its major contributors.

[Age 29] abt. February 1911. Publication of *The City of Shadows: A Romance of Morocco* (London: Everett and Co.). According to historian Geoffrey Pocock, Beadle's novel offers the "best account" of the Battle of Marrakech. Source: private communication with Pocock, 12 September 2022.

[Age 29] 2 April 1911. Resides at 69 Antrim Mansions, Hampstead, London. Source: 1911 English census, which identifies Beadle as "author."

[Age 29] July 1911. Café La Rotonde opens at 105, Boulevard Montparnasse. (Source: Luc Bihl-Willette, *Des tavernes aux bistrots: Une histoire des cafés*, Paris: L'Age d'Homme, 1997, p. 174.) The Rotonde is prominently featured in Beadle's novels, *The Esquimau of Montparnasse* and *Dark Refuge*.

[Age 30] 23 September 1912. Picasso leaves Montmartre to rent a flat in Montparnasse, at 242, Boulevard Raspail. His studio is a ten-minute walk from La Rotonde, which he patronizes along with Modigliani, Max Jacob, André Salmon, and many other artists and writers, including Beadle.

[Age 31] October 1912. Publication of Beadle's second novel, *A Whiteman's Burden* (London: Stephen Swift and Co.).

[Age 32] 1914. London. Elected as Fellow of the Royal Geographical Society.

[Age 32] 14 March 1914. British Consulate General, Paris. Marries Sylvia Hornsby (1891 – 1915), daughter of Edmund Hornsby (1861 – 1908) and Teresa Ashwell (1866 – 1940). The couple resides at 4, rue de la Grande Chaumière, a few doors away from the famous Académie de la Grande Chaumière (located at 14, rue de la Grande Chaumière), where Modigliani, Gauguin, and many other artists drew from the model. Source: certified copy of marriage certificate, in possession of Beadle's great-niece Patricia, who recalls having a Picasso print in the house, "for which Sylvia probably modeled."

[Age 32] 3 June 1914. Posts a letter from Sussex to New York's *Century Illustrated* magazine, submitting "3 short stories & an article (a piece of humorous biography)." A watermark at the top-right corner of the stationery reads: "Creek Cottage, Bosham, Sussex." Source: New York Public Library, Century Company records, Series I.

[Age 32] 28 July 1914. Austria-Hungary declares war on Serbia.

[Age 32] 1 August 1914. Germany declares war on Russia. The French General Staff issues the Order for Mobilization.

[Age 32] August 3, 1914. Germany declares war on France. The following day, Britain declares war on Germany.

[Age 33] c. 1915. Modigliani creates a pencil drawing of Beadle, composed in Beadle's flat at Place du Tertre. Titled *The Pilgrim,* the portrait is described in detail in Beadle's Modigliani biography, *Artist Quarter*. (See Illustrations, above.)

[Age 33] January 1915. The hallucinatory drink absinthe is banned in France by presidential decree.

[Age 33] 8 Jul 1915. Birth of daughter, Jane Owen Beadle (1915 – 2002), in Saint-Tropez.

[Age 33] 20 August 1915. Letter from former U.S. President Theodore Roosevelt to Charles Beadle, addressed to Beadle's residence at Villa Robinson in St. Tropez, thanking him for sending his book (probably the forthcoming *A Passionate Pilgrimage*).

[Age 33] September 1915. Publication of Beadle's third novel, *A Passionate Pilgrimage* (London: Heath, Cranton, and Ouseley), while Beadle resides at Villa Robinson, St. Tropez. Source: Last Will and Testament of Sylvia Beadle.

[Age 33] 13 September 1915. Death of Sylvia Beadle, in Cannes. According to her death certificate, she died at the Hotel Beau Rivage (now known as the Hotel Majestic) during a period in which the villas and hotels of Cannes were requisitioned as hospitals, especially for the soldiers of WWI.

[Age 34] 13 November 1915. D. H. Lawrence's novel, *The Rainbow*, is banned in Britain. Censors burn over 1,000 copies.

[Age 35] 30 October 1916. Embarks from Cadiz, Spain aboard the SS *Montserrat*, heading to New York. On the ship's manifest Beadle lists Beatrice Hastings as his "closest friend living in country of departure," noting her address at 13, rue Norvins, Paris (Montmartre). His contact information in Manhattan is Paul Tausig, 104 East 14th Street. An ad for the company Paul Tausig & Son appears in the 28 July 1910 issue of New York's *The Call* newspaper, advertising "Steamship tickets to all parts of the world. Railroad tickets to all parts of the United States and Canada. Money orders and drafts sent to all parts of the world. Foreign money bought and sold. Located in the German Savings Bank Building." The manifest indicates that it's Beadle's first trip to America.

[Age 35] 14 November 1916. Arrives in New York City.

[Age 36] March 1918. Outbreak of the Great Influenza Pandemic, with the first documented case occurring in Kansas. By the end of the pandemic in 1920 about 500 million will be infected worldwide, resulting in fifty million to one-hundred million deaths, with 675,000 fatalities occurring in the United States.

[Age 36] 3 April 1918; 3 May 1918. *Adventure* lists Beadle as a travel expert in its "Ask *Adventure*" column. ("A Free Question and Answer Service Bureau on Information on Outdoor Life and Activities Everywhere and Upon the Various Commodities Required Therein." His area of expertise is Africa: "Transvaal, N. W. and Southern Rhodesia, British East Africa, Uganda and the Upper Congo ... Covering geography, hunting, equipment, trading, climate, mining, transport, customs, living conditions, witchcraft, opportunities for adventure and sport." Beadle's contact info is still c/o Paul Tausig & Son. This is the first of many mail-drop locations that the peripatetic author will provide to *Adventure*: a useful resource for tracking his whereabouts.

[Age 36] 18 May 1918. Publishes "The Christman," the first of twenty-six stories that Beadle will publish in *Adventure*. His contact info is still c/o Paul Tausig & Son.

[Age 36] August 1918. Residing in, or traveling through, Grand Isle, Jefferson, Louisiana. (Source: announcement in *Adventure*, 18

August 1918.) Around this same time Beadle may have visited nearby Mexico.

[Age 36] 12 September 1918. A draft registration card in San Francisco notes that Beadle was living at the King George Hotel on 334 Mason Street, and that he would soon be moving to 119 Central Avenue, in nearby Sausalito. Under "Description of Registrant" it says that he's of medium height with a slender build, blue eyes, and gray hair. His occupation is "Novelist."

[Age 36] 3 October 1918. Contact info in *Adventure* is still Authors' League of America, New York. (Repeated in issues 3 January – 3 February 1919.)

[Age 37] 11 November 1918. Armistice. End of World War I.

[Age 37] 23 April 1919. Departs from New York aboard the SS *Rotterdam*, traveling second class, headed for Paris. His address is registered as 7, Place de Tertre, Paris. Source: Rotterdam, Netherlands, Passenger Lists of the Holland-America Line, 1900-1969.

[Age 37] Late April or early May 1919. Arrives in Paris and resides at the Grand Hotel. Source: Rotterdam, Netherlands, Passenger Lists, etc.

[Age 37] 15 March 1919. *Adventure* publishes the first installment of Beadle's *Witch-Doctors* (a four-part serial appearing between March 15 and May 1, 1919). Published in book form in 1922 by Jonathan Cape (UK) and Houghton Mifflin (U.S.).

[Age 37] 3 April – 3 May 1919. Contact info in *Adventure* is still Authors' League of America, New York.

[Age 37] 18 August – 18 September 1919. Contact info in *Adventure* changes to 7, Place de Tertre, Paris. Repeated in the 3 December 1919 and 3 March 1920 issues.

[Age 37] 19 October 1919. Corresponds with novelist Theodore Dreiser while residing at 8 East 9th Street in Manhattan. Source: University of Pennsylvania, Kislak Center for Special Collections, Rare Books and Manuscripts.

[Age 38] 8 January 1920. Spotted in Paris by occultist Aleister Crowley: "I ran around Paris, and walked into Lapérouse for lunch to find Beadle and Willy!" (The latter was the Pulitzer Prize-winning journalist Walter Duranty.) Source: Aleister Crowley, *The Magical Record of the Beast 666. The Diaries of Aleister Crowley, 1914 – 1920* (London: Duckworth, 1972), p. 90.

[Age 38] 17 January 1920. Volstead Act goes into effect in the United States, prohibiting manufacture and sale of alcohol. Prohibition Era continues until 1933.

[Age 38] 18 January 1920. *Adventure*'s "Camp-Fire" column publishes a letter from Beadle postmarked from Paris.

[Age 38] 24 January 1920. Death of Modigliani.

[Age 38] 25 January 1920. Death of Modigliani's companion, Jeanne Hébuterne, by suicide.

[Age 38] 3 August 1920. Residing in Westminster. Source: announcement in *Adventure*, August 3, 1920: "Care Society of Authors and Composers, Central Buildings, Tothill St., Westminster, London." This same info is repeated in the 18 October 1920 and 16 March 1921 issues.

[Age 38] 3 October 1920. The "Camp-Fire" column publishes a letter from Beadle, postmarked from Paris.

[Age 39] 6 October 1920. Hôpital Cochin, Paris. Death of Modigliani's lover, Simone Thiroux, from tuberculosis.

[Age 39] 18 January 1921. *Adventure*'s "Camp-Fire" column publishes a letter from Beadle, postmarked from Paris.

[Age 39] 21 February 1921. After *The Little Review* publishes excerpts from James Joyce's *Ulysses* in its 1920 issue, the magazine is successfully prosecuted for obscenity, effectively banning *Ulysses* from publication in the U.S.

[Age 39] 3 May 1921. "Camp-Fire" column publishes a letter from Beadle, postmarked from Paris.

[Age 39] 1921. Max Jacob is portrayed by Picasso as a monk in his two large paintings of the *Three Musicians*.

[Age 40] 2 Feb 1922. Sylvia Beach publishes Joyce's *Ulysses* in Paris.

[Age 40] June 1922. After serialization in *Adventure* in 1919, *Witch-Doctors* is issued as a book by Jonathan Cape in London and by Houghton Mifflin in Boston.

[Age 40] 20 June 1922. Beadle's contact information in *Adventure* is now "Île de Lerne," a small island off the northwest coast of France, in the Gulf of Morbihan.

[Age 41] 1923. The Dingo Bar opens at 10, rue Delambre in Montparnasse: the site where Hemingway will meet Fitzgerald, two years later. One of the only all-night pubs in Paris, it will eventually become one of Beadle's favorites. Frequented by artists and writers during the 1920s and Thirties, the clientele includes

Pablo Picasso, Aleister Crowley, Nancy Cunard, and Isadora Duncan, who lived in a flat across the street.

[Age 45] April 1927. Publication of Beadle's fifth novel, *The Blue Rib: A Romance of the Riviera* (London: Philip Allan and Co.).

[Age 45] August 1927. Residing in the vicinity of Nice. Source: Beadle's letter to his niece Isabel.

[Age 46] July 1928. An unexpurgated edition of D. H. Lawrence's *Lady Chatterley's Lover* is privately published in Florence. The novel is subsequently declared "obscene" and banned in Britain until 2 November 1960; and in the States until 21 July 1959.

[Age 47] Fall 1928. Publication of Beadle's sixth novel, *The Esquimau of Montparnasse* (London: John Hamilton). A quasi-autobiographical satire about Parisian expatriates, it includes characters based on Modigliani, Beatrice Hastings, Simone Thiroux, and Beadle (as the "Esquimau").

[Age 48] 29 October 1929. A stock market crash ushers in the Great Depression.

[Age 48] February or March 1930. *The Esquimau of Montparnasse* is republished as *Expatriates at Large* (New York: Macauley).

[Age 48] 18 May 1930. The *Sioux City Journal* features a fuzzy image of Beadle, standing in profile, which accompanies a review of *The Esquimau of Montparnasse*, "Paris Quartier Latin Sans Romantic Gloss."

[Age 49] Circa 1930. Teaching English as a second language at the International School, located at 1, Avenue St-Hilaire, Grasse, Côte d'Azur, France. Source: letter to Isabel.

[Age 49] 19 February 1931. Residing in the vicinity of Nice. Source: letter to Isabel.

[Age 50] Circa October 1931. Visits Paris but doesn't return again until circa May 1933. Source: letter to Isabel, circa spring 1933.

[Age 50] 1 January 1932. Breaks his ankle. After recovering, works as "a cabin boy on a yacht." Source: letter to Isabel, circa spring 1933.

[Age 51] Circa May 1933. Returns to Paris after an absence of "about 18 months." Source: letter to Isabel, circa spring 1933.

[Age 51] May 1933. Paris. The Palais-Royal Press publishes Beadle's seventh novel, *The White Gambit*.

[Age 52] 5 December 1933. End of Prohibition in America.

[Age 52] May 1934. The Dingo's charismatic barman, James "Jimmie" Charters, publishes *This Must Be the Place; Memoirs of Montparnasse*, edited by Morrill Cody, with an Introduction by Ernest Hemingway. Beadle is included in a list of notable patrons mentioned at the back of the book; his favorite drink is said to be a glass of white wine.

[Age 52] 1 September 1934. Jack Kahane's Obelisk Press publishes Henry Miller's novel, *Tropic of Cancer*, which is banned in the U.S. until 1964.

[Age 53] October 1934. Beadle writes a letter to Isabel addressed from the Promenade des Anglais, Nice, which includes the remark: "The few friends I have are as broke almost as I am. Others don't know me ..."

[Age 56] June 1938. Jack Kahane publishes Beadle's eighth and final novel, *Dark Refuge*. It features thinly disguised portraits of

Modigliani, the art dealer Léopold Zborowski, Max Jacob, Beatrice Hastings, and others from the Parisian demimonde.

[Age 57] 6 June 1939. Beadle visits Aleister Crowley at Crowley's home in Chiswick, England: the first of five dinner engagements there, lasting through 23 October (see below).

[Age 57] 1 September 1939. Germany invades Poland.

[Age 57] 2 September 1939. Publisher Jack Kahane dies from heart failure, possibly induced by a suicidal consumption of alcohol.

[Age 57] 3 September 1939. Two days after Germany invades Poland, both France and England declare war on Germany.

[Age 57] 29 September 1939. Beadle is residing at 331 Homewood Road, St. Albans, Hertfordshire. Source: 1939 England and Wales Register. The National Archives; Kew, London; 1939 Register; Reference: RG 101/16681.

[Age 57] 23 October 1939. Chiswick, England. After Beadle's fifth dinner engagement chez Crowley, the occultist notes in his dairy: "Here to pick my brains regarding Montparno" (Montparnasse). Beadle is gathering material for his only nonfiction book, later published as *Artist Quarter*.

[Age 58] 14 June 1940. German troops enter Paris and march on the Champs-Élysées as Nazi tanks rumble around the Arc de Triomphe.

[Age 58] 20 June 1940. Death of Beadle's mother-in-law, Teresa Ashwell, at La Maison Jaune, Chemin de St. Claude, Antibes. She leaves behind an estate worth £113, 17s, 1d. Source: England and Wales, National Probate Calendar (Index of Wills and Administrations), 1858-1995.

[Age 59] June 1941. Faber and Faber publishes *Artist Quarter: Reminiscences of Montmartre and Montparnasse in the First Two Decades of the Twentieth Century*. Coauthored by Charles Beadle and Douglas Goldring under the portmanteau pseudonym "Charles Douglas," the chronicle will eventually be recognized as a seminal work on the life of Modigliani.

[Age 62] October 30 or 31, 1943. Convinced that she's suffering from a terminal illness, Beatrice Hastings commits suicide in Worthing, Sussex. Shortly afterward, Beadle and Goldring receive a manuscript from her estate: a surrealist novella titled "Minnie Pinnikin," written by Hastings in French, which dramatizes her relationship with Modigliani. According to Modigliani scholar Kenneth Wayne, the curator of the Museum of Modern Art, William Lieberman, was preparing for a 1951 exhibit of Modigliani's work "when he was put into contact with Goldring and Charles Beadle by the art historian Douglas Cooper," and "through them he obtained a copy of Minnie Pinnikin." Source: Kenneth Wayne, *Modigliani and the Artists of Montparnasse*, New York: Harry S. Abrams, 2002, p. 205; and private communication with Wayne.

[Age 62] 24 February 1944. The Gestapo arrest Max Jacob in France.

[Age 62] 5 March 1944. Two days before being shipped to Auschwitz, Jacob dies at the Drancy internment camp.

[Age 63] 2 September 1945. End of World War II.

[Age 64] 7 August 1946. Birth of Beadle's granddaughter, Elizabeth Owen Bely, daughter of Jane Owen Beadle and Igor Bely, in Bournemouth, England.

[Age 65] 10 June 1947. *Short Stories* magazine publishes "Nameless Spy," Beadle's last known original publication.

[Age 70] February 1952. *Short Stories* republishes Beadle's "The Idol," a tale that first appeared in their 10 October 1933 issue.

[Age 75] 27 January 1957. Beadle's death certificate states that he passed away at 20, avenue de la voie Romaine, Nice (which was probably part of the Hôpital Pasteur Urgences complex). It also notes that he was residing at 4, avenue Victoria, Nice. Neither the cause of death nor his burial place are mentioned. The date and location of Beadle's death remained a mystery until 14 May 2025, when Céline Cardon located his death certificate in France. A reproduction of the document appeared for the first time in our newly revised edition of *A Whiteman's Burden*, in August 2025.

Charles Beadle Publications

Literary and genre fiction novels:

— *The City of Shadows: A Romance of Morocco*. London: Everett and Co., 1911.

— *A Whiteman's Burden*. London: Stephen Swift and Co., 1912.

— *A Passionate Pilgrimage*. London: Heath, Cranton and Ouseley: 1915.

— *Witch-Doctors*. London: Jonathan Cape, 1922. Boston: Houghton Mifflin, 1922.

— *The Blue Rib: A Romance of the Riviera*. London: Philip Allan and Co., 1927.

— *The Esquimau of Montparnasse*. London: John Hamilton, 1928. Later republished as *Expatriates at Large*. New York: Macauley Company, 1930.

— *The White Gambit*. Paris: Palais-Royal Press, 1933.

— *Dark Refuge*. Paris, Obelisk Press, 1938.

Nonfiction:

— *Artist Quarter: Reminiscences of Montmartre and Montparnasse in the First Two Decades of the Twentieth Century* (with Douglas Goldring). London: Faber and Faber, 1941. Published under the pseudonym "Charles Douglas." Later republished as *Artist Quarter: Modigliani, Montmartre and Montparnasse*. London: Pallas Athene Arts, 2018.

<u>Short works of fiction and nonfiction in journals and periodicals:</u>

— "Our Trip Down the Zambezi" (nonfiction). *The Wide World Magazine: An Illustrated Monthly of True Narrative, Adventure, Travel, Customs and Sport*, May 1907.

— "A Talk with the New Sultan of Morocco" (nonfiction). *Pall Mall Magazine*, October 1908.

— "What Has Happened to Muley Hafid" (nonfiction). *The Sphere*, 3 July 1909.

— "Two Close Calls" (nonfiction). *The Captain: A Magazine for Boys and "old Boys,"* June 1910.

— "My Narrow Escape From a Lioness." *The Brooklyn Daily Eagle*, "Junior Eagle" section (nonfiction), 7 August 1910.

— "In the Heart of the Kopje. A Story of the Mashonaland Rebellion." *The Wide World Magazine* (nonfiction), June 1912.

— "The Triumph of Tony." *Windsor Magazine*, July 1912.

— "The Better Man." *The London Magazine*, March 1913.

— "Romance for Sylvia." *Cassell's Magazine of Fiction*, March 1913.

— "A Decade of Christmas Dinners." *The Badminton Magazine of Sports and Pastimes* (nonfiction), December 1914.

— "A Pinch of Fever." *The Badminton Magazine*, June 1915.

— "An African Love Song." *The International*, October 1917. This piece appears to be a translation into English of a traditional African poem. (The same issue of the *International* features a lead story by Aleister Crowley titled "Cocaine.")

— "NQO," *The International*. December 1917.

— "The Palm Tree and the Window." Originally slated to appear in the March 1918 *International*. (In the February issue, under the feature "Jugging the March Hare," Aleister Crowley remarked: "Mr. Charles Beadle brought out his Eastern comedy, "The Palm Tree and the Window.") However the story never made it into print.

— "A Doctor of Men. *The International*. April 1918. (In the March issue, under the title "April Showers of Amusement," Crowley writes: "Charles Beadle contributes a delightful sketch of life in the Latin Quarter of Paris with its curious mixture of religious fervor and debauchery."

— "The Christman." *Adventure*, 18 May 1918.

— "The Autocrat." *Everybody's*, June 1918.

— "The Idol of 'It.'" *Adventure*, 3 July 1918.

— "John O'Damn." *Adventure*, 3 August 1918.

— "The Double Scoop." *Adventure*, 18 August 1918.

— "The Cave." *Adventure*, 3 October 1918.

— "The Winged Avenger." *Adventure*, 18 October 1918.

— "The Black Lure." *Adventure*, 18 November 1918.

— A story in *The International*. December 1918. (In the November issue, in a feature titled "The Editor Boosts the Next Number,

Aleister Crowley writes: "A story of African magic by Charles Beadle is really better than any of Kipling's African tales. That's going some, but it is true."

— "Rabbit: Philosopher" (novelette). *Adventure*, 18 January 1919.

— "Witch-Doctors" (novella). *Adventure*, 18 March 1919 (part one); 3 April 1919 (part two); 18 April 1919 (part three); 3 May 1919 (part four).

— "Uncle." *Ainslee's*, April 1919.

— "The Breaker of Idols." *Ainslee's*, May 1919.

— "Red Infidel" (novelette). *Adventure*, 18 May 1919.

— "Through Rabat's Eyes." *Argosy*, 2, 16, 19 August 1919.

— "The Tree of Life" (novella). *Adventure*, 3 August 1919.

— "The White Frog." *Adventure*, 18 August 1919.

— "Through Rabat's Eyes" (3-part serial). *Argosy*, 2, 9, 16 August 1919.

— "Captain Tristtam's Miracle." *Adventure*, 18 October 1919.

— "The Inner Hero." *Romance*, November 1919.

— "The Brothers." *Romance*, December 1919.

— "The Woman Courageous." *Ainslee's*, January 1920.

— "The Alabaster Goddess." *Adventure*, 3 January 1920.

— "Technique." *The Blue Magazine*), February 1920.

— "The Spell." *Adventure*, 18 February 1920.

— Untitled. *The Editor: The Journal of Information for Literary Workers* (nonfiction contribution to the forum "Contemporary Writers and Their Work." A discussion of Beadle's writing process), 25 February 1920.

— "An African Love Song." *Coterie* No. 4, 1920. (Reprinted from *The International*, October 1917.) The *Coterie* journal, a quarterly of art, prose, and poetry, boasted an impressive editorial board, including Conrad Aiken, T. S. Eliot, Richard Aldington, and Aldous Huxley. This particular issue features a poem by Douglas Goldring, who would later coauthor the book *Artist Quarter* with Beadle. It also hosts work by several of these contributing editors, poetry by Amy Lowell, and drawings by Zadkine and André Derain.

— "The Singing Monkey" (novella). *Adventure*, 3 March 1920.

— "The Picture." *The Blue Magazine*, June 1920.

— "The King's Sword." *Adventure*, 3 August 1920.

— "The McIntosh" (novella). *Adventure*, 3 October 1920.

— "The Bowl of Alabaster." *Adventure*, 18 September 1920. (A sequel to "Alabaster Goddess.")

— "The City of Baal." *Adventure*, 18 January 1921.

— "Buried Gods," (novella). *Adventure*, 3 September 1921.

— "The Land of Ophir" (3-part serial). *Adventure*, 10, 20, 30 March 1922.

— "Gifts of Diamonds." *Adventure*, 20 June 1922.

— "The Lost Cure" (novella). *Adventure*, 30 January 1923.

— "Sparklers and the Rascals" (novella). *Top-Notch Magazine*, 1 March 1923.

— "The Ghost of Fat Lung." *Argosy Allstory Weekly*, 4 August 1923.

— "Toll of the Jungle." *Tip Top Stories of Adventure and Mystery*, January 1924.

— "The Alabaster Goddess." *The Regent Magazine*, June 1924. (Reprinted from *Adventure*, 3 January 1920 or 1921.)

— "The Philanthropist" (novella). *Short Stories*. 10 June 1924.

— "White Medicine." *Short Stories*, 10 August 1924.

— "The Blond Spiders" (novella). *Adventure*, 20 December 1924.

— "The Wild Man." *Short Stories*, 25 February 1925.

— "White Magic." *The Frontier*, March 1925.

— "Romance," *Adventure*, 20 April 1925.

— "The Mark of the Leopard." *Short Stories*, 10 May 1926.

— "Hashish," "Voyage," and "Small Body." Bob Brown. *Readies for Bob Brown's Machine*. (Cagnes-sur-Mer: Roving Eye Press, 1931), p. 105.

— "Black Velvet." *This Quarter*. March 1932.

— "The Idol." *Short Stories*, 10 October 1933.

— "Mr. Burnjack's Crime." *The 20-Story Magazine*, January 1935.

— "Magic Head." *Short Stories*, 25 October 1938.

— "The King of Many Voices." *Short Stories*, 10 November 1939.

— "The Explorer's Graveyard." *Short Stories*, 25 April 1941.

— "The Baboon's Paw." *Short Stories*, 10 December 1945.

— "Ant Island." *Short Stories*, 10 October 1946.

— "Lost Heritage." *Short Stories*, 25 December 1946.

— "Nameless Spy." *Short Stories*, 10 June 1947.

<u>Posthumously reprinted stories and collections:</u>

— *The City of Baal*. Introduction by John Locke. Castroville, CA: Off-Trail Publications, 2007.

— *The Land of Ophir*. Introduction by John Locke. Castroville, CA: Off-Trail Publications, 2012.

— *The Blond Spiders* (e-book). Good Press, 2020.

— *The Double Scoop* (e-book). DigiCat, 2022.

Commentary in *Adventure*'s "The Camp-Fire" column:

— 3 July 1918. A detailed five-paragraph autobiographical sketch, from which we can draw various threads from Beadle's early life, including childhood trips into Asia and various titles of employment later in Africa. (The letter was composed circa May 1918. See John Locke's "Introduction" to *The City of Baal*, p. 13.)

— 18 January 1920: A commentary on the walled cities of Zululand (with a passing reference to Sir Richard Burton).

— 3 October 1920. Describes the events that inspired "The McIntosh."

— 18 January 1921. Some remarks about "The City of Baal."

— 20 June 1922. Provides biographical background to "Gifts of Diamonds."

Commentary in *Adventure*'s "Ask Adventure" column:

— "Diseases of East Central Africa." 18 September 1918.

— "The Rhodesian Mounted Police." 18 September 1919.

Letter to *Romance* magazine's "Meeting-Place" forum:

— January 1920. Beadle remarks that "Personally I have a theory that a writer should only use material which he has more or less actually lived. Anyway, I work on that principle." And he adds: "That is all writing is (to me); a mania to tell other folk what I see in my walks abroad."

Reviews of Beadle's Novels

<u>*The City of Shadows* (1911)</u>:

— *The Times* (London).

— *Manchester Courier*.

— *Daily Mirror* (London), 7 April 1911, p. 7.

— "Moorish Revolution." *The Guardian Journal* (Nottingham), 7 March 1911, p. 15.

— *Westminster Gazette* (London), 11 March 1911, p. 1.

— *Croydon Chronicle and East Surrey Advertiser* (London), 18 March 1911, p. 20.

— *The Globe* (London), 7 April 1911, p. 6.

— *The Bookseller* (London), 14 April 1911, p. 11.

— "A Story of Morocco." *Evening Express* (Liverpool), 20 April 1911, p. 3. (Copied verbatim from the *London Globe*.)

— *The Academy and Literature* (London), 6 May 1911, pp. 555-556.

— "A Moorish Romance." *Sheffield Daily Telegraph* (Yorkshire, England), 25 May 1911, p. 3.

— *The Queenslander* (Brisbane, Australia), 3 June 1911, p. 20.

— "New Books," *The Age* (Melbourne, Australia), 10 June 1911, p. 3.

— *The Australian Town and Country Journal* (Sydney), 14 June 1911, p. 55.

— "Morocco Bound," by Charles Lowe. *London Daily Chronicle*, 21 July 1911, p. 6.

<u>*A Whiteman's Burden* (1912)</u>:

— *The Athenaeum: Journal of Literature, Science, the Fine Arts, Music and the Drama* (London), 26 October 1912, p. 477.

— *The Scotsman* (Midlothian, Scotland), 4 November 1912, p. 2.

— *The Review of Reviews* (London), 1912, vol. 46, p. 696.

<u>*A Passionate Pilgrimage* (1915)</u>:

— *Freeman's Journal* (Dublin), 2 October 1915, p. 8.

— *The Devon and Exeter Gazette*, 2 November 1915, p. 6.

— "Echoes from Everywhere: What Men and Women are Talking of." *Liverpool Echo*, 11 November 1915, p. 4. (A list of quotations from various books, including three from *A Passionate Pilgrimage*.)

<u>*Witch-Doctors* (1922)</u>:

— *The Scotsman* (Midlothian, Scotland), 13 July 1922, p. 2.

— *The Times* (London), 28 July 1922, p. 13.

— *Punch* (London), 16 August, 1922, p. 168.

— "An American God." *Westminster Gazette* (London), 29 August 1922, p. 12.

— *The Province* (Vancouver), 30 August 1922, p. 6.

— *The Kingston Whig-Standard* (Kingston, Ontario), 2 September 1922, p. 4.

— *Calgary Herald* (Calgary, Alberta), 2 September 1922, p. 2.

— *The Topeka State Journal* (Topeka, Kansas), 9 September 1922, p. 8.

— *The News Journal* (Wilmington, Delaware), 9 September 1922, p. 8.

— *The Kansas City Star* (Kansas City, Missouri), 9 September 1922, p. 6.

— *Evening Public Ledger* (Philadelphia), 12 September 1922, p. 18.

— *Liverpool Post and Mercury*, 13 September 1922, p. 9.

— *New York Herald*, 17 September 1922, p. 19.

— *Buffalo Morning Express and Illustrated Buffalo Express* (Buffalo, New York), 17 September 1922, section 7, p. 4.

— "Fiction Snapshots," *New York Times Book Review and Magazine*, 17 September 1922, p. 7.

— *Buffalo Courier* (Buffalo, New York), 24 September 1922, p. 15.

— *New York Tribune*, 24 September 1922, section 5, p. 7.

— "Charles Beadle Tells Something about Himself." *Deseret News* (Salt Lake City), 30 September 1922, section 5, p. 3.

— *Detroit Free Press*, 15 October 1922, p. 12.

— *Daily Arkansas Gazette* (Little Rock, Arkansas), 15 October 1922, p. 4.

— *Hartford Courant*, 15 October 1922, p. 13.

— *Democrat and Chronicle Rochester* (Rochester, New York), 15 October 1922, unpaginated, section B.

— "The Witch Doctors." *Oakland Tribune* 15 October 1922, section S, p. 8.

— *The Chattanooga News*, 28 October 1922, p. 8.

— *Omaha Daily Bee*, 5 November 1922, p. 8.

— *The Buffalo Times*, 26 November 1922, p. 45.

The Blue Rib: A Romance of the Riviera (1927):

— *Aberdeen Press and Journal*, 21 April 1927, p. 3.

— *Montrose Standard* (Angus, Scotland), 22 April 1927, p. 6.

— *Birmingham Post* (West Midlands, England).

— *The Observer* (London), 15 May 1927, p. 8.

— *Sheffield Daily Telegraph* (Yorkshire, England), 11 June 1927, p. 10.

The Esquimau of Montparnasse (1928):

— *Sheffield Independent* (Yorkshire, England), 12 November 1928, p. 3.

— *Birmingham Daily Gazette* (Warwickshire), 22 November 1928, p. 3.

— *Northern Whig* (Antrim, Northern Ireland), 24 November 1928, p. 11.

Expatriates at Large (1930):

— *Argus-Leader* (Sioux Falls, South Dakota), 9 March 1930, p. 14.

— *Saturday Review of Literature*, April 1930).

— *Buffalo Times* (Buffalo, New York), 6 April 1930, p. 6-B.

— *Buffalo Evening News* (Buffalo, New York), 19 April 1930, p. 4.

— *Kansas City Star*, 19 April 1930, p. 8.

— *San Francisco Examiner*, 20 April 1930, p. 10 E.

— *Boston Globe*, 26 April 1930, p. 13.

— *Sioux City Journal* (Sioux City, Iowa), 18 May 1930, unpaginated. Features a photo of Beadle standing in profile.

— *The Minneapolis Star*, 3 June 1930, p. 15.

— *Birmingham News*, 8 June 1930, p. 4.

— *The Gazette* (Cedar Rapids, Iowa), 22 June 1930, p. 5 A.

— *New York Times Saturday Review of Books and Art*, 22 June 1930, p. 9.

— *St. Louis Post-Dispatch* (St. Louis, Missouri), 2 July 1930, p. 3 C.

— *Atlanta Constitution*, 3 August 1930, p. 8.

— *Detroit Free Press*, 17 August 1930, part four, p. 4.

— *Los Angeles Evening Post-Record*, 19 August 1930, p. 2.

— *Brooklyn Daily Eagle*, 10 September 1930, p. 18.

— *Book Review Digest*, 1931, volume 26, p. 62.

<u>*The White Gambit* (1933):</u>

— *The Daily Times-News* (Burlington, North Carolina), 10 June 1933, p. 2.

<u>*Artist Quarter: Reminiscences of Montmartre and Montparnasse in the First Two Decades of the Twentieth Century* (1941):</u>

— *The Observer* (London), 13 July 1941, p. 3.

— *Birmingham Post* (Birmingham, West Midlands, England), 22 July 1941, p. 2.

— *News Chronicle* (London), 1941.

— *Western Mail* (Cardiff, South Glamorgan, Wales), 5 August 1941, p. 2.

— *Time and Tide* magazine (London), 1941.

— *The Gazette* (Montreal), 29 November 1941, p. 21.

Posthumous Reviews and Commentaries:

"*Dark Refuge* appears in print for the first time since its original publication in 1938, presenting a world traveler's experiences with bohemian life in Paris in a novel that also serves (thanks to Rob Couteau) as a biography of Beadle's life. Extensive annotated references link Beadle's experiences to his fictional representations, offering a literary backdrop for understanding both the atmosphere and progression of his fiction and its roots in reality. Readers should be prepared for a sexual romp that is ribald, explicit, and thoroughly steeped in Beadle's personal experiences of the times....Whether exploring drug experiments and the revelations that follow them or descending into the sordid and colorful world of bohemian Paris, Beadle flavors all of his impressions with the same attention to flowery detail that makes his writing so timeless.... Pair this with the extensive notes and annotated references Couteau injects to not just explain but expand the story, for a sense of the unique literary and historical importance of this reappearance of Beadle's rare classic, which has been out of print for far too long. Libraries seeking literary representations of the marriage between fiction and nonfiction will find *Dark Refuge* a fine example. The 200+ annotated notes come from previously unpublished letters and documents, combining with photos and historical reviews to represent a hallmark of not only literary fiction, but biographical research. *Dark Refuge* deserves a place in any library strong in works of literature that represent the intersection between fictional devices and biographical inspection, whether or not there is prior knowledge of or interest in Beadle's works and importance." – **Diane Donovan, Senior editor,** *Midwest Book Review*, **November 2022**.

"There is no doubt in my mind that *Dark Refuge* deserved to be reprinted, especially in its present form which reinforces the text with numerous annotations, a long afterword which charts Beadle's life and activities, photographs, a bibliography, and additional material. Rob Couteau, who is largely responsible for discovering so much about Beadle and his publications, deserves our thanks for all his hard work." – **"Three Curious Interwar Novels," by Jim Burns,** *The Penniless Press Online*, **October 2023**.

"This new publication of *Dark Refuge* is a helpful addition for all those interested in the adventurous life of bohemian author Charles Beadle … His book *Artist Quarter* is the source of both fictional and nonfictional stories about Modigliani still prevalent today. In this book expertly edited, annotated, and commented upon by Couteau and Sawyer-Lauçanno, we gain greater insight into Beadle's life and the origins of his novel, *Dark Refuge*, that thankfully is once more available to the public." – **Dr. Henri Colt, Emeritus Professor of Medicine at the University of California and author of** *Becoming Modigliani*, **January 2024**.

"*A Passionate Pilgrimage* was first published in 1915, when it earned the acclaim of being one of ten books blacklisted for years by Britain's Circulating Libraries Association. Modern readers may be puzzled by this fact when they read this novel; but its descriptions of free-ranging sensual encounters between the protagonist and a host of consenting women made it a scandalous piece at the turn of the century. Why reissue *A Passionate Pilgrimage* now? The introductory notes (which are extensive and vital to understanding the novel's continuing importance) state that the novel: 'provides a variety of clues about Beadle's early life.' In so doing, it reveals the essence of social and psychological transformation, toeing the line between autobiography and a fictional discourse containing many topics vital to understanding not just these times, but modern morals and values. Its subjects and considerations make for thoroughly engrossing reading, presented in a way that builds the character's focus, emphasizes his differences, and ultimately creates a captivating tale of transformation and insight. Libraries that choose *A Passionate Pilgrimage* will find it highly recommendable to students of literature; teachers seeking novels that hold lively debates about not just banned literature, but banned ideas; and book clubs that will find *A Passionate Pilgrimage* thoroughly thought provoking." – **Diane Donovan, Senior editor,** *Midwest Book Review*, **March 2025**.

"*A Whiteman's Burden* was first published in 1912, when African sleeping sickness raged through the sites of Charles Beadle's various African expeditions. The fictional representation of this milieu and his experiences in *A Whiteman's Burden* creates a thought-provoking story set in 1904-06, the time frame of Beadle's own journey. It brings to life the contrasts between and dilemmas of the white man's expeditions into deepest, darkest Africa.

Here, a deadly illness has ravaged the native population and is now making headway among colonists who had believed themselves immune to the disease. Issues of survival and racial perceptions of life and death rage alongside the illness, adding existential strength and depth to a tale of adventure, exploration, and angst.

An unexpected focus on points of co-mingling, contrasting viewpoints, shared experiences that bring to light different ways of confronting life and death, and the disparate experiences and insights of men and women are transmitted through characters whose perceptions are oftentimes surprising. Embedded within these encounters are social and political reflections which emerge from privilege and African native encounters alike.... By including the reflections and observations of women as well as men, Beadle expands the potential of understanding this environment in a valuable manner....

Libraries seeking literary works about turn-of-the-century Africa and the colonists and natives whose lives intersected around illness and struggle will find *A Whiteman's Burden* exceptional. This stems from both its setting and its juxtaposition of characters buffeted as much by their own prejudices and perspectives as by an illness which feels unconquerable.

Replete with philosophical, cultural, moral, and historical insights, *A Whiteman's Burden* is highly recommended not just for leisure readers seeking an adventure story of African exploration, but to book clubs interested in thought-provoking existential examinations that can provoke lively debates and discussions about hazardous worlds and equally deadly prejudices." – **Diane Donovan, Senior editor,** *Midwest Book Review*, **August 2025.**

ALSO BY ROB COUTEAU

Fiction:

Doctor Pluss
Afterword by Jim Feast

Essays and Interviews:

Collected Couteau

More Collected Couteau
Introduction by James Dempsey

*Portraits from the Revolution: Interviews with the
Protestors from Occupy Wall Street*

Biography:

*A Blind Man Crazy for Color. A Tribute to Leon Angély: Illustrated by
Picasso's Model and Muse, Sylvette David*

Poetry:

The Sleeping Mermaid
Introduction by Christopher Sawyer-Lauçanno

Selected Poems
Introduction by Ed Foster

Memoir:

Intimate Souvenirs
Introduction by Robert Roper

EDITED AND ANNOTATED BY ROB COUTEAU

Charles Beadle:

*A Passionate Pilgrimage. Edited with an Introduction
and Afterword by Rob Couteau. Postscript by John Locke*

*A Whiteman's Burden. Edited with Annotations and an Afterword by Rob
Couteau. Introduction by John Locke*

*Dark Refuge.
Edited with Annotations and an Afterword by Rob Couteau.
Postscript by Christopher Sawyer-Lauçanno*

Francis Carco:

*From Montmartre to the Latin Quarter.
Edited with Annotations and an Introduction by Rob Couteau.
Afterword by Christopher Sawyer-Lauçanno*

Stanley J Marks:

*Murder Most Foul! The Conspiracy That Murdered President Kennedy:
Edited with an Introduction by Rob Couteau*

*Two Days of Infamy: November 22, 1963; September 28, 1964
Introduction by Rob Couteau*

*Coup d'Etat! Three Murders That Changed the Course of History. President
Kennedy, Reverend King, Senator R. F. Kennedy
Introduction by Rob Couteau*

*A Murder Most Foul! A Three-act Play about the JFK Assassination.
Introduction by Rob Couteau. Afterword by James DiEugenio*